SCOT ON THE ROCKS

SCOT ON THE ROCKS

Catriona McPherson

This first world edition published 2020
in Great Britain and 2021 in the USA by
SEVERN HOUSE PUBLISHERS LTD of
Eardley House, 4 Uxbridge Street, London W8 7SY.
Trade paperback edition first published
in Great Britain and the USA 2021 by
SEVERN HOUSE PUBLISHERS LTD.

British Library Cataloguing in Publication Data
A CIP catalogue record for this title is available from the British Library.

ISBN-13: 978-0-7278-9031-3 (cased)
ISBN-13: 978-1-78029-739-2 (trade paper)
ISBN-13: 978-1-4483-0461-5 (e-book)

This is a work of fiction. Names, characters, places and incidents
are either the product of the author's imagination or are used fictitiously.
Except where actual historical events and characters are being described
for the storyline of this novel, all situations in this publication are
fictitious and any resemblance to actual persons, living or dead,
business establishments, events or locales is purely coincidental.

All Severn House titles are printed on acid-free paper.

Severn House Publishers support the Forest Stewardship Council™ [FSC™],
the leading international forest certification organisation.
All our titles that are printed on FSC certified paper carry the FSC logo.

Typeset by Palimpsest Book Production Ltd.,
Falkirk, Stirlingshire, Scotland.
Printed and bound in Great Britain by
TJ Books Limited, Padstow, Cornwall.

This is for Sharon Tenbergen, with love and thanks.

ONE

'It's the most lud-i-crous taaaaiiiime of the year!' I sang to myself as I traipsed through the streets of downtown Cuento, en route to the Yummy Parlor Szechuan Restaurant and Takeaway.

When I was a kid, back in Dundee – or Dundee, Scotland, as they call it here – St Valentine's Day meant a card if someone fancied you, knew your address and had a stamp; a bunch of flowers if you had a boyfriend who hadn't worked off whatever he did at the New Year's Eve party; or a white furry teddy bear with a red satin chest if you were really slow on the uptake and the sickening Christmas present you got from the guy who'd buy a teddy bear for Valentine's Day hadn't made you dump him yet. Maybe some wives put love notes in the lunch boxes of some husbands. Maybe some husbands put chocolates on the pillows of some wives. My dad bought my mum a card once. She opened it at the breakfast bar, frowned, said, 'For crying out loud, Keith,' and ripped the front off to use for a shopping list.

She would keel over in her tartan slippers and hit the ground stone dead if she could see Cuento on Valentine's Day. Every shop window had a mammoth eruption of bright red and bright pink – two colours that, newsflash, do not go – and it didn't matter whether the eruption was balloons, ribbons, fabric, flowers, table linen, stuffed animals, stationery, garden tools (because of course the hardware store had got in on the act) or iced cakes, the result looked like a giant shiny haemorrhoid. A new kind of giant haemorrhoid that could also give you a migraine if you looked at it too long.

The bars and restaurants were worse than the shops. Every table on every covered patio and in every show-off window was set for two, with a cheap red candle already dripping wax on to a fake red rose, and two deluded numpties gawping at each other across a hiked-up plate of dodgy oysters while a server twisted the cork out of a hiked-up bottle of domestic fizz.

Some of the girl numpties were ripping open tiny pink and red packages and popping open the velvet lid inside with the practised flick of a gel tip. To be fair, these scenes could be quite entertaining. I stopped at La Cucaracha and pretended to look at the menu purely to watch one of them play out. The gift in question was silver earrings and either the male numpty who had bought them, or a sociopath in the jewellery shop, had been dumb enough to put them in a very small, square, white-and-gold-for-God's-sake box that looked, even to my inexpert eye, like it had been conceived and manufactured expressly to house a diamond solitaire. She held it, still closed, against her heaving chest, gazing at him with shiny eyes. He realized – a second too late – what she was thinking. She saw him realize – also a second too late – just as she was lifting the plump, white lid on its little gold hinge. And there they were, the pair of them: dismayed, mortified, furious, resentful, ungrateful, hate in their hearts and still a whole evening to get through. Happy Valentine's Day!

It was almost enough to make me glad I getting myself a Chinese takeaway for one to go home and watch Britbox. Almost.

But the rot had spread even here, to my favourite of Cuento's eateries. I loved this place. For a start, there was the glamour – irresistible to all foreigners – of Chinese food in one of those waxy little decapitated pyramids, just like in the movies. Truly, it made me feel like the lost seventh Friend to pluck one from my fridge, sniff it, wince and eat it anyway. Also, their meals were blistering hot. I had got mightily sick of lukewarm, litigation-avoiding food in the just-over-a-year I'd lived here and I'd come to appreciate deeply the way the cooks at the Yummy Parlor handed over soup that would still be bubbling when you got it home, seeming to say, *Sue us if you like, ya wimp. It won't put the skin back on your tongue.*

I was guessing at what they said, of course. And that was the last reason I adored the Yum. The customer service was appalling. They were surly, unbending, pretty sarcastic even in English and obviously hilarious in Cantonese, flinging around judgements about the customers and not trying to pretend they weren't. Whenever the endless beaming smiles and bottomless obliging service of the typical Californian really started to unsettle me, there was nowhere like the Yum to remind me of home. With a curled lip and a rolled eye, they could cure my homesickness before they'd licked their pencil and laughed at my order.

So, obviously, I had told myself after work, no one would be clueless enough to bring a Valentine's date here. I could get my honey-and-walnut prawns and my nuclear soup without any pink, any red, any roses or any pity.

Ha. What I had forgotten was that – unrelated to the misanthropy of the staff, the temperature of the sauces and the shape of the containers – the food was good. And, even on this insufferable day, there were a few courting couples in Cuento who cared. The Yum had done their best to make clear the establishment's contempt for the holiday. The tea lights were slapped straight down on the Formica and they'd made ten roses do thirty tables by chopping them into three pieces, crossways. Twenty tables had sections of stalk in shot glasses, while ten had flower heads with no stalk. Truly, pie shops in Glasgow could learn disdain from these masters.

Still, I should have been able to tough it out. I *would* have been able to tough it out. If only I hadn't seen in the usually dead eyes of the Yum's counter-order taker something that undid me.

'Hot sour soup and honey walnut shrimp, please,' I said, translating effortlessly into American.

'For one?' she said, and that's when I saw it. It wasn't pity, nor empathy, nor kindness, nor concern. But it was, unmistakably, human. And she didn't shout anything scathing over her shoulder towards the kitchen either.

'No, for tw—' I started to say, then I put my hand to my back pocket and prised out my phone. Yes, I was wearing very tight jeans. Yes, I had changed into them twenty minutes ago. Just in case. 'One minute,' I told the order taker as I put the phone to my ear. 'You're just in time,' I told it. 'I was going to get you the same as me. What do you want? OK. OK. Open a tinny for me. I'll be there soon.' I put the phone back in my pocket and said, 'The soup and shrimp for one, plus a general chicken and fried rice. Four crispy wontons. Thank you. And two fortune cookies,' I added, in case she still hadn't got the message.

'You're a sad, sad, sad, sad, sad, sad, sad little sack,' I sang as I traipsed home again, using the tune of 'When the red, red robin'. I was disgusted with myself for pretending to have an imaginary boyfriend, for pretending my useless imaginary boyfriend sent me out for takeout on Valentine's Day, for pretending my useless, uncommunicative imaginary boyfriend ignored all my texts asking him what he wanted, and most of all for pretending that my useless, uncommunicative, *boring* imaginary boyfriend ate general chicken and wontons, when I could either have ordered him something lovely that I would have welcomed tomorrow for lunch, or something properly awful, like congee and frog curry, that I wouldn't be tempted to cram into my lonely, bitter face tonight with my second bottle of wine and third romcom.

I even found myself looking at a man walking ahead of me, alone, not carrying chocolates or flowers, not dressed up or reeking of aftershave and not – I saw the lack of a reflective glint on his left hand as he passed a lighted hairdresser's salon – married. Was he also lonel— No! Was he also *single*, maybe? I knew he was straight, from the clothes – truly pitiful, but I didn't mind a fixer. And he had a walk that said, *I'm fine with who I am; ain't life grand?* If I were to overtake him in my skinny jeans, then he were to catch up again at the pedestrian crossing, and I smiled, and he smiled back, and the lights were broken and we were stranded there . . .

As it happened, he sailed across the road when the walky man appeared and strode into the phone shop on the other corner, going straight past the sales area and in through the staff door. That was that then. A phone-shop staff member would never look twice at me, with my unused apps and overpriced chump plan. Men didn't want fixers.

As if all of that wasn't bad enough, the downtown florist was still open and, as I passed, a woman in a pink overall, with a red ribbon tied round her head then done up in the kind of rosette you can only learn to make from a YouTube video, was putting out a sign saying, *Sold Out of Red Rose's*, and I was too depressed at the thought that Phone-shop Guy and me were the only solitary people in Cuento tonight to ask, *Red Rose's what?*

And then the tin lid was applied and tamped down all round with the handle of a sturdy screwdriver. I noticed, outside the only residential property on my route – from the Yum, under the railway line to the (literal) wrong side of the tracks, past the police station, drive-through coffee shack and self-storage facility, to the Last Ditch Motel where I make my humble home – a pile of what they call 'yard waste'.

It's a great service provided by Cuento City Waste Management and Recycling. When you're doing your garden, you just scrape all the crap you don't want – everything from palm branches to grass clippings – down on to the street and leave it there for someone to take away. It's a hell of a waste of parking spaces and it's not much fun for the odd cyclist who somersaults into piles of jaggy stuff, but you've got to love such a celebration of extreme laziness. It's right up there with the drive-through bank.

I had never seen anything to trouble me in this pile. Usually it was prunings, punctured lemons, weeds and the odd rotting squash. Tonight, though, right on the top, there was a bunch of slightly wilted, not-quite-decaying roses. I stopped and stared, feeling the tub of soup hit me in the calf with a hot smack. I'd never wondered about the people who lived in this one little house jammed between a fro-yo and the multistorey car park for the cinema. Students, I'd have guessed. Or maybe an original owner from the fifties, hanging on, shredding the offers from developers that had to come through the letterbox thick and fast now that the zoning was commercial on this block. Whoever they were, I now saw, one of them bought roses so regularly that the old bunch could go out for the binmen when a fresh lot turned up on Valentine's Day.

So I was in the mother of all slumps when I trudged across the Last Ditch car park, heading for the corner where the path led round to the motel's namesake slough in which my little houseboat sat bugging the life out of the city planners. I purposefully avoided looking upstairs towards Todd and

Roger's room, even though they were bound to be either out somewhere fabulous or already in bed with lobsters. I even more purposefully avoided looking into the office, where the owners, Kathi and Noleen, were bound to be either lovingly sharing a curry on a card table or having a romantic game of darts and a margarita.

Unfortunately, two doors opened while I was right in the middle of the asphalt; not a chance of a getaway. Room 101 was the lair of Devin, a kid who'd moved out of his college accommodation when he couldn't stand the bullying and moved in here to try and live off the buffet breakfasts for three meals a day. Room 105 was the permanent home of Della and her six-year-old, Diego, as well as two cats, a rabbit, a seahorse and an expanding family of tropical fish.

'He sleeps!' Della was calling along to Devin. She hadn't even noticed me.

'Cool!' Devin said, and pulled his door shut behind him with his foot. He loped along the walkway under the overhang, his arms bursting with . . . looked like some kind of board game . . . and a six-pack swinging by its plastic from one finger.

'Oh!' I said. 'You two having a game night? You should have told me. I've over-ordered Chinese and I've got a bottle of . . . can't remember, actually, but I'll get it.'

'Hi, Lexy,' Della said. She was staring at me with a weird, penetrating look on her face that I couldn't begin to decipher.

'Yeah,' said Devin. Della swung round and treated him to the look now. 'I–I mean, "Yeah, hi, Lexy," not, "Yeah, Chinese food and mystery booze,"' he said. 'Hi, Lexy. Yeah.'

He always talked like this. Noleen had burst into his room every day before they legalized it, looking for evidence of a hydroponic grow, but I reckoned he was just made that way.

'So . . .?' I said. I really did. I was that slow.

'See you tomorrow!' said Della. 'Have a lovely evening. Thank you.'

'Wait,' I said. I looked at what Della was wearing and noticed at last that there wasn't much of it. And I looked at Devin's armload and realized that the board game was Twister.

'Wait,' I said. 'Are you . . .? Are you two . . .? Is that even . . .?' *Legal*, I was going to say. Thank God I stopped myself in time. But seriously, Devin was a student, a child, and Della was a woman, a mother.

'Legal?' Della said. 'Were you asking, "Is it legal?"'

'Jeez, Lexy,' Devin said. 'I'm twenty-one.'

'I wasn't going to say "legal",' I lied. 'I was going to say . . . "legal". Sorry. Why not? What's it got to do with me? Joan Collins . . . I mean, isn't Madonna . . .? I mean, Demi Moo—'

'I'm twenty-five,' Della said. 'Have a lovely evening, Lexy.'

'*Hasta pronto!*' I said, even though I knew my accent hurt Della's teeth, then I went round the back of the motel to eat two dinners and try to feel proud, because this stupid manufactured holiday really needed a Grinch of its very own and I was ideal. Clearly.

TWO

No matter how depressed, carb-stuffed and hammered you go to bed, waking up to find that it's still California outside always helps. February the fifteenth, I thought to myself, stretching in bed. Well, I say stretching, but it's more like bracing. I put my hands against the wooden wall at the top of my box bed and my feet against the wooden wall at its base to see what creaked first: me or the boat.

The sun was shining through the bare branches of the hackberry trees and a Cinderella wardrobe department of little birds was chirruping away as they all took their morning dip in the slough. There was good coffee waiting at the Swiss Sisters drive-through, and fresh bagels too if I wasn't still full of takeaway. In Dundee, in mid-February, the rain would be turning to sleet – horizontal sleet, at that – the pigeons would be pecking at frozen sick and the coffee would be instant. It didn't go down well when I mouthed off to Alison about instant coffee: 'What's wrong with us? We've got the cheek to whine about American tea and then suck down that bilge. We might as well eat tinned potatoes and drink powdered OJ.'

'*OJ?*' Alison had said, with scorn seeping out of every pore. '*OJ!*' She's my best friend, or at least my oldest one, so she gets to say what she likes to me.

Life, I told myself sternly, wasn't too bad. I had my health, I had Obamacare while it lasted, I was living in a democracy in a time of local peace. I had good friends and an interesting job where I was my own boss, flexible hours, all that. I just needed to tweak that one last little thing. I just needed to meet the man of my dreams. Even the man of one wild weekend would do.

Todd had started asking intrusive questions about a week after I first met him. He could hardly be expected not to: for one, he was happily married and, like all happily married people, he'd turned into Mrs Bennet before the end of the toasts at his wedding and now wanted to marry off everyone in his life, starting with me. For another thing, he was Todd. He had no boundaries. He didn't recognize the category 'boundary' as part of life. He couldn't spell 'boundary'. Didn't know how to pronounce it. Got nothing but a short burst of static if anyone said it. With a gun to his head and a set of magnetic letters, he couldn't write 'boundary' on the door of a fridge.

But Roger, Todd's husband, was at it too. He was a doctor, a paediatrician, and he met a lot of other doctors in the course of a day, including a widowed thoracic surgeon who attended a whisky-tasting club every fourth Friday.

'I hate whisky,' I said.

'I know,' said Roger.

'Everyone hates whisky. It's the world's best-kept secret.'

'I know,' said Roger. 'But you understand it. You know it's not bourbon. You can name distilleries. You wouldn't drink it with ice.'

'I'd drink it with Dr Pepper if it would take the taste away,' I said. 'What are you up to?'

Roger smiled and said nothing until Todd had floated up to the other end of the Last Ditch's swimming pool, where we were all trying to survive a triple-digit day. When his beloved was out of earshot, Roger said, all in one breath, 'If you don't go out with him to this whisky tasting Todd's going to try to get you to go to the Scottish games and make me go too to grease the introduction please Lexy I can't be near all those bagpipes I'll cry.'

'Scottish games?' I said. '*Highland* games, you mean? Cabers? Sword dancing? People who know their family tree back to the fourteen hundreds? Jesus Christ, why didn't you say? When's the whisky thing?'

My God, it was dull. And the smell!

The surgeon was well groomed and well dressed, attractive in a surgeon-y sort of way, which was mostly an air of extreme confidence from always being in charge of everything. He had an encyclopaedic knowledge of Scottish geography, based entirely on whisky production, and a strange earnest literalness that it took me two hours to realize was a complete lack of a sense of humour. He truly had no sense of humour at all, as if it had been neatly excised by a skilful colleague. And once I started to suspect as much, I had to keep checking.

'I thought a thorax was a Dr Seuss character,' I said.

'No, that's a Lorax,' he said. 'The thorax is the area of the body . . .' I assume he kept talking until he'd produced a whole sentence, but I stopped listening so I can't be sure.

'But of course, I thought Dr Seuss was a TV therapist,' I tried next.

'No, that's Dr Ruth,' he said. 'Dr Seuss was a writer of . . .' I think he got a paragraph out of that.

I told him about the time a lorryload of dried soup-mix fell into the River Tay and what the newspapers managed by way of headlines. He voiced concern for the wildlife. I told him about the time I said Ted Bundy was my favourite poet, when I meant Ted Hughes, but Edmund Blunden had got in the way and confused me.

'I don't recall that Ted Bundy published any poetry,' he said.

There was no second date.

Later in the summer, when Noleen said she had the perfect man for me, I said nothing could be worse than what I'd been through already and agreed to meet him. I think it was an act of lesbian revenge. At least if I tell myself that, I can just about manage not to smack Noleen every morning as soon as I'm up to punish her. Before she and Kathi met and married, I'm sure they had years and years of being set up with 'the perfect woman' by straight friends who thought the main indication of some woman being perfect for some other woman was that she was a woman who was into women. And was single. And breathing.

This perfect man Noleen shoved me at with a foot in the small of my back was indeed a breathing, single, straight male. Perfection. He was forty years old, lived alone, ran a business that provided filtered water for offices (and, I'm assuming, motel reception areas) and was – he told me – the number-one fan of California's most famous competitive dog groomer. Whose name is Cat. He showed me a photo on his phone of a poodle groomed to look like the front of a tiger and the back of a flamingo.

'Amazing, isn't it?' he said.

'And this is . . . your dog?'

'I don't own a dog. I do have a shadow-puppet theatre.'

I filed that for the time being and carried on with my main line of questioning. 'So the owner of the dog lets you . . . pays you . . . You pay to . . .?' Now I was looking at a poodle that seemed to have a koala bear climbing its back leg and a snake climbing its front, or maybe it was a snake and a koala who were posing on a poodle-shaped climbing frame; it was hard to say.

'No, I'm not a groomer. Just a fan. I follow the pros – Cat and the rest of them – around the dog shows. I'm going to South Carolina next weekend. I don't suppose you're free?'

To fly 3,000 miles to watch my date watch a woman make a poodle look like a magic-eye picture of Dory and Nemo? 'Damn it,' I said. 'I've got clients all weekend. Otherwise, you know . . .'

I batted open the door of the Last Ditch reception with the flats of both hands, making Noleen flub the handful of fishbowl business cards she was sorting into alphabetical order for the mailing list. 'Did you know?' I said.

'Heh heh heh,' she said.

'Sicko,' I said.

'What sicko?' said Noleen. 'He's an innocent lover of lovers of animal art. Don't be so closed-minded.'

'Not him,' I said, with an involuntary shudder. 'You.'

So, when Kathi told me to be in the Skweeky Kleen Laundromat attached to the motel at six p.m. one late-autumn day and went as far as to insist I put on some mascara and pull a comb through my 'nest' – her word – I told her I wasn't interested in whisky bores, shadow-puppet-cum-poodle-dyeing fans or any other kind of documentary-worthy freak she might have unearthed.

'Guaranteed freak-free,' she said. 'Twin brothers, coming to pick up ten Eton shirts, five blue and five white, like they do after work every Thursday. They're lawyers. They need good shirts.'

'OK,' I said. 'Which one of them is it you're throwing me at?'

She lifted her eyebrows and tucked her lips in, a very Kathi expression, but one which would take many years of study, high on a mountain in Nepal, to decode.

'Either?' I guessed.

Kathi's lips disappeared completely.

'Oh God. Both?' I said, backing away.

'I didn't think you were so . . .' she began, the cheeky cow.

'That's incest,' I said. 'That's disgusting.' I had got to the door and I stopped dead. 'Wait, they're not conjoined, are they? Sorry. I didn't mean to be horrible.'

'No, they're not conjoined,' Kathi said. 'They're just very close. They're lovely guys.'

'I think their shirts might be their best feature,' I said. 'Say, Kathi, if you ever *do* meet anyone you find freaky, please don't tell me, eh?'

Thus, I didn't really have a leg to stand on, the day in midwinter when Todd announced he couldn't stand to see me 'dicking around' any longer and was taking over. The only surprise was that he announced it and gave me some warning. After all, when he and Kathi had mounted a coup on my business, neither of them had found *that* worth mentioning. It was only when I saw three names on one of my own business cards as I handed it over one day that I realized what had happened.

As a relationship counsellor, with a consultation room at the back of the houseboat, in what was probably meant to be a parlour, while I worked towards state accreditation and, in the meantime, listened and clucked, offered tissues – the good ones, with aloe vera – and tried not to give advice like 'dump him', because it's bad for repeat business, I didn't think there were any loose ends in my professional life for two new partners to pull on.

But I reckoned without Todd and Kathi. Kathi can't help it; she's a germophobe, so of course she was going to check whether anyone in the throes of life improvement was willing to include their house in the general detoxification. As for Todd? Well, he's got his own problems. He lives at the Last Ditch Motel with his paediatrician husband, instead of in their art deco five-bedroom up in the suburbs, because of a rampant case of cleptoparasitosis and because there's nothing like a germophobe motel owner for making sure there are no bugs – crawling, flying, burrowing or even imaginary – to trouble the faintest cleptoparasitastic heart. But that doesn't explain why he's offering makeovers to my clients instead of practising as the anaesthetist he is. Well, only in a roundabout sort of way. The hospital board won't let him back while his delusions are rampant, so he's bored stiff. Add to this what we already know about his boundaries (lack of, total) and I suppose it does make sense, if you half shut your eyes and turn sideways.

It was just before Christmas that he really laid into me, asking me to sign an agreement to go on a date per month for three months if he offered six choices, four dates from eight choices, or five out of ten, and a penalty involving body-hair removal (boundaries) if I flaked for more than two consecutive weeks out of any seven, or any three weeks at all out of nine.

He had printed it out and stapled it together. He had brought a pen.

'You *can't* flake out of more than two weeks without flaking out of three,' I said. 'That's very inefficient contractual language. Make it four out of nine and we've got a deal.'

Todd sucked at maths. Sometimes it made me glad he wasn't doling out fractions of three different anaesthetics depending on body weight and minutes taken per procedure. At that moment, he pretended to consider the deal, then nodded.

I amended the wording, got him to initial the changes, signed the bottom and post-dated the whole thing for after the holidays – which to Brits like me means January the sixth, the fifth being Twelfth Night; no matter that to Todd it would mean the 26th of December because Americans fail so badly at Christmas they don't even have Boxing Day.

He started nagging me nice and early anyway, which was as big a surprise as the sun going down and then – major twist – coming up again, but I had managed to wriggle out of consequences until now, telling him that the two-week flake was moot, given the four-in-total clause, because he hadn't specified *and/or* over *either/or* and any vagueness in a contract is settled in favour of the party who didn't write it.

When I had got through four dateless weeks on that basis, he really thought he had me on the second clause, going as far as to drop an 'Aha!' as he burst into my bedroom on the relevant morning, boundary-free as ever.

'Four weeks since you signed, Lexy,' he said. 'I've set you up for tonight with a—'

'Does the contract say seven-day period or calendar week?' I croaked from the depths of my duvet.

'Neither.'

'See you Monday, then.'

'This is some bullshit right here,' he said, standing over my bed and glaring at me.

'Any vagueness in the wording of a contract,' I said, 'as we've discussed before—'

He banged the door behind him.

Then he tried again, but I got him on four-week periods versus calendar months, forward projections of nine-week periods as yet undetermined with respect to numbers of hook-ups completed, threw in a leap-year loophole that gave him a headache behind one eye and almost made me feel guilty, and finally arrived at today.

When he let himself into my bedroom on the morning after Valentine's Day, still in his early-morning caffeine-run ensemble of draped cashmere, I had come to terms with it all and was telling myself that, (a) I had to have some sort of up-to-date relationship experience if I was going to keep being a relationship guru with any self-respect, (b) Todd was married to a gorgeous hunk of baby doctor and had inevitably high standards as a result, and (c) I had seriously considered sitting on one of the washing machines in the Skweek a couple of days back, when the load was unbalanced and the drum starting bucking. It was time for me to put my toe back in the socket, come what may.

'Coffee,' Todd said. 'Tall, hot, black and slightly bitter. You like your coffee like I marry my men.' It was an old joke, its job being to celebrate our closeness. I opened one eye. Why was he being nice to me?

'Cheers,' I said, reaching out a hand for it.

'What did you take your mascara off with last night? The pillow again? Don't you care about eyelash mites?'

'Eyelash mites are microscopic, unrelated to make-up and completely natural,' I said.

'Ew,' said Todd. 'Rather you than me.'

I don't know if he really believed he was free of them, or if he pretended as much in an act of self-soothing, but he sat down a long way off and blinked quite a bit.

'OK,' I said. 'Hit me. Do your worst. I'll be a good little sacrificial lamb and do what I'm told.'

'What are you talking about?' Todd said. 'I've come to break some bad news.'

I sat up.

'It's none of us,' he added hastily. 'Roger, Kathi, Nolly, Diego, Della – all fine.'

'My mum and—?'

'—dad are both fine,' said Todd. 'As far as I know.'

'Who isn't?' I said. 'Tell me, before I throw this coffee over you. Who died?'

'Mama Cuento.'

'Who?'

'*What?* Mama Cuento.'

'I didn't know she was still alive,' I said. There was a massive statue of Mama Cuento where First Street crossed Main Street; I assumed – coming from a land where most statues were of dead monarchs and admirals – that the original was long gone.

'What?' said Todd again. 'We saw her not three nights ago. Drink some coffee and wake your brain. She was standing proud as ever until last night and then sometime in the small hours someone knocked her off her plinth.'

'The statue!' I said. 'Got it. A drunk driver? Isn't there a camera?'

'Not a drunk driver,' Todd said. 'At least, yes they must have been driving and they might have been drunk, but not too drunk to get a strap round a gazillion tons of bronze and winch her on to the back of a monster truck.'

'Hang on – she's gone?' I said. 'Someone *stole* her?'

'I saw the news van heading up there when I was in line for coffee, so I followed. Quite a crowd, a lot of weeping, laying of flowers, all that. So I flirted my way in front of the camera and said Trinity was offering free counselling to anyone affected by this . . . What did I say . . .? Blow to the civic heart of our town.'

'That's the bad news you've come to break?' I said. 'The fact that I'll be working for nothing all day, mopping tears of grief about a nicked statue?'

'So cynical,' said Todd. 'No, the bad news is that there's been an assault on an important cultural emblem. The free publicity's a silver lining. But you need to get your lazy ass up there to First and Main, and get your picture taken before the newshounds melt away.'

'Because I'm so much more camera-ready than you?' I said.

'Because we can't have people seeing me and getting their hopes up then finding out it's your shoulder they'll be sobbing on,' Todd said. Can't fault his honesty.

Can fault his memory, though. He was so busy drumming up business and inserting us into the heart of the tragedy he'd forgotten all about my love life. Take the win, Lexy, I told myself, throwing back the covers and heading into my midget shower room, hot coffee still in hand.

THREE

'd assumed Todd's take on statue-grief was bogus, although I hadn't bothered arguing: when he gets that look in his eye, it's easier to go along. So, I let him pick an outfit for me, French-plait my hair, apply three individual false lashes on each eye and a slick of nude gloss on my lips, cheeks and what he insists on calling my 'crease' – he means eyelid – to finish me off with a winter glow that would pop for the camera. I'm quoting.

Twenty minutes later, we were in the heart of downtown, right by the patio of La Cucaracha, looking at the plinth where Mama Cuento's broad bare feet usually stood. And it wasn't bogus at all; I found myself buying one of the tealights in glass holders that an even more enterprising individual than Todd was already selling from a cart for five bucks a pop and adding it to the impromptu altar growing just outside the crime-scene tape.

Just *inside* the crime-scene tape, Soft Cop – a walking marshmallow of a police officer – and Detective Molly 'Mike' Rankinson, the closest thing I had in town to an arch nemesis, were standing close together, I assume discussing the case. The cold February air plumed around them as they spoke and lent a noir-ish touch, as if they were smoking. I couldn't imagine what there was to speak about. Mama Cuento was gone. The perps must be caught on some camera somewhere. And the insurance would surely replace her. Unless the cops were hashing out the best method to take plaster casts of unusual footprints, this looked a lot like making sure they got on the evening news. But the cameraman from the local NBC affiliate was resting against his van, while the reporter sat warming up inside, drinking what looked like hot chocolate through a straw.

'That woman's drinking hot chocolate through a straw,' I said to Todd. 'Do you think she hates sea life that much?'

'Lip line,' Todd said. 'You should see what slurping your joe on the hoof has done to yours, Lexy.' He speeded up as we got close to the van. 'Hoyt?' he said. 'Lola? This is my colleague I was telling you about. The counselling expert. Lexy? Lola from the news. And Hoyt.'

It took her less than a minute to find her mark, flip her glossy black hair and get her smile in gear. Todd shoved me into position beside her.

'I'm joined now by Dr Lexy Cameron, who has volunteered clinical time to help any Cuento-ite affected by the desecration of the cultural treasure at the heart of this close-knit community. Dr Cameron, before we get into that, can you tell me what Mama Cuento means to *you*? And how you feel to have lost her?'

'Uh,' I said. 'It's Lexy Campbell. And I'm not a doctor.'

'We understand you're not a medical doctor,' Lola said. Her eyes narrowed although her smile stayed as wide as ever. 'But tending to the emotional needs of the grieving Cuento community at this time is just as important. So tell me, what does the lost icon of Mama Cuento mean to you personally?'

'Uh,' I said again. What could I say? She was useful to navigate by in the grid of streets that otherwise sometimes fuddled me; she looked great yarn-bombed every year; I loved how there were hardly any pigeons in California towns so she wasn't covered in bird shit. 'I liked her feet,' I said. 'You hardly ever see public statues with bare feet.'

Lola opened her mouth to respond, but understandably came up empty.

'What Dr Campbell-Cameron means,' said Todd, 'is that it's a unique feature of Mama Cuento that she's as down to earth as the children who play around her. She speaks to a yearning for true connection to the land and for humble heroes who are just a step ahead on the path, showing us all the way.'

Swear to God, if not for her lip line and her dedication to preserving it, Lola would have drooled. 'Thank you, Dr Kroger. And you *are* a medical doctor, I believe?' She asked it in a tone of, *Please run away with me and make babies.* It's not the first time I've heard Todd affect someone that way. 'Anyone who turns to Trinity Solutions for grief counselling and advice on handling anxiety is going to be in very good hands,' she went on, but there was some kind of commotion taking place over at the shrine and we had lost her interest.

I looked over too and saw a young guy in a business shirt and tie, with a lanyard of keys round his neck, holding a piece of paper and talking excitedly to a gathering crowd of school-run mums, retired dog-walkers and a few buskers. It was too early for students.

Showing her nose for news, Lola set off at a sprint, with her cameraman following as if he was tied to her with a stout rope. Todd and I shared a look and scampered after them.

'It's a note,' the lanyard guy was saying, waving the piece of paper around like a surrender flag. 'Look, look, it's a note! Look.'

Lola jostled her mike into her left hand and reached to steady the sheet of paper, turning it to face the cameraman. 'Breaking developments, live from the scene of the Mama Cuento theft, as Aaron Tulpen' – God, she was good; she had read the guy's name tag from his lanyard – 'from the local Bank of America' – she had read the logo, too – 'discovers this bombshell.' It was a gamble. She hadn't read the note yet. She read it for the first time on air, her voice an octave lower as she reached for gravitas: '"Listen to our demands or you will never see her again. There are nine more where this came from." That's the cryptic ransom note discovered by bank clerk Aaron Tulpen and shared in an exclusive with this station, as developments in the Mama Cuento kidnap case come thick and fast.' She was a genius!

'It's not cryptic,' Aaron said, opening his hand to reveal a huge bronze toe.

The next half hour was chaos. Mike tried to arrest the bank guy, but two carpool mums linked arms around him and wouldn't let go, swearing he picked the note up, swearing he hadn't put it there himself. In all the commotion, he dropped the toe. A Labradoodle snaffled it, sucking on Aaron's salty sweat probably, and had to be bribed with a jam doughnut to spit it out again. The note tore as Mike was putting it in an evidence bag and the toe steamed up *its* evidence bag with dog saliva. Which made Mike angry enough to demand that the officers get rid of us riff-raff and loiterers. But the doughnut had made the dog puke and Soft Cop, rushing to clear the scene, skidded in the sick and grabbed the cameraman to steady himself.

So the footage that would play on a loop on the local news for the rest of the day, and feature on regional in the next three bulletins too, included shots that looked – even to me, who knew better – like police interference with the free press via an act of actual bodily assault. Lola was having a big day.

Todd and I were having a big breakfast, tucking into steak and eggs (me) and a chicken apple egg-white scramble (him) at the Red Racoon while we mulled it over.

'Who kidnaps a statue?'

'What demands?'

'Was she a real person? Is it like a land thing?'

'Sovereign nation? Was she a native leader?'

'How do you snap off a bronze toe?'

'What about those soccer moms forming a human shield?'

'Do we have any connections to CCTV in the downtown area?' That was me.

'What do you mean?' said Todd. 'Can we hack into a feed, you mean? I couldn't. We could ask Devin, I suppose.'

'Speaking of Devin . . .' I said, but this was no time for Last Ditch gossip. 'No, I meant, did you have a handy ex in one of the bars, or maybe your mum's got a pal in the bike repair shop over the road. Someone who'd let us watch the footage from last night.' Todd, being born and bred in Cuento, could often come through with an opportune acquaintanceship.

'Why?' he said. 'What makes you want to see footage of a statue being stolen?'

'Nothing,' I said. 'Nosy, that's all.'

'You are such a terrible liar, for a therapist. Tell the truth. Why do you want to see footage of a statue being stolen?'

'Because,' I said, 'I wouldn't trust the cops in this town to solve the riddle of where all the seeds went and what's wrong with the budgie.'

Todd leaned to one side and pulled out his phone. He hit a

button and held it out to me, the way Lola had held out her fluffy mike.

'Say that again,' he commanded. 'Say it on tape that you want to get involved in this and see if we can help find Mama Cuento.'

'Why are you being so weird?' I said instead. I had no idea why he'd gone all WikiLeaks receipts on me.

'Because,' Todd said, 'after we solved that murder that time, you did nothing but bitch and whine. And then after we solved that other murder that other time, you did nothing but bitch and whine.'

'This. Isn't. A. Murder,' I said. 'It's. A. Statue.' Then I found my integrity. 'But a hat-trick would be nice. Yes please,' I added, to the server who was offering coffee refills.

'You heard the news?' she said, as she plied the jug. 'You think it's a climate protest? A political thing? Think it's those damn Canadians again?'

'It's hard to say,' I plumped for. Which, unbelievably, seemed to satisfy her. 'What damn Canadians?' I asked Todd, when she was gone.

He shrugged. 'At least it wasn't "damn Mexicans". Makes a change.' Todd was half Mexican on his father's side – Kroger was his married name and Todd was short for Théodor – and, if you were going to diss a national neighbour around him, Canada was definitely the one to go for. 'How can you drink that over-roasted bile?' he said, nodding at my thick white mug of warmish, cloudy brew.

'I like my coffee like I like my men,' I said. 'Average but free refills.' Then, just too late, I remembered I shouldn't be making jokes that hinged on me and the men in my life.

Todd's eyes flashed fit to dim his diamond earrings and he whipped his phone back out again. 'What date is it today?' he said. 'Lexy, Lexy, Lexy, did you really think I'd forget?'

'I really knew you'd forgotten,' I said. 'Till I just reminded you.'

'And that's why you tried to distract me with some hare-brained scheme about investigating the kidnap?'

'Theft,' I said. 'Not kidnap. It's a lump of bronze.'

'Say that to anyone who comes for free grief counselling,

why don't you?' Todd said. '"It's a lump of bronze!" I thought you had learned something by now. "Your miscarriage was a clump of cells." "Your granny was a can of ash."'

'I didn't say either of those two things, for the five thousandth time. I said that an even later miscarriage would have been even more traumatic, and there was comfort to be taken. I said her grandmother's earthly remains weren't her essence, and that memories were perhaps more precious than a spilled . . . And, anyway, what did *you* do?'

'I took her shopping for better maternity clothes for next time and I scraped up enough granny to make a ring,' said Todd. 'Stop changing the subject. Right. Tonight, at seven thirty p.m. – I'll text you the name of the restaurant once I've confirmed. His name is Earl.'

'Ooh,' I said. 'That's promising.'

'He's an ER nurse. His sister works on Roger's ward.'

'This is actually sounding quite good. I don't suppose you've got a photo?'

Todd shook his head, his eyes wide and innocent.

'What's wrong with him?'

'What are your deal-breakers?' he asked me, instead of answering. What a sneaky move that was. Of course I'd sound shallow if I said there were any physical lines in the sand.

'Halitosis,' I suggested, for an easy start.

'Doesn't show up in pictures. Nice try.'

'Obscene tattoos? Utility kilt? Mullet?'

'All clear. Mullets are coming back, by the way. Anything else?'

'Suppurating pustules, vestigial twin, acid sweat.'

'Anything in the body-art department you've got a problem with?'

'What's pierced and how the hell do you know?' I asked.

'Just his ears,' Todd said. I watched as he finished his egg whites, dabbed his lips with a napkin and meshed his knife and fork neatly on his plate, drawing them slightly to one side, like a debutante's ankles.

'He hasn't got those stretchers in, has he?' I said.

'He's a nice guy!' said Todd.

'How big are they?'

'He's a great guy. Kind, funny, solvent. Loves kids and dogs obviously I'm making it up now but he really is.'

'How big are they?'

'I don't know. He has to take them out and roll the flaps for work, keep a bandage on them in case one of the ER drunks gets hold and rips his whole ear off.'

'So you can get your hand through,' I said. 'Why do you hate me? What did I ever do to you, except put up with you quietly? And keep your mum out of jail that time?'

'Is it so bad? When the rings are in—'

'Yes! It *is* so bad. Todd, you're not supposed to be able to throw something at a person and have it go through! Jesus.'

'By the terms of our agreement, though . . .' he said.

'I need to go on a date this week and next or I'm in breach of contract and liable for a waxy forfeit. Would he be willing to wear a hat with flaps, do you think?'

'I'll ask Roger to ask his sister to ask him, and get back to you.'

I paid the bill from the Trinity account and we left, a tentative peace stretched thinly over us.

'What *about* Devin, anyway?' Todd said, as we reached the motel again.

'He's got a girlfriend,' I said.

'Swine,' said Todd. 'Does Della know?' He couldn't have looked more chuffed to have trumped my gossip. To soothe myself, I decided to look in on Noleen as I passed the office. She couldn't care less about gossip, or my love life either. It was sometimes hard to say what Noleen did care about, actually, beyond Kathi's happiness and Devin's nutrition.

'Seen the news?' she asked, as I entered. She was behind the desk, as ever, but keeping a close eye on the continental-breakfast area: a basket of instant oatmeal, three apples and a microwave. 'Some sick fucker that hasn't got the balls to face a real woman has started defacing us in effigy. I'd like to see him take his pliers to *my* toe!'

'That's a theory,' I said. 'Misogyny. Did you hear they've sent a ransom note? Once they list their demands, we'll have a better idea what's behind it, I reckon.'

'A creep with mommy issues,' Noleen said. 'Dollars to donuts.'

'Does that mean the same as "heavens to Betsy"?' I asked her.

She laughed, which probably meant no, but she didn't enlighten me. Instead, she clicked her fingers as if only just now remembering something. 'There was someone in here, asking for you. I sent them to the boat.'

'Client?' I said, thinking of Todd's freebie offer. 'That was quick.'

'Nope, this looked personal.'

'Cop?'

'What a life you do lead, Leagsaidh.' I can always tell when she's saying my name in Gaelic rather than English. 'No, not a cop. Not a bailiff, not a bondsman. If I had to guess, I'd say he was a sexy doctor. Or maybe not quite a doctor.'

'A sexy nurse?'

'Coulda been a sexy nurse,' said Noleen, pushing her lips forward thoughtfully and nodding.

'Did you see his ears?' I asked. 'Was he wearing a hat?'

'I don't want to know about your fetishes,' said Noleen. 'I'm not judging. I just don't want to know.'

As I made my way round the side of the motel through the undergrowth, I really did try to open my mind. I had holes in my ears. Who was I to—? No, no, no, no, no. I had necessary holes in my ears, to hang pretty things from without squashing my lobes. He had to use plumbing bits to keep the holes in his creepy, floppy ears open.

He was still there. I knew that as soon as I reached the bottom step leading up to the front porch. I could tell there was a couple of hundred extra pounds somewhere on deck. Big guy, then. Big Earl, the ER nurse, so almost perfect for me.

He wasn't in the living room that stretches across the width of the boat and half the length. And he wasn't – why would he be? – in either of the midget bedrooms, with their box beds and Lilliputian wardrobes that sit on either side, just behind. The shower room was empty – I can only dream of a shower room so lavish anyone could hide behind its door – and there was no bum sticking out of the kitchen into the passageway, the way there would have been if someone was at the sink in there. It's really not that roomy.

So he was in the consulting room. I grabbed the door handle, told myself I needed a man – and what were earlobes anyway? I could get used to it, depending on the rest of the package – and opened the door.

He was facing the other way, looking out the window. Tall, white, short hair, nice shirt, bad jeans, terrible watch, but absolutely normal ears. Ears of the utmost averageness. Ears so unremarkable they even looked familiar. He started turning. His profile looked familiar too. One granite cheekbone, an eye, his high, strong nose, the other eye, the other cheekbone, the soft shadow that settled in the dimple in his chin.

It was Branston Lancer, my ex-husband: the reason I live in California, instead of cosily at home in Dundee.

'Lexy,' he said. And a tear rolled down one of those granite cheeks and dripped off the sheer cliff edge of his jawline.

I had never seen Bran cry before. I'd seen him happy; annoyed by waiters; angry at squirrels; gutted about a golf shot (his) or a touchdown (not his); transported in sexual ecstasy, close up, while we were on our honeymoon and during our brief marriage; and – crucially, if we're taking stock – transported in sexual ecstasy, from behind, while I watched him deciding he preferred his last wife, Brandeee, to his current wife, me. But that was the first tear I'd ever seen roll decoratively down his cheek.

'There's tissues,' I said, pointing at the box. 'What else can I do for you?'

'I'm sorry,' he said. He didn't take a hanky. Maybe he was too upset or maybe he knew bits of it would get caught in his perfect stubble. He shaved the stubble to that length every day.

'What for?' I said. 'We're all square. You've apologized already for everything you did and you haven't done anything new. Have you?'

'I'm sorry for this,' he said, raising his arms as if to display himself standing here in my house. Maybe to display his helplessness and his silent plea for mercy. Or maybe to display the bottomless oceanic entitlement it took to come here and cry at me as if I still owed him something. Cry just three perfect, Swarovski-style tears at me, by the way; no snot, no blubbing.

'How's Brandeee?' I said, not even having to try to get my voice as hard as gum on tarmac.

Bran closed his eyes and nodded, as if to acknowledge that I had every right to remind him. Or as if he'd forgotten his wife again, like I'd seen him do that time before.

'Brandee's gone,' he said. 'Lexy, I need you.'

FOUR

Hear me out.

Yes, he had married me to get back at his ex-wife for dumping him. And yes, he could have chosen someone who didn't need a green card to shack up with him while the spat played through. And yes, it only took a matter of weeks *for* the spat to play through. And the divorce was no fun. Actually, that's not true. The divorce was the most fun I'd ever had, holed up in a suite in Nevada, waiting six weeks for the paperwork to clear.

But I'd fancied him a year and a half ago and we'd had fun. And he would get Todd off my back. Or make Todd's eyeballs bleed with impotent fury at how dumb I was being. Win, win.

I opened my mouth to say . . . I dunno . . . maybe, *Kiss me, you fool*, like Maxim de Winter. Thankfully, the one brain cell that was still on self-respect duty, while the others headed south for a party, piped up just in time. 'So . . . did Brandeee leave because you need me? Or do you need me because Brandeee left?'

He frowned at me, puzzled. It should have been off-putting. Men looking stupid is usually off-putting to me. Seriously, some of the so-called heart-throbs you get on the cover of *People* magazine look so dumb it's creepy – like if you tried to point something out to them, they'd look at your finger.

But Bran looking at me with that out-of-depth expression only reminded me of our early days, before I'd picked up fluent American and he had not the slightest shred of Dundee. Those were the days when he would ask me about joining his 40l(k) and I'd say that was far too far and what a strange mile-count anyway; the days when I would say I thought I could smell Calor gas in the utility and he'd say he reckoned there was a skunk in the laundry room, and we'd both think our problem should be dealt with first.

'I don't understand,' he said, as he had so often in our whirlwind romance and extended honeymoon, about biros and Bramleys and the actual *The Office*, long after I'd got to grips with Sharpies and college lines and learned that no one went to sea in an HMO.

'Try,' I said.

'I don't trust the police,' he began. I think I managed to hide the mixture of surprise and delight, at hearing him in tune with me while not getting why it mattered. 'And I don't want to go to a private detective. It's so tacky. But I have to find her, Lexy. I'll die without her. And if someone's hurt her . . . If someone's harmed her . . .' Now he really was crying. He sucked in a big fluttery breath that made his bottom lip wang against his teeth and blew a bubble out of his left nostril as he let it go again.

'Brandeee's gone,' I said. Unbelievably, he still didn't twig. He thought I was sharing his pain or thinking aloud. He nodded and gave me a watery smile. This man, I often reminded myself, was a dentist. He'd been to college and passed exams in chemistry. He was one notch off being a doctor. I remembered Noleen agreeing my visitor might be a nurse and reminded myself to give her props for intuition when I saw her next.

'And I know you sorted out that thing,' he said. 'And then you sorted out that other thing.'

'How did you know that?' I said. 'And that?'

'From all the publicity,' said Bran. He took a tissue at last and blew his nose with an elephantine honk and a lot of success. 'You were in the *Voyager*. All three of you.'

I stared at him. Trinity Life Solutions got a good deal of positive press. Todd saw to that any day the sun came up. And we *had* been mentioned in passing in connection to two suspicious deaths as well, but I truly did not know until that moment that we had gained a reputation around town as . . . whatever Bran thought we were.

'There would be a cost,' I said. 'If it was up to me then mate's rates all the way. But my partners are hard-headed businesspeople.'

'I thought you were in with that disgraced knockout jockey,' said Bran. 'And the chick from the laundromat.'

Ah, there he was! There was the man I divorced, so very happily, so very recently. 'Yes, Todd is an anaesthetist,' I said. 'You have to have one doctor to do the anaesthetic when the other doctor's doing more than pull out a grey molar. And he's not disgraced, Bran. He's diversifying. Now, do you have time to come to the Skweeky Kleen with me and call Kathi a chick to her face or will we do it next time?'

'Gotcha,' he said. 'You won't help. Still too bitter. Gotcha, Lexy. Coming through loud and clear.'

'Oh, I'll help you,' I said. 'I'll work my buns off to find Brandeee and bring her home to you. I'll even eat my personal cut to do it on the cheap, if you need a break on your bill.'

'Thank you,' he said. He smiled and did that thing he always did, hitting himself in the forearm to bounce the wet tissue out of his other hand and into the bin. Or rather, at the bin. He missed every time. This time included. 'Thank you,' he repeated as he stooped to retrieve it. 'You've no idea what this means.'

But he was wrong. *He* had no idea what it meant, but I was very clear. It meant that I still hated him so much that I was willing to track down the tedious, prattling, shallow puddle of ketogenic me-time he was lumbered with by his own efforts and plop her back in his life to ruin every day until one of them dropped dead from the crushing weight of their own vapidity. How dare he call me bitter.

'We've got a case,' I said to Todd, as he said it to me, as we met on the doorstep of the Skweeky Kleen ten minutes later.

'Snap,' said Kathi. She was inside at the big table, folding shirts on to card and pinning them. 'Did anyone come for grief counselling, Lex?'

'Nope,' I said. 'Not yet, anyway.'

'And have you knocked out your five hundred yet?' she added.

Behind me, Todd was gesticulating lavishly. I could see him in the reflection off the washing-machine doors along the back wall. Kathi kept this place too clean for surreptitious gestures.

'I might not have mentioned that yet,' he said. 'But, since Kathi brought it up, the *Voyager* wants a piece on our attachment to symbols and emblems, and how to heal after desecration. For tomorrow.'

'Well then, let's hope the person who agreed to submit it is feeling creative,' I said. 'I'll read it over for you and check the spelling, if you get it to me before teatime.'

'You mean happy hour?' said Kathi.

'Leave me alone,' I said. 'That's not on the list.'

'Should be,' she mumbled through a mouthful of pins.

'Todd?' I said. 'Pick a side.'

'I don't care,' Todd said. A win for me. We were trying to annoy each other a bit less by not saying the words that bugged us all most – super-cute, binmen, mindfulness, that sort of thing – and there were fines involved.

Kathi blew a quick raspberry but accepted the result. 'And when you say "a case",' she asked, 'you don't mean a client, right?'

We already had plenty of clients. At first, it had been a revelation to me, the number of people in emotional distress who also wanted new clothes and a tidy kitchen, but I was getting used to it now. There was Marsha, whose depression went away along with her collection of gift bags and lidless Tupperware; Roy, the lonely mailman, whose head cleared as soon as Todd got him to stop hitching his trousers up to his windpipe, as if it was his belt that had been keeping him from speaking to women in coffee shops, offering them biscotti. Personally, I thought we had gone too far with Roy. He was getting to be a bit of a menace, and no one in his sixties should be in low-rise skinnies.

'I don't know what Lexy means,' Todd said, 'but I mean a case. I got the manager of the smoke shop to let me see the CCTV footage.' He was scrolling on his phone again. It was just as well for his dignity that he didn't have even the first hint of a bald spot, because he'd be showing it to the world most of the time. 'Huddle in and watch this,' he said, joining Kathi behind the folding table. The film was already running. Mama Cuento stood with her bare feet spread and her broad arms on her hips, gleaming very faintly here and there as the light of the nearest lamp post found its way to her forehead, chin, breast, knee and fateful toe.

'Did she say you could film it?' I asked. 'This manager.'

'He,' said Todd. 'He'd have let me film him in his bubble bath, if I'd asked. Seriously, is there a straight person left in this state?'

'Yeah, but did he?' I asked. In the course of our first two adventures Trinity had made the Cuento cops look a bit more Keystone-esque than they'd cared for and Detective Mike was itching to stick something on us.

'At the moment only I know,' said Todd. 'Do you want to know too, in case it comes up later?'

'I don't,' said Kathi. 'When does something happen? Oh!'

Something was happening right now in the gloom produced by the street trees, the midnight hour, the crappiness of the smoke shop's camera and the inevitable added crappiness of Todd filming it off the screen with his phone. 'Atmospheric' was an understatement. It was like those seasons of *The X Files* when Gillian Anderson was pregnant and they just dimmed the lights instead of having her stand behind things.

But as near as I could make out, someone had sidled up beside Mama Cuento and was festooning her. It looked a lot like a yarn bomber caught in the act except that whatever was being festooned had glints of metal about it here and there.

'Tow straps,' said Kathi. 'But unless that's the world's strongest man . . .'

'Wait,' Todd said.

The festooner strolled nonchalantly into the street light and off along the road. I scrutinized his black beanie, black sweats and black shoes. And it was about as worthwhile as that sounds, believe me. A moment later, someone else turned up in the shot, carrying a bulky load over one shoulder.

'Is that a grenade launcher?' I said, squinting hard at the tiny image.

'Jeez, drama queen of the month is in the bag,' said Todd. 'It's a chainsaw.'

'It's a skill saw,' said Kathi. 'A chainsaw would have woken up the neighbourhood.'

I wasn't so sure. By the time anyone who lived in the downtown had woken up, nudged their partner and said, 'What's that racket?' it would all have been over. Even the skill saw made short work of the bolts holding Mama Cuento to her plinth.

There was one interesting moment. The guy paused, bent down for a closer look, swiped something up off the ground and pocketed it. Then he finished the job, put the saw over his shoulder like a rolled umbrella and went the same way as the first one. Black beanie, black sweats, black shoes. Also black gloves, I noticed, pointlessly.

'Maybe the toe was an accident then,' Todd said. 'Maybe he found it in his pocket later and thought he'd have some fun.'

'Maybe,' I said. 'When do they actually—?'

Todd shushed me. 'You're going to want to watch this next bit.' The intersection had been deserted throughout the strapping and sawing, but now a pickup truck, one of the ones with a fat arse and double tyres that they call a 'doolie', came along the street towards the smoke-shop camera. It had no front number plate but then there's a lot of that about. In less than the time it would take the average driver to stop at the fourway, check for pedestrians and get going again, it had mounted the pavement and pulled up close to Mama Cuento, unfurling a crane from the middle of its truck bed, like a fern head in stop-motion. Someone who'd been lying down in the bed jumped up and did something out of sight of the camera, but it didn't take Sherlock to guess they were attaching the tow straps to the hook on the crane. When the truck started moving again, Mama Cuento leaned forward, as if she was keening, yearning for it to stay, then she rose up into the air, clear of the trees that usually sheltered her, and sank gently down beside the crane as it fell flat. The guy in the truck bed swung a tarp over the whole lot with a practised swirl of his wrist and, as the doolie raced away, the last thing we saw was him swinging himself round the back of the cab and in through the passenger-door window. We watched the tail lights until they dwindled to nothing and the tape stopped.

'The back plate was covered,' Kathi said.

'We'd never have been able to read it anyway,' said Todd.

'But they wouldn't have wanted to go far like that is my point,' she went on. 'They must have stopped somewhere else pretty soon and uncovered it. I hope you're right about every man in downtown gagging for you with his tongue out, Todd, because we're going to need to see more CCTV.'

'The police will be so far ahead of us,' I said, 'I think we should attack it from another angle.'

'Such as?' said Todd.

'No clue,' I said. 'Kathi?'

'Such as,' Kathi said, 'look at the way they got Mama Cuento out from under the trees, up in the air and down on to the truck bed without smashing her against anything. They must have practised. Scoped it out. I think we should ask the wait staff at the Cockroach if they've seen anyone hanging about.'

'Ssshh!' I said, pointing furiously at Todd. It wasn't like Kathi to be so thoughtless.

'It actually freaks me out less in English,' Todd said.

'I can't believe they named a restaurant that in any language,' I said.

'This was before your time, Lexy,' said Todd, 'but it never got above third place in the Worst Name in Cuento competition.'

'El Mono always scooped second,' Kathi said.

'Was the Last Ditch Motel the winner?' I said.

'Not even an honourable mention,' said Kathi. 'First place went to El Salmòn. Their name's picked out on a roundel with a bit of a squiggle between the two words so it looks like Salmonela, no two ways about it. And like they can't spell.'

'Which is why the competition got shut down,' said Todd. 'Three Mexican restaurants winning all three prizes? Between the woke brigade, who think Latins can't laugh at ourselves, and the old-school racists, who hate us winning anything, it got ugly.'

'Do you think *that's* got anything to do with *this*?' I said. 'I mean, Mama Cuento isn't Caucasian, is she?'

'And the guys in the beanies must be white,' Todd said. 'Carrying a chainsaw through town in the night and not getting stopped?'

'Skill saw,' said Kathi again.

'I've just thought of something,' I said. 'Wind it back to when they're driving away.'

'Wind!' said Todd, scraping the frames backwards with a finger until the beanie boy was throwing the tarp over Mama Cuento, then slithering round the edge of the cab and in through the passenger-door window.

'Can you open the doors on a low-rider?' I said.

'That's not a low-rider,' Todd said. 'Learn the culture, Lexy!'

'No, but look at him!' I insisted. 'Could *you* get yourself out of a truck bed and in through a window, on the move, in the dark? I was just thinking he must do it all the time.'

'Why wouldn't you be able to open the door on a low-rider?' said Todd.

'In case you scrape it on a high kerb,' I said. 'It was just a thought. Don't bite me.'

'Yes, you can open the door on a low-rider. And of course I could do that in-the-window move.'

'Let's see it,' I said. 'Show me. On Noleen's truck. Because I don't believe you.'

We spent ten minutes in the car park, with Todd standing up in the back of Noleen's Ford F-150, thinking it over, assessing the challenge and looking at the angles. Kathi and I watched him. Even Noleen came to the office door and watched him. A couple of tourists who were staying at the Last Ditch en route to Napa came and watched him.

'Yeah, I can't do it,' he said at last. 'Come up and look at it from here. You'll see.'

I swung up on to the bed and marched purposefully to the front. How I wished I could launch myself, à la the guy on the footage, slipping into the cab like a greased eel and bowing to the applause, but even thinking about it made me start to sweat.

'Certain death, right?' Todd said.

'Maybe it's easier if it's moving,' I said. 'Compensating . . . G-force . . . or counter . . .'

'I'll drive it round the parking lot,' Todd said. 'But I'm not driving you to the ER if you're dumb enough to try.'

'So,' Kathi said, 'this is a bona fide clue. Whoever that was has either been practising a whole lot or they took Mama Cuento away to the Cirque du Soleil.' Then she glanced at her watch. Kathi always wears a watch. She thinks it's more hygienic than forever touching your phone. As if she'd ever touch her phone. She keeps it in a disposable sleeve and still puts a latex glove over one finger, chopping off the contaminated bit of the glove afterwards and binning it, until all five are used up. Then she gets a couple of phone touches out of the palm section before she's done. 'For the environment,' she said, the first time I saw her at it. She wasn't joking. 'Right, gotta go,' she said. 'Big day for sheets, the day after Valentine's Day.'

'Bleurgh,' said Todd. 'But you better go too, Lexy. Big day for people finally getting therapy, I imagine. And you've got a date tonight, remember.'

'Yes, I have,' I agreed. 'But not with Earl. I've made my own arrangements. Ask Nolly.' I'd pay later when he pieced it all together, but later was better than now. 'Oh, and by the way,' I said, as I headed back to the boat. 'I've got a case for us too. Let's all have lunch at the Cockroach and I'll tell you.'

FIVE

had told Bran I would go round to his house – my ex-house! – later in the day, on two conditions. One: he had to tell the police that Brandeee was missing. I agreed that they wouldn't take it very seriously, since she was an adult and no one who ran away from him could be blamed, but they'd be able to do something, surely: check to see if her cards had been used or if she'd left her bag on a cliff with her driver's licence inside. Two: I was bringing my partners with me. Which shouldn't have been controversial, but Bran felt such an extreme level of shame about his woman taking off that he could only bear to discuss it with his other woman who'd also taken off. I think.

'No deal,' I'd told him. 'Trinity, Bran. Clue's in the name. It's all of us or none.'

'I'd be happier if I could talk to you alone, Lexy,' he said.

'Is there something that'll be tough to say in front of strangers?' I made my face very open and welcoming. I even put my head slightly on one side.

'Kinda,' he said.

'I see. Well, I can assure you Todd and Kathi are the most accepting, least judgemental individuals you could ever hope to meet.' In truth, Todd rated everything about everyone, from who-wore-it-besting babies in pull-ups to ranking multiple wives on how decoratively they all cried at a bigamist's funeral (Bravo channel's got a lot to answer for), and Kathi's withering stare could strip the white off rice. The point was that I loved them both and Bran had hurt me.

'Before we get there,' I said, 'I'd like you to assemble contact numbers for Brandeee's friends, colleagues, relations, acquaintances. I'd like a copy of her appointment diary for the last couple of weeks and any recent text exchanges with you. You said she'd taken her phone, right?'

'I said her phone's *gone*,' said Bran. 'I don't think she took it, because I don't think she left.'

I'd forgotten how pedantic he could be. He was so pedantic that the one and only time I called him a pedant he corrected my pronunciation.

'Until then – we should be there about three-ish – why don't you go to work and keep busy?' I hesitated over that advice, actually. Was a distracted dentist such a great idea?

'Yes,' he said. 'I need to keep the practice afloat for her to come back to. That's what Brandee would want.'

'She would,' I said. If she had skipped out on him, she most definitely wouldn't want the business to lose value before they split it.

I was still thinking that over as I waited for my first actual client of the day. *I* hadn't tried to get much of a settlement out of Bran, here in our sunny community-property state. It didn't seem fair, since we had only been married ten minutes and I should have known better. But Brandeee, from the few times I had met her, struck me as a very different kind of gal. She had bored me rigid talking about swapping credit cards to get interest-free months and changing insurers to screw out better deals. No way she'd walk away from her own half of a business and her share of Bran's horrible house. Unless she was the one with the serious wedge. Lord, these were going to be ticklish things to ask. Thank God Todd and Kathi were coming with me.

And thank God for my morning clients too. At ten o'clock, I had the third hour with a straight-up unemployed loner trying not to sink into depression while he was on a job search. All I had to do was listen to him weigh up the challenge of abandoning his dream career – tree surgeon – against the challenge of another month eating instant noodles and mending his shoes with gaffer tape. At least that's what I thought, but then he switched it on me.

'What would you do?' And he didn't want to hear about positive thinking or affirmative self-talk either. He wanted me to tell him what to do. A lot of people want someone to tell them what to do. And since this guy's parent-provided mental-health insurance was just about to run out on his twenty-sixth birthday, he wanted me to tell him today.

'I'd do two things,' I said. 'Put together a forty-hour week on whatever you can get – Starbucks, Walmart, call centre – while volunteering at the arboretum for another five hours and doing all your job applying in your down time. Red Bull, if you need to keep awake. Tell the people you're applying to that you're self-supporting and you're proud of it. And take the first job you get offered, no matter where it is. Even Alaska.'

'How will I get there?'

'Ask them for relocation expenses. Or hitchhike. You're twenty-five. Soon enough you'll be needing new knees and wondering why you never see your grandkids.'

'Are you sure you're a therapist?' he said.

'Yes, and my ambition is to go out of business because everyone's OK.'

'Have you ever been depressed yourself?'

'Not yet, thank God and all His angels. It's scary stuff. So that was all the first thing. I also think you should go and see your doctor and get a ninety-day prescription of something good and strong before your insurance goes *pfft*. Then hang on to it in case you need it. You can Google dosage and all that. Unless you've ever felt suicidal. In which case please don't get a hundred and eighty pills and hoard them. Have you?'

'Of course I have. Haven't you?'

'Hasn't everyone? But you know what I mean.'

'*Are* you a therapist?'

I thought about getting insulted but managed to convince myself it was a compliment. He looked a bit chirpier as he left anyway.

'Keep in touch,' I said. 'Send me a postcard from Anchorage.'

My eleven o'clock was a woman in her forties, on her third marriage, who thought she was a crap mother and a lazy friend, and wished she could talk to her parents about how she was feeling before it was too late.

'What would you say?' I asked her.

'I don't know.'

'What would you say if you did know?' I asked her.

'I'd say, "Why did you never tell me I was special or clever or pretty or welcome or precious?" Why did they never tell me they loved me? Or tell me I was safe? Or that they'd always be there? Or that I could tell them anything and they'd believe me?'

'What did you want to tell them?' I asked her. 'That they wouldn't believe?'

'I don't know.'

'What would you have told them if you did know?' I asked her.

She stared at the floor for a bit. Then she raised her eyes and stared at me.

'Those fuckers!' I said.

I didn't nudge the box of aloe-impregnated tissues towards her when she finally started to cry. Sometimes it's important to feel the tears run and drop. Sometimes nothing else will do but ropes of snot hanging from your chin.

She didn't say much more that hour. She mostly listened to me swearing. But she did promise out loud that she would go to the matinee of *Frozen II* with a box of cashew brittle before she went home to make the dinner. I told her I was holding her to it, on her honour.

'Your children can eat toast and jam for one night,' I said.

'I'm supposed to be baking an eggplant,' she said. 'I can't make them suffer for my problems.'

'If your kids would rather eat baked eggplant than toast and jam, they've got bigger problems than you anyway,' I said. And I managed to get a laugh out of her. Not that I compete against myself on that index and keep a tally in their files or anything.

I hugged her goodbye. 'You're great,' I said. 'You're a bloody marvel. I know that doesn't help. I know you being a marvel means everyone else got lucky. I know you'd rather *they* were marvellous and you just soaked it up like a lucky sod. But think about how much worse life might feel if you were shit. Eh?'

She sort of half-laughed again. 'Sometimes it's hard to believe you're a trained clinician.'

'Thank you,' I told her. 'Remember that next time, when I start digging. Now go. Cashew brittle! *Frozen II*!'

So I was feeling pretty in tune with the universe – OK, smug – as I headed up to La Cucaracha for lunch. I reckoned I'd earned myself some refried beans and cheese. Or a vat of hot soup with hominy and bones floating in it.

Maybe I was going native at last. I tried to imagine whether I'd call today chilly and be thinking about soup in Dundee, or whether I'd be in a T-shirt and sandals, thinking spring had sprung. I certainly wouldn't be muffled up in a lined hat, furry gloves and Uggs, like half the Cuento-ites I was passing. I'd definitely swum in the North Sea on colder days when I was a nipper.

'I've just worked something out,' I said to Todd and Kathi as I slid into the booth they had snagged at the restaurant. They were always early everywhere, to check for bugs and dirt without anyone tutting and rolling their eyes. 'You lot run for the wellies and balaclavas as soon as the weather dips below blistering, just like we're all in our spaghetti straps as soon as the frost clears. I thought you were wimps but it's not that at all, is it? It's just so you can make sure and wear it, since you've bought it. In Dundee, if you don't wear a sundress one day in May when it stops raining, the next dry day might be Christmas Eve, ten below zero.'

'What's a balaclava?' said Kathi.

'Would I suit one?' said Todd.

'It covers your face,' I told him.

'Oh well no,' he said. 'That wouldn't be fair on everyone else.'

I reached for the menu, but Todd told me he already ordered, which meant I was going to be lunching on salad. Again. He had inadvertently seen me naked just after New Year – what a shocker, that bursting into a woman's bedroom might find her déshabillé – and decreed that I had seven pounds to lose before he could face any friend he set me up on a date with.

Kathi had a jumbo burrito with everything and two baskets of tortilla chips. Woman doesn't have an ounce of spare flesh on her anywhere. Todd had ceviche and pickled carrot. He'd be necking the Pepto by teatime.

'So,' I said, when we had been served, 'as well as the case of the nine-toed bronze giant that we seem to have decided to horn in on, I've got some interesting news for you. We have just landed an actual paid investigative gig. Waddaya thinka that?'

'What is it?' Kathi said.

'A missing person, but what I really meant was, how *amazing* is that? The last couple of times were accidental, or inadvertent, anyway, but this is a job. A case. I've quoted an hourly rate and a retainer, negotiated expenses. Pretty incredible, eh?'

Kathi took a gargantuan bite. She was into the middle bit of the burrito now, where you've really got to commit to proper mouthfuls if it's not all going to fall apart. Todd bent low over his plate of ceviche and picked away with his fork like an archeologist brushing dust from the face of a pharaoh.

'What don't I know?' I said. 'What did I miss?'

'No idea,' said Todd. 'You're in charge of how up to date you choose to stay. Not Kathi and me.'

I ate a couple of bites of salad. It was the really annoying kind where the bits are too big to scoop up on your fork and too thin to be speared. It was more like Whac-A-Mole than eating. 'So . . . I've not been keeping up to date,' I said, hoping if I spoke in a threatening voice one of them would crack, 'and Bran managed to suss out that we might be up for finding a missing person. And you two look as guilty as . . . I haven't seen anyone look as shifty as you two today, since . . . Oh my God!' I whipped my phone out and punched the shortcut for the Trinity Solutions website. I knew when I'd seen them looking like that before. When they unilaterally upped and joined my counselling practice to their obsessions, they'd looked exactly that way: like butter would sizzle to black in a second in their mouths.

Trinity for Life, I read off my phone. *Trinity for Home. Trinity for You.* At least they had eventually put me first, after a lot of bickering. But I was right. There was a new one: *Trinity for Trouble: whether it's a stray cat or a long-lost loved one, Trinity offers affordable, dependable investigations. Try Trinity for Rapid Results!*

'Wh—?' I managed to get out, before the enormity of it winded me.

'After the press we got, it seemed like a no-brainer,' said Kathi.

'Oh it's a no-brainer!' I said. 'It's a no licence, no training, no experience no-brainer!'

The server was instantly at our table, smiling and frowning simultaneously. 'Everything OK here?'

I hadn't realized I was shouting.

'Fine,' said Todd. 'This ceviche is like velvet. Tell the chef.' He turned to me as she walked away. 'Do you know how you *get* a licence? Same deal as your state board of shrinks thing. You rack up hours. So, we start counting today.'

'I don't want to rack up hours as an investigator,' I said. 'All my hours are going on the rack I'm already racking them on, Todd. And you're a doctor! You can't give up on the idea of going back one of these days. You can't distract yourself this much.'

'He's not,' said Kathi. 'I am. Unless you think I shouldn't aspire to get out of the laundromat and do something more with my life?'

'You love that launderette,' I said. 'What do you mean, "something more"?'

Kathi looked at me with a pained expression on her face. 'Where did you get the idea that I love the laundromat?' she said. 'I prefer it to scuzzy bedrooms full of strangers' toe jam. And I do believe the phthalates in the softener keep my sinuses clear. But "love"?'

That stopped me dead. Had I been ignoring my friend dying of boredom in a dead-end service job, just because she was stoic and never complained about it? Just because she was such a marked contrast to Noleen, who moaned all day long about everything to do with the motel business, from the city taxes falling due in December to the guest cars with oil leaks messing up her car park.

'I need something new, Lexy,' Kathi said. 'Now more than ever. Noleen won't even consider a family and I need a way to fill the void in my life where a baby will never be.'

'Ohhhhh!' I said. 'Riiiiighhht! It's a wind-up. Well, fuck you for giving me heart failure, you evil bastard.'

'Admit it,' said Kathi. 'I got you!' She took another mammoth bite and grinned through it at me.

'For one second, you got me. Half a second more like. So what's the real story?'

'If you're not expanding, you're falling behind,' Todd said. 'First rule of business. I was looking at the city and county business records.'

'Why?'

'To monitor closures of counselling, clutter and clothing concerns,' said Todd. 'To see if we're beginning to have a monopolizing effect on our competitors. I'd like to see every other counsellor in Cuento shut up shop and leave town with a duffel bag.'

'Lovely,' I said. 'Heart-warming. And are they?'

'No,' said Todd putting his fork down. 'It really is just raw sour fish, when you get right down to it, ceviche.' He pulled Kathi's second basket of tortilla chips closer and scooped up a blob of cheese that had plopped out of her burrito despite her expert handling.

'Hey!' she said.

'No sniffles, no stomach troubles, no cold sores, no need to worry,' he said. 'Can you squirt some more out? I'm starving.'

'Todd,' I said. 'Not to be a fusspot or anything, but what you've just said in no way explains why I am now a private detective.'

'It does,' he said. 'Because it's the fastest-growing business category in Beteo County for companies smaller than ten employees, and I didn't want to miss out when we've got such a head start in name recognition and goodwill.'

I whacked another seven calories' worth of limp lettuce up on to my fork tines and went wild with it. 'I'm just glad it wasn't septic services,' I said. 'Or pool cleaning.'

'Or martial-arts centres,' said Todd. 'Those doboks look like cotton, but a lot of them are a polyester blend. Can you imagine how sweaty they get?'

'I don't have to,' said Kathi. 'You think those people wash their own? I see them and smell them every day.'

'But,' I said, just checking, 'you don't hate the launderette. You were only messing with me.'

'I love the laundromat,' Kathi said. 'It kept us afloat when the motel was struggling. However, when I'm Beteo County's only master launderess and licensed private dick, I'll be even happier than I am now.'

'Absolutely no way,' Todd said. 'Ten-dollar penalty. Agreed, Lexy?'

'Agreed.'

'Master launderess and licensed gumshoe,' Kathi said, after a moment's thought. 'So . . . this missing person, Lexy?'

Todd was still crunching his way through the tortilla chips and he choked himself a little, while gasping. 'Hang on!' he said, spluttering and turning streaming eyes on me. 'Rewind. Did you say "Bran"? Does that mean who I think it means?'

'I've said we'll go there this afternoon and take the details,' I told them. 'You two and me, on a trip down memory lane.'

SIX

I hadn't lived in Bran's Beige Barn for very long, but going back kicked up a complicated storm of emotions all the same. After all, it was the backdrop to the toughest day of my life, when I'd admitted to myself I had turned my entire existence upside down for a man who wasn't worth a second date and I was now penniless, friendless and thousands of miles from home. On the other hand, it was the first American house I had ever been inside and I could remember with affection how it felt to be that close to one of those cavernous fridges like in the movies, and a garbage disposal in the sink ready to take me off at the elbow, a ceiling fan straight from Tennessee Williams, a top-loader washing machine the size of a Mini Cooper. I had been happy here. More than once.

'Jesus,' said Todd when we were parked outside. 'You never told me it was a McMansion.'

'I probably didn't know the word when I moved out,' I said. 'And, after that, it wasn't relevant. I always called it the Beige Barn. It's the most ferociously open-plan house that's ever passed a building inspection – hence "barn". And everything inside it? If it comes in beige, it's beige.'

'I believe you,' Todd said. 'Are those beige flowers up the sides of the walkway?'

'Probably,' I said. 'But have you really never seen it? Have you never idly driven up here to have a neb at where I used to live? I'm hurt.'

'Why the hell would I do that?'

'Huh,' I said. 'You really are a guy. Sometimes – what with you being gayer than a G.I. Joe salt shaker – I forget.'

'Offensive,' said Todd. 'But inventive. Back me up here, Kathi. It's nothing to do with gender.'

Kathi shrugged. 'Noleen and I might have done a drive-by to see what you were giving up, Lex,' she said. 'We ate fish tacos and put the wrappers in his shrubbery for you.'

'I'll never understand women,' Todd said, climbing out of the car. 'Between this and that midwife show. Space aliens.'

'I love me some nun on a Sunday night,' said Kathi, following him.

So I was left alone to steel myself. It's only a house, I repeated. It's here every day when you get up and go to bed again. It has no power over you. It's not magic. But still, as I walked up the path between the billows of flowers that – Todd was right – weren't quite pink or yellow, but something in between, I couldn't help remembering floating in a pool of clean blue water instead of in a boat on a slough full of algae, driving my air-conditioned car to my rented office instead of hoping my clients couldn't smell last night's curry while they were baring their souls. And I couldn't forget the moment when Bran said, 'I need you, Lexy,' and I had wavered, so briefly and so invisibly, but so undeniably too.

The door was opening. I stiffened my spine and resolve, ready to show off to my friends with a barrage of subtle trolling and put-downs. But what was this? Bran lurched out on to the doorstep, pure white and shaking. He had a letter in his hand and his other fist was clutched tightly around something too small to see.

'Oh God,' he said. 'Oh God. She's been kidnapped! Someone's taken her! Look, look!'

The way he was shaking the piece of paper in our faces was far too familiar for my liking. I shared a panicked glance with Todd and then stepped forward.

'"Agree to our demands or you will never see her again",' I read out loud. A look pinged around Todd, Kathi and me.

'Is that it?' Todd asked, wincing.

I shook my head and read the rest of it. '"There are nine more where this came from."'

'Brandee!' Bran wailed. 'Oh, Brandee, ba-aby!' His voice broke and he fell on Todd's neck, sobbing like a child. Todd patted and shushed and even smoothed Bran's sweaty hair back from his face, but all the while with his other hand he was pointing at me and at Bran's clenched fist, trying to get me to . . . I don't know what he was trying to get me to do. Keep it away from his cashmere jumper, maybe?

It was Kathi who stepped in. 'Branston?' she said, in a gentle voice I had never heard her use before. 'Can you open your hand and let that drop into this baggie I've got here? There might be evidence on it. There might be DNA or even fingerprints.'

I looked away as I saw Bran's fist start to loosen, then found myself looking back. What is that about us? Why have we got that impulse? You'd think once it had brought us Dr Pimple Popper we would have tried a bit harder to put it out of commission.

In this instance, the repulsive beast that lives inside didn't get much of a feast. Barely a snack, actually. Because it wasn't one of Brandeee's toes that dropped into Kathi's outstretched baggie; it was one of her nails. And not even one of her real nails. Just one of her acrylics.

At least I assumed so. 'Bran?' I said. 'Is that definitely Brandeee's?'

He lifted his head and glared at me. 'Would that matter?' Good point. 'But yes it is. We go together. I have a citrus power pedi; Brandee has a butter pedi, a head massage and a spa manicure. She gets all three at the same time so she's finished when I'm finished. She's low maintenance.'

He meant it. It was touching in a funny sort of way.

'And have you called the police?' Todd said, finally letting Bran go, with one last manly pat on his shoulder. 'Because this changes everything.'

'I know,' said Bran. His tone was hard to decipher. It might have been that he didn't like some other guy telling him things. 'I haven't had the chance. I only got it two minutes ago. Come inside and I'll call them now.'

Kathi was bagging the note, and Todd was squaring up to Bran for some bizarre male reason, so it looked like I was expected to lead the way, walking back into the Beige Barn, the scene of my downfall, the backdrop to my heartbreak. Besides, even if I had hung around until Todd stopped the chest-beating and Kathi finished the bagging, I knew they'd both find something else to do. Minuscule as the chances were of a dentist living in squalor or of my ex-husband having a tank of tarantulas I'd never mentioned, Todd and Kathi didn't want to be the first ones across the threshold of a stranger's house. I forget sometimes what a daily dose of debilitation their conditions are. So, I readied myself for a pang of regret or a wave of nostalgia and opened the door.

I should have known nostalgia and regret couldn't survive the beigeness of these floors, walls, ceilings, art, furnishings and fruit accent on the kitchen island. Seriously, there was a bowl of Asian pears set out, as if an estate agent's stager lived here. The only beige fruit in the world. I was going to be fine.

Todd led Bran to the pair of stone-coloured couches facing each other across an oatmeal-coloured coffee table – I'm trying to be kind – where a book of photographs celebrating deserts of the world lay open at a double-page picture of a sandscape. Earth tones, inevitably.

'Lexy, you know where everything is,' Kathi said. 'Can you get him a glass of water?'

I did indeed know where the complicated equipment might be found that would allow one to produce a glass with some water in it. Glaring at Kathi, I headed over to the kitchen area, to where the taupe carpet gave way to sepia vinyl. I took a tumbler from one of the ecru cabinets and set it down on the fawn tiles of the worktop.

But I'm not a monster and Bran really was in a bit of a state, so instead of turning the tap on and starting the inevitable round of carping about the filtered water in the fridge, the exquisite safety of the Cuento water supply, the toddlers in Indonesia dying of dysentery who could be saved for the price of a Brita cartridge . . . I decided to honour my ancestry and make him a cup of sugary tea. The teabags were where I had left them – the way that Brandeee's cuticle oil had been where she'd left it when I moved in – and although the kettle was long gone, I microwaved a mugful, telling myself we hadn't been together long enough for him to find it insulting. There was no sugar, of course, because they're dentists. But there was honey, because they're morons, and I stirred in a good big dollop before rejoining the three of them at the couches, where Trinity for Trouble's first official investigative interview was already underway.

'No, I didn't hear a car or footsteps,' Bran was saying. 'I

went to the door because I was looking out for you all arriving. And I looked down and saw the envelope on the mat.'

'Where's the envelope now?' Kathi said.

'Recycling,' said Bran.

'Lexy?' Kathi was really milking the fact that I knew this place. I went out to the laundry room, leaving the door propped so I could hear what was said, and fished a plain brown envelope out from the top of the paper box, using a sheet of kitchen paper.

I brought it back and laid it on the coffee table face up. It finished the colour scheme off to a T.

'Hand delivered,' Todd said. 'We can ask the neighbours if anyone saw anything.'

'It's not that kind of neighbourhood,' I said.

'Not what kind of neighbourhood?' said Bran, still very upset but recovered just enough to pick me up on a cross word.

'They tend to leave their garages in their Miatas and check texts until they reach the junction with the main road,' I said. 'I nearly got mowed down a couple of times when I was out walking.'

'We had a state-of-the-art treadmill for walking on,' said Bran. 'And it's only two blocks to the park for leisure walking, with free two-hour parking. What do you expect?'

'I'm just saying,' I told him, 'that the neighbours wouldn't notice a life-sized unicorn, unless it was selling cookies without a permit. Anyway, you saw the envelope . . .?'

'Picked it up, opened it, read it and was going back outside to see if I could . . . I don't know. For help? To look in case whoever left it was still out there? And you were arriving. What size is a life-sized unicorn anyway, Lexy?'

He had a point.

'I'm so glad we *were* arriving,' said Todd. 'We can support you. Now, are you ready to call nine-one-one?'

'Would *you* do it?' said Bran. If I didn't know from my own unforgettable lived experience that he was right up one end of the sexuality continuum, with an interest in the contents of women's knickers second only to the World Gynaecologists' Association's Annual Gathering and Bingo Night, I'd have said he was flirting. He had certainly done the Princess Diana chin-dip and eye-raise. I cast a glance at Kathi to see if she had noticed, but I knew from the way she was staring at her hands that she was lost in thoughts of what she'd been touching and how she could get into a bathroom without coming into contact with its door handle, and what she would do if the taps were the kind you had to twist on and off with a tight grip.

Todd was dialling. 'Police,' he said and waited.

Bran sipped his tea. It was putting some colour back in his cheeks, which, when he'd paled under his tan, had turned quite – you guessed it – beige.

'Yes, I want to report a missing person. Well, a kidnap.' Another pause. 'Because there's a ransom note . . . A wife . . . Her husband . . . No, I'm not. He's too upset to talk. I'm a . . . friend.' Another pause. This one lasted long enough for me to start gesturing at him to hand over the phone.

'Who am I talking to?' I said, when I'd got the phone in my hand and Todd was glowering at me.

'Oh. You're back,' said the despatcher.

'What?'

'Did you have an argument? Are you safe, ma'am, or should officers attend?'

'What? Oh! No, I'm not the wife. I'm the ex-w— doesn't matter. Brandeee Lancer of three-one-four-five Camino Loop has been kidnapped and we think it's the same people who took Mama Cuento and left her toe.'

'She left her toe?' said the despatcher, with her voice rising to a squeak.

'Not Mrs Lancer! Last night. Someone left behind Mama Cuento's toe. And the note's the same. *What?*' That was to Bran who was waving at me trying to butt in.

'She's a doctor and she combined her names,' he hissed at me.

'Sorry,' I told the despatcher. I dredged deep into my memory of our divorce papers and found what I was searching for. 'Her name's not Mrs Lancer. It's Dr Rumsfeld-Lancer.'

'Are you high?' said the despatcher. I'm sure it wasn't one of the questions on her checklist.

'I know!' I said. 'Imagine not ditching Rumsfeld. Be that as it may— *What now?*' Bran was waving again.

'Kowalski-Lancer,' he said. But I couldn't face the scorn of the despatcher if I switched it again.

'This toe injury,' she was saying. 'Do you need an ambulance? Do you have it iced? It might be quicker to take her to the emergency room in your car, but I can call and tell them you're coming. What insurance does Dr Rumsfeld have? Are you a family member?'

I shoved the phone at Kathi, unbagged and straight into her gloveless hand. 'We're looping,' I said. 'You try.'

'We need an officer at three-one-four-five Camino Loop,' Kathi said, 'for a two-seven-three-D. Thank you.' She hung up. 'I need to wash my hands,' she said. 'Lexy, you know where it is, don't you?'

'What was that?' I said as I led her along the bedroom corridor to the half bath.

'That was ten years in the motel business,' she said. 'Two-seven-three-D is police code for a felony domestic abuse.'

'Kathi!'

'I know. I'll tell them I got the code wrong. But, (a) it's the quickest way to get a cop here without saying "officer down", and (b) I don't know what number kidnap is, anyway. Back me up if it gets ugly, OK?'

She had run the hot water and now she was applying germicidal handwash as if prepping for surgery.

I can't be in a loo without peeing and Kathi can't be close to someone else's pee because of the completely imaginary risk of a non-existent infection, so I went back to Todd and Bran.

'When did you last see Brandee?' Todd was saying.

'She was in bed with me when I fell asleep on Valentine's Day Eve,' Bran said.

'So you came to me the very next morning?' I said. 'How hard did you try to find her?'

'Not Valentine's Day in the evening, Lexy,' said Bran. 'Valentine's Day Eve. The day before.'

'That's not a thing,' I said. 'And it's still pretty quick to be getting help. Thirty-six hours?'

'Thirty-six Valentine's Day hours,' said Bran.

'That's not a thing either,' I said. 'You said it like it's dog years.'

'Valentine's Day is Brandee's favourite holiday,' Bran said. 'It's her birthday. And it's the day we met. The day we married—'

'No, it's not,' I said. 'You were still— Oh. The first time, you mean?'

'When I woke up and she was gone, I thought she had slipped out of bed to arrange a surprise for me. So I didn't get up and go looking for her, in case I spoiled it. It was only around seven forty-five, when I hadn't heard a sound, that I started searching.'

'And you did search right through the entire house, I suppose?' said Todd.

Kathi was back. 'The police will, anyway,' she said.

'Of course I did,' said Bran. 'I knew she hadn't left, so I thought she was hiding somewhere, perhaps in a costume or . . . you know, not . . . so I went looking for her. House, garage, pool, yard . . . I even went into the roof space, in case she had prepared . . .'

'A sex dungeon?' I said.

'As long as I live in California,' said Kathi, 'I'll never stop missing basements.'

'And what has she taken with her?' Todd asked next, getting the same answer as I had.

'She didn't *take* anything *with* her. She didn't *go*. Not by choice. Her phone's gone but that's because whoever took her took her phone too.'

'Did they take her wallet? Her keys? Her ID?' said Kathi.

'Who cares if they took a stupid wallet!' said Bran. 'They took my wife!' He was getting himself so upset I wondered which one of us would be brave enough to ask the next question. But thankfully we were all saved by the sound of a car pulling up outside, doors slamming and feet tramping up the path with a determined tread.

An unmistakable police knock sounded at the door and a voice shouted, 'Po-lice! Open up!'

Of course it was Mike. Of course it was. There were other detectives in the Cuento squad, but, if I was anywhere around, Mike came down on me like she was attached to a pulley.

'Does anyone need medical assistance?' she asked as she

swept past Kathi, walking with that gorilla-style lope, shoulders bundled forward, that some police think gives them what
they call – pitifully – 'a strong command presence'. It would
have helped if Mike wasn't five foot four with a mop of curls
and a figure like a mini Jessica Rabbit. Or maybe that just
made it all the more important for her to try to look intimi-
dating. I managed not to say 'Bless!' and chuck her under
the chin.

'I'm all right, officer,' said Bran. 'I was a little faint but my
ex-wife got some sugar in me.'

Mike was slowly taking in the cast of characters in Bran's
living room, while a uniformed officer I didn't recognize
stood behind her, gawping at the fittings. The Beige Barn,
admittedly, has got some swank about it, albeit swank that
looks as if it's been soaked in weak tea.

'And who hit who?' Mike said. 'Which two of you are
domestic partners anyway?'

The uniformed officer cleared his throat.

'Godammit,' said Mike. 'I mean, which of you are domestic
participants?'

She'd been on a course about new family structures, I
reckoned. It wasn't fair to laugh, but I didn't know which
of the three – Bran, Todd or Kathi – looked more horrified
by the very suggestion.

It didn't take too long to straighten out. Mike was happier to
think that Kathi had made a mistake with the police code than
to think they'd peeled up here because a civilian played them
and, when she saw the note and nail, all that went out the
window anyway. She asked the same questions as Todd had
about the timing of Brandeee's disappearance, and she sent
the uniform to search the house with a subtle jerk of her chin
while Bran had his head briefly in his hands. But then she
asked a few extra questions too: had Bran and Brandeee been
getting along? How was business? Any trouble with co-workers?
And did he have any recent connections to La Cucaracha?

'To what?' said Bran. 'Is that a gang?'

'It's a taqueria,' said Mike. 'Downtown. You know about
the other incident, don't you?'

Bran swallowed hard. 'There's been another kidnap?' he said weakly. 'When?'

'Doesn't matter,' said Mike. The uniform was back, giving her a subtle shake of the head. 'Mr Lancer, we're going to take the note and nail away for testing and we'll be sending someone out to ask you more detailed questions later today. In the meantime, do you have someone who can stay with you?' She flicked a glance at the three of us, sitting in a row on the other couch like three wise monkeys. Or possibly stooges. 'Any family?'

'Blaike!' I said suddenly, only just now remembering about Brandeee's son. 'Where is he?'

'School,' said Bran.

'He's OK enough to go to school?' I said. 'The poor boy must be—'

'Boarding school,' said Bran. 'I haven't told him yet. I didn't want to worry him.'

'We'll have to speak to your son, Mr Lancer,' Mike said. 'Your wife might have been in touch with him after her last contact with you.'

'Of course,' said Bran. 'I'll give you his contact details, but can I ask you to wait until I've had a chance to break the news to him?'

'Absolutely,' Mike said.

'Meantime, we'd better be getting off,' I said. 'Unless . . . Bran, *have* you got someone else who could come and be with you? Or one of us could stay, if you'd prefer?'

'I'll call Elise.'

'Daughter?' said Mike. 'Mother? Sister?' She was going to make him choose a way to describe this woman whose name had come so effortlessly to mind as soon as he was pressed to find someone he could lean on. That was my first inkling that she suspected him.

'Dental receptionist,' Bran said. 'Co-worker and very close friend of us both. And, since we will have to close the practice, I know she's not working today.'

'Aye right!' I said, as we walked down the path. 'What do you bet there's no way Elise would get her white crocs over the door if Brandeee was there?'

'But he sounded genuinely freaked out by the ransom note,' Kathi said. 'Genuinely upset all around. And you said he was crying when he came to see you at the Ditch too.'

'Genuinely upset?' said Todd. 'You mean when he said, "Brandee! Oh, Brandee, ba-aby"? Jesus, have you never seen *Grease*? That was the stagiest thing I've ever heard and I've heard the Sacramento Gay Men's Choir doing *Oklahoma!*'

'You're just pissed off because he can't speak Spanish,' I said.

We were back at the car and, as Todd climbed into the driver's seat, he gave me a solemn look in the mirror. 'No, Lexy,' he said. 'I'm pissed off because he thought some random Spanish phrase he didn't recognize was a gang name. Seriously, why did you ever marry him?'

'Same reason you wore denim dungarees in the eighties,' I said. I had seen a lot of Todd's old photos by now. 'We all make mistakes.'

'And Brandee made the same mistake twice,' said Kathi. 'But do you think he's capable of harming someone?'

'He's capable of sending a kid to boarding school,' Todd pointed out. 'And those were grievous sins against taste going on in there too.'

SEVEN

Funny old world, I thought, as I walked up the path of the next-door neighbour. I'd decided that there was no time like the present and had got back out of the car again, leaving Todd and Kathi to go downtown without me.

I'd never knocked on this door when I lived at the Beige Barn and so I had no idea who was going to answer it, my Cuento expertise not being well honed enough yet to hazard a guess based on planting and window treatments. Prayer flags and flag flags I knew, and I was starting to get a bead on cactuses versus geraniums – put it this way: you'd be surprised to find a Trump lawn sign snagged on a prickly pear – but this garden had lots of rocks and a couple of Japanese maple trees, with a swing on the porch . . . Hard to call. I rang the doorbell and waited, composing an opener that didn't sound too mad to deliver.

'About time.' A man answered the door, practically pulling it off its hinges. 'Are your shoes clean?'

'Uhhh,' I said.

'Let's go round.' He came out on to the porch beside me, bustled past and headed off towards the back of the house before I could think of a thing to say. I scampered after him.

It was quite a big garden for these parts, with enough space for him to have disappeared by the time I got round there.

'Hello?' I called. 'Are you . . .?' On strong medication? In the middle of an episode? Mistaking me for someone else?

'Are you coming?' his voice was rising up from somewhere inside a covered walkway made out of white-painted wood. Like a . . . bower, I suppose. A gravel path led into it. But it would take more than a gravel path to lead *me* into it.

'Sir?' I said. 'Can you come back out here and tell me what's going on, please? I came to ask you about your neighbour—'

'Ohhhhh,' he said, appearing at the mouth of the . . .

pergola – is that the word? 'You think it's my neighbour? Which one?'

'Think what's your neighbour?' I said, feeling a slight chill that was more than the pathetic California attempt at winter.

'Come and see,' he said. 'She's right there, as dead as a dodo.'

I stared at him. He didn't look mad or ill or dangerous. He looked like an upright citizen of Cuento: Jason Momoa hair and Roy Cropper fashion sense. He turned to look behind him. And I couldn't help myself, I wanted to see if it was true. I told myself I could scream bloody murder if it was and bring Mike and the uniform flying to my side. And I'd be able to comfort Bran by telling him she looked peaceful, whether she did or not.

I stepped off the grass on to the gravel and followed the path as it wound in under the white painted . . . trellis? It didn't take long. A big garden for Cuento is still not a very big garden, and this wasn't the Hampton Court Palace maze, by any means. Another ten paces brought me alongside the guy again. He was standing, looking down at . . . nothing.

'Wait,' I said. 'You told me someone was dead.'

'She is,' he said, pointing at absolutely nothing. 'Barbra Streisand – dead as disco.'

I took a couple of breaths, wondering how to play this. 'Do you have someone who can come and be with you?' I asked, taking a leaf out of Mike's book. This guy had some serious problems and – although he didn't look all that distraught at imaginary-invisible Streisand's demise, here in his backyard – at the very least, he shouldn't be driving.

'What?' he said. 'Are you mocking me?'

Uh-oh, I thought.

'My mother said you were the right people to call,' he added.

'Who is it you think I am?' I said, reckoning the answer could be absolutely anything.

'The Beteo County Master Gardeners' on-call trouble-shooter,' he said, which proved me right. 'Aren't you?'

It took me a couple of beats, nodding and smiling, before I made sense of it. 'A gardener?' I said at last. 'I thought you thought I was the police.'

'Oh my God!' he said. He wiped a hand over his forehead. 'She called the *police*? I'm sorry, officer. Please don't punish her for wasting your time. She's not as young as she was and she has bad days.'

'I'm *not* the police though,' I said. 'I'm the ex-wife of your neighbour across the way, whose current wife appears to have been kidnapped. And a counsellor.'

It took *him* a couple of beats this time, nodding and smiling, while he wondered how to cope with being trapped in a . . . gazebo? . . . with a complete nutter.

'Your neighbour across the road?' I said. 'Lancer? His wife's gone missing and she might have been kidnapped. So I came to ask if you had seen anything. And you said, "She's dead," and I thought—'

'Oh my God!' he said, again stuck between gasping and laughter. 'No, not a neighbour!'

I relaxed a bit and laughed with him.

'Barbra Streisand's dead,' he said.

I might well have stopped laughing again.

'Look!' Once more, he pointed down at nothing. 'My mother said so yesterday and I thought she was having a senior moment, but there's no hiding it today.'

'Sir,' I said. 'Barbra Streisand isn't here. Barbra Streisand is probably at home in Santa Barbara, alive and well.'

He stared at me a moment, but he didn't use the nod and smile this time. Then light broke over him. '*Rosa* "Barbra Streisand",' he said, pointing for the third time at nothing, or rather at some brown twigs poking up out of the ground. 'Someone has killed my mother's favourite hybrid tea.'

'A rose?' I said.

'Dead,' he said, reaching down and breaking off a piece of twig with a snap like a cracker.

'But don't roses die *every* winter?' I said. 'I'm really not a county garden master, see?' I added, as he gave me a withering look.

'Right,' he said. 'You're the counsellor for the ex-wife of the guy who's missing from across the street.' Some people have no mind for detail. 'Tell me, do you really think roses die and come back to life? Do you think all plants do that?

Any animals?' I supposed when he put it like that it did sound a bit unlikely.

'Ha,' I said. 'I might have used the wrong word.'

'You know how the leaves fall off the trees and then the trees grow new ones?' he said, stepping way over the sarcasm line. 'The trees are still alive. Look.' He reached out and pulled a low-hanging bare twig towards him, then bent it double like a hairpin and scratched the bark, showing me a bright lime-green underneath layer. To be fair, it was very different from the biscuit snap of the dead rose.

'What a shame for your mum,' I said. 'She'll have to plant a new one.'

'If it's a horrible disease she might not be able to,' he said. 'That's why I was trying to get a diagnosis.'

'Right,' I said. 'Well, I hope the garden trouble master guy can help you, when he gets here. Meantime, *did* you see anything funny going on over the way? The night before last?'

'Me?' he said. 'I don't live here. What, you thought I lived with my mother?'

'Ah,' I said. It wasn't the worst insult I could have dreamed up. Those would all have involved his dress sense.

'I don't live with my mother,' he said. He was protesting a bit too much, to my mind.

'OK,' I said. 'Me neither. Yay us. So could I speak to your mother, maybe? *She* might have noticed something.'

Reluctantly, it seemed, he agreed to let me in the house and question the old lady. He made me take my shoes off at the door, like a mother-living old fussbudget, then took me through a maze of big, heavy walnut furniture towards the back of the open-plan layout, where an incredibly spindly old woman sat in a glassed-in neuk, looking out over her garden. Here was where her son had got his knack for snazzy dressing. She was wearing a mustard-coloured velour lounge suit, looking like something from *The Sopranos*.

'She's dead, isn't she?' was the greeting I got, as she turned a blank gaze my way. I couldn't see her eyes behind the shine on her bottle-bottom glasses but her lip was wobbling and she held a hanky in one fist.

'I'm not the gardener,' I said. 'But your rose didn't look

too good, if I'm honest. I'm sorry.' There was a short pause.
I expected her to ask who I was, giving me a good opener.
But she was lost in horticultural grief or something and the
silence stretched. 'I'm actually here on another matter,' I said,
when it had stretched to twanging. 'You know your neighbours
across the way? The Lancers?'

'Cautious drivers, smell like mouthwash,' she said.

It was an odd description, but not untrue. 'That's the
ones,' I agreed. 'She's gone missing.'

'Again?' said the old lady. I was beginning to like her. 'He
doesn't have much luck with wives. This is the third one, I
think.'

'I mean, she's disappeared and it might have been kidnap.
I was just wondering if you saw anything the night before
last.'

'Do all the other pencils in the box make fun of you?' she
said. 'For not being as sharp as them?'

'Um,' I said.

She leaned forward and this time I did see what lay behind
her thick lenses. 'I'm blind,' she said. 'I haven't seen anything
for seven years.'

I suppose it explained the lounge suit, if not the heavy
glasses. Maybe they were wishful thinking.

'Do you sleep at the front of the house?' I said. 'Maybe
you heard something?'

'Because my other senses have developed to make up the
difference?' she said. 'I'm eighty years old. I can't hear what
I used to, my knees are shot, I'm a prune-juice junkie and
even at that it's a red-letter day if I'm out of the bathroom in
under an hour. And my heart sounds like modern jazz.'

I sat down, thinking that I liked this woman more and more
and wanted to hang out. Also, how would she know?

'Take a seat, why don't you?' she asked me.

'There's nothing wrong with your hearing at all, is there?'
I said. 'But I'm sorry I annoyed you.'

'I was being honest. I don't hear as well as I did ten years
ago. But I can hear traffic on the street. Two nights back, you
say? Two nights back. Last night, I read late – audiobook,
you understand – and it must have been midnight when I put

my light out – just an expression. The night before . . . Now, then, what was I doing the night before . . .? No, I can't say I recall much. They came home about eight, parked on the drive instead of in the garage. He took the garbage out at ten and put the car away then. She opened the powder-room window around eleven, just after flushing her toilet – strange time of day to need to air out a bathroom; I was always trained to go in the morning. But that's the modern way – the twenty-four/seven lifestyle.'

'Did someone close it again?' I asked. I was thinking to myself that if I ever had a blind neighbour I'd make sure and have a loud fountain too. She'd practically been on a stake-out.

'I fell asleep,' she said. 'I couldn't say. But I will say this: I'd be surprised if the wife just up and left him. They seemed very happy, if you get my drift.'

'No noisy arguments?' I said, guessing.

'Not that so much as they never closed their bedroom window. And they seemed very happy at least three times a week.'

'Ah,' I said. I was glad she couldn't see me blushing.

'Don't be embarrassed,' she said. 'My son's single,' she added. 'Are you?'

'Ahhhhhhh,' I said, standing up and going into a fast reverse. 'I think I heard someone outside. That might be your garden guru.'

'Oh calm down,' she said. 'There's no harm in mentioning it.'

'Of course not.'

'It's just that I want grandchildren before I'm too decrepit to pick them up.'

My mouth literally dropped open of its own accord. 'Aaaaanyway,' I said, to shut her up before she asked me about my religion or menstrual cycle. 'Sorry about your rose bush.'

'My favourite of all roses.'

'It's an odd choice for a blind person, isn't it?' I said. 'They're not exactly tactile, what with the thorns. And it's not as if—'

'I can see them? That's no loss. I think Barbra Streisand is a very cold purple-ish blue, like blackberry ice cream. But her scent! She smells like the Arabian Nights. Her perfume is enough to make you drunk with delight.'

'Would it interest you to know,' her son said, having come back into the room silently in his stockinged feet, 'that roses don't have thorns?'

'Oh yes?' I said, wondering how long he'd been standing there and how much he'd heard, wondering if this was his idea of a chat-up line.

'Those things are prickles.'

'Oh. Well, in that case no.'

'A thorn is a pointed section of stem. A prickle is an outgrowth of bark.'

'How is that helpful when there's blood running down your arm?' I said. 'Anyway, I'd better be off. I need to tell the police to take a close look at that bathroom window for footprints in case she climbed out that way. That was a good tip. Thank you.'

I jammed my feet into my shoes and shuffled off at double speed, in case he came after me to tell me that a tomato didn't have seeds or a lily wasn't a flower.

The person I passed halfway down the path looked a lot more like a gardener than me. She had a lot of pockets on the outside of her clothing and boots you could wear up a mountain.

'Watch out for the son,' I said, as we passed. '*And* the mother. Unless your clock's ticking.'

I didn't stop to see what effect my words would have on her, because across the road Mike and the uniform were coming down Bran's path as if to leave.

'Hey!' I said. 'Have you looked for signs of entry around the window of the downstairs loo?'

'What?' said Mike. 'It's all downstairs, Lexy. It's a single-storey house.'

'Half bath,' I said through gritted teeth. I couldn't bring myself to speak the words 'powder room'.

'Did your ex-husband tell you to say that?'

'What?' I said. 'No. I've been over there.' I pointed. 'The neighbour heard suspicious noises on the night Brandeee disappeared and she happened to know there was a window left open.'

'Was that where he was heading when he came out to howl up at the heavens and you found him?' said Mike. 'The neighbour's house?'

'What?' I said. 'You've lost me. Look, never mind. Have you checked for prints around that window?'

'Specialized work. We'll send forensics,' said Mike, but in that dry way of hers that means she's being sarcastic. Bran was standing in the doorway, white faced and damp around the eyes. I let Mike go and rushed up to try him instead.

'Do you still shut all your windows at night, except the room you're sleeping in, like a paranoid little old lady?' I asked him. It had been a bone of contention during our short marriage. Bran liked to seal the house against the few California elements and manage the temperature by means of the air-conditioning unit. I preferred my air with a few mosquitoes and a bit of barbecue smoke in it and I hated trying to sleep through the racket of the air-conditioning fan rumbling away outside the window. Bran suggested a white-noise machine to mask it. I suggested more noise wasn't the answer to noise. Bran asked me why I thought white-noise machines were on the market if they weren't useful. I directed his attention towards patented melon slicers and we left it there.

'Why?' he said.

'Because your neighbour across the road thinks there was a window left open the night Brandeee disappeared.' I veered away from him into the shrubs that hugged the front of the house. The one nearest the downstairs-loo window was a . . . well, who knows what it was, but it had a single thick stem and left a good lot of soft bare earth between it and the wall, perfect for footprints if someone had scrambled into the house this way. I peered at the ground but couldn't see so much as a dent.

And inside, when we got there, the windowsill showed not a scrape nor a smudge.

'Of course I didn't leave this window open!' Bran said. 'Cuento isn't the place it used to be.'

'When Cuento was the place it used to be, this was all fields,' I said. 'What did Mike say? What are they going to do? Do you still need us to chip in or do you think they've got it taped?'

Bran sat down on the closed toilet lid and put his head in his hands.

'That detective thinks Brandee left me,' he said. 'She thinks the note's a fake.'

'What?' I said. I said it quite loud and it rang out uncomfortably in the little loo. The echo made me realize that, only two days after Brandeee had left (or been taken), the number of decorative guest towels was down to nil. A bit of me wanted to go and count the decorative pillows on the master bed. But instead I patted Bran awkwardly on the shoulder nearest to me. 'She probably didn't mean it,' I said. 'The wording is the same as the note left at Mama Cuento corner. She does realize that, doesn't she?'

'She does,' said Bran. 'That's the whole point. She thinks I copied the wording to make them take it seriously.'

'But you didn't know,' I said. 'Did you? You didn't seem to know about Mama Cuento being missing, when we turned up.'

'I was kind of busy with my wife disappearing,' Bran said. 'I haven't been following human-interest stories on the local news, no.'

'I suppose it could be worse,' I said. He gave me a look as if to say, *Could it?* 'At least they think Brandeee left and you faked the note to make them investigate. They don't think you got rid of her and faked the note to throw the suspicion off of you on to a kidnapper. That would be really bad.'

Bran went so pale and so clammy-looking, I was glad he was near a toilet. But he didn't puke. He stood up and took hold of me with both hands. 'If she doesn't escape, though,' he said, 'if no one finds her, eventually those dumb cops will have to agree there's something wrong, won't they?'

'If she doesn't turn up, or use her cards or get in touch with Blaike,' I said, 'eventually, yes.'

'Blaike!' said Bran, close to wailing. 'But you think, when they finally accept she's missing, they're going to come after me?'

'Probably,' I said. 'For thoroughness, they've got to. Like they looked through the house in case you had her tied up and gagged somewhere. It's just a process of elimination.'

That got him going. He was up on his feet, trying to pace

in this titchy little toilet with someone standing in his way. After two tight turns, he gave up and went out into the hallway. 'So, yes, I still need you,' he said. 'I need you to find Brandee and . . . I really need you to go to Idaho and break the news to Blaike.'

'I can't . . .' I said. 'Wouldn't it be better coming from you?' I was trotting after him as he paced now, up to the opening at the main room, back to the master-bedroom door, back to the main room again. He still hadn't hit on the prime pacing location in the house, in my opinion. A circuit round the living area would have been a lot more satisfying.

'Blaike hates me,' he said.

'Palming off something like this isn't going to help,' I pointed out. 'And I've got a practice, Bran. A job, just like you.' He had always thought his work was more important than my work when we were married. Just because he earned four times more than me in my best month and didn't run his business from a suite that rented out offices by the day.

'This *is* your job,' he said. 'I'm paying Trinity Solutions to take care of this.'

'Oh yeah,' I said. I had forgotten. 'But still, I can't go flying all over the country to take care of your personal family business.'

'I'll pay for your flights, obviously. And hotel.'

'First class?'

'Extra legroom.'

'And priority boarding. OK, I'll discuss it with my partners. And now I better go. Did you give Todd and Kathi—?'

'Everything I could think of – friends, appointments, usual haunts, all the paper, notes, forms, bills . . . I have to get her back, Lexy. After everything we've been through, I couldn't bear to lose her now.'

EIGHT

*A*fter everything we've been through, I repeated to myself as I embarked on the long walk down from the posh suburbs to central Cuento, the railroad tracks and the Last Ditch. It was hardly flattering, since a lot of what Bran had been through was me. But his devotion to Brandeee was just as puzzling on its own merits. She didn't strike me as the sort of person to spark major passion. She was . . . I mean, I wished her no harm but she was . . .

Actually, I had no idea what she was, beyond committed to grooming and fond of a lot of little towels and cushions. I was actually looking forward to interviewing her friends and colleagues to finally get a handle on this woman who was responsible – in a roundabout way – for upending my life. There must be more to her than I had ever seen, because I was far from sure anyone would come reeling out of the house to – what was it Mike said? – howl at the heavens, if *I'd* been stolen away.

Without meaning to, I found myself walking slower and slower, as if my batteries were running out. That was a very strange thing for Mike to have said, actually. And it was a very strange thing for Bran to have done. He didn't call the cops when he found the note. He didn't even call me to see how close we were. He came outside and happened to find us just arriving. And the only reason he'd found the note was that he'd come outside minutes beforehand to look for us once already.

That, as Mike had seen and I had not, wasn't like Branston Lancer. He was an app-downloader extraordinaire, an online booker, an other-end-of-the-sofa texter. I couldn't remember him ever having to ask a barista for his drink; he would sit in the car park and order it, then wait till he could see it before he opened Starbucks' door. So there was no way on God's earth Bran would react to bad news by rushing out into the street to look for an actual human being to help him. He would be googling ransom notes and FBI stats with one hand while he sent a message via speech-to-text and uploaded a scan of the nail to a subreddit with the other.

And was it possible he hadn't known about Mama Cuento? Wouldn't he have been glued to the local news if he thought his wife had gone missing by foul means?

I still hadn't puzzled it out when I arrived at the corner of First Street and Main Street, where the floral tributes had now spread across the whole corner, banked up against La Cucaracha's wall and filling the pavement to the kerbside. A couple of students from UCC were reading messages and taking pictures of them.

'It's very sad, isn't it?' I said.

One of them looked up and frowned. 'It depends on the issue,' he said. 'If it's a protest against colonization, then the selection of Valentine's Day to stage it was a great moment in the march to freedom.'

'Right,' I said, in place of the *Huh* I felt. 'Was it? A protest.'

'It had to be,' he said with a shrug. 'Why else would you steal a symbol?'

'Have there been any more notes from the kidnappers?' I asked him.

'Nope,' said the female student, shaking off a determined bunch of lilies that she'd got tangled up in. 'We'd know. We're recording and transcribing the emerging text.'

'Right,' I said, in place of a snort. 'Aren't there police doing it too, though? I mean, isn't this still a crime scene?'

'Isn't everywhere?' said the boy.

'Right,' I said a third time, instead of a raspberry. California still regularly made me feel like a retired colonel from Agatha Christie.

I dragged my feet past the police station, in case Mike looked out, saw me and decided she wanted to chew over the case and give me lots of useful information by the by. But she must have been on the other side of the building.

Back at the Last Ditch, I checked my watch and decided I had just enough time for a brief catch-up with Noleen. I don't need meditation, spa days or alcohol, as long as I check in with Noleen every now and then. She's like a salt rub with a shamanic loofah, in her own quiet way. She sorts me out even as she flays me.

Or maybe I'm more in tune with my deeper self than someone from Dundee has any right to be. Certainly, I didn't know what I wanted to find out when I pushed open the office door. I was just going where my instinct took me. And I was right.

Nolly was in the middle of one of her periodic reorganizing drives. Usually the motel office was in marked contrast to the Skweeky Kleen, being rather more filled with discarded clothes, half-done crosswords, burst lamps, accidentally printed-out room bills that still had one blank side and would be useful for scrap paper if we ever got locked in the office for a month and needed to write out our wills and a three-volume novel before we pegged it. But every so often a tower of paper would fall, or Noleen would find her favourite base-ball cap just after she'd ordered a replacement one, or a potential guest would put a head round the door, curl their lip and go away without booking, and then Noleen would blitz the place, throwing out everything that wasn't her own coffee mug or a new inkjet cartridge, until there was no junk left at all and the office was revealed in all its tatty lack of splendour.

She was facing away from me, wearing a sweatshirt I hadn't seen before – it read, *Nobody asked you* – and upending the stationery drawer over a black bin bag. Elastic bands, bulldog clips and pens cascaded down. I think I saw some postage stamps go in there.

'Wow,' I said. 'Are you going paperless?'

'I'm starting over,' she said, turning. The front of the sweat-shirt said, *Shut up*. Blunt, even for Noleen. 'I'm going to OfficePro, after Della gets here to tag me, and buying just what I need and nothing else. None of this . . .' She stirred the very dregs of the drawer contents, then tipped it higher to shoot the lot into the bin bag.

'Is that foreign currency?' I said. 'Because it looks like quarters. Nolly, you're binning money.'

'I'm letting go,' she said. 'And I'm going to start locking

this drawer so no one can put hairbands and thumb tacks in it when I'm not looking.'

'No one . . .' I began. 'OK. But you know what I think?'

'Don't want to,' she said. 'Don't want your opinions stinking up my head any more than I want random strangers' Canadian change stinking up my drawer.'

'I'll tell you anyway. I think that drawer is like a coral reef, or maybe a compost heap. It's a functioning ecosystem that will keep finding its own equilibrium, no matter what.'

'All this time, I thought you had to study psychology to be a therapist,' Noleen said. 'Now, I find out you've got a master's degree in bullshit.'

There she was! There was the Noleen I knew and loved, the insults as much a part of her as her tidy-up blitzes. That thought sparked another one and I let it run as I stood there watching her tie the binbag and then set about the empty drawer with a Clorox wipe. She'd caught that habit from Kathi. Kathi adored a Clorox wipe. It was neck and neck whether the floating island of plastic she alone was responsible for building in the ocean was more wipes or gloves; she had to have one or the other over her hand before she'd touch most things.

'What?' Noleen said, when she'd had enough of being watched.

'People don't change,' I said. 'Or they change slowly, for reasons. Kathi's rubbing off on you and you're probably rubbing off on her. But people don't do things they don't do.'

'You aced that Bullshit MA.'

'Bran *would* have called someone, or texted someone,' I said. 'He'd never have run out into the street to look for succour.'

Noleen put down the drawer and regarded me through narrowed eyes. 'They told me,' she said, 'he was looking out for you and he found it on the doormat. Then he went outside again to see if you were on your way.'

'Yeah, but we hadn't texted or anything,' I said. 'We'd only said we'd be there today. It doesn't ring true. Much as it pains me to say it, I think Mike might be right. He staged it. He was acting. He knows more about it than he wants us to think he does.'

'He was real upset when he came here looking for you this morning,' Noleen said.

'He sounded "real upset" when he wailed "Oh, Brandee, baby!" too,' I said. 'But he didn't hang around in the car park, waiting and watching, did he? Oh!' A light bulb had just gone on in my head. 'Where did you say I was, Nolly? Where did he think I was when he went to wait on the boat for me to come back?'

'I said you were up at First and Main, where Mama Cuento had gotten stole away. Why, where were you?'

'Bingo!' I said. 'We've got him. He said he hadn't heard the news about Mama Cuento. But he had. Bugger it, Mike *is* right. He really did fake a copycat ransom note.'

Noleen whistled. 'He's chopped her up and fed her to the hogs?'

'Possibly,' I said. 'Not very flattering that he employed me to investigate in that case, is it? Or maybe he just wanted to make the cops pay attention to her disappearance. I wonder why he doesn't want to tell Blaike face to face, or even phone the school and get a sympathetic teacher to break the news.'

'Maybe he's hoping she'll come back before the kid needs to hear,' Noleen said. 'If he hasn't chopped her up. Or, if he has, he wants people to think he's hoping she'll come back.'

'No, he wants Blaike to know,' I said. 'But he wants *me* to go and tell him. He's willing to pay for me to fly to . . . somewhere . . . Is Idaho a place?'

'Maybe Blaike can tell when he's lying,' said Noleen. 'If he's chopped her up. Or maybe – if he hasn't chopped her up – he doesn't want to be away from home. Or he doesn't want to take the blame for her disappearing. This is if he hasn't ch— You know what? We need a shorthand. "Chop" and "no chop". OK?'

'Absolutely not,' I said. 'For God's sake. I don't think it's anything so dramatic, anyway. Whether we're looking at—'

'Chop,' said Noleen.

'Or no chop. It's just that Blaike hates him and Bran hates the poor kid right back. He's hopeless with kids. And dogs.'

'I gotta ask,' Noleen said. 'What were you thinking?'

And I couldn't wheel out the dungarees-in-the-eighties riposte again, because I'd seen all Noleen's photographs from all her sixty years by now, and she had dressed exactly the same, with the same hairdo, since she left school and burned her little kilt and white knee socks.

'The question is, should I go flying all over the country to break it gently or is that Bran trying to get me out of the way? Or does he think so little of me he doesn't realize what a risk he's taking, letting me talk to his arch-enemy?'

'Wow,' Noleen said. 'You want some incidental music to punch this scene up a little? Arch-enemy? All over the country? Where do you think Idaho is, Lex?'

'Uhhhhh, the middle? Chicago.'

'That's Illinois.'

'Cleveland then.'

'That's Ohio.'

'That's the same damn word. That's barely even an anagram.'

'Keep guessing,' Noleen said, as the door opened to admit Todd and Kathi. 'Cool new game, guys! Lexy don't know shit about these our United States. Ask her where Iowa is. Funniest thing you ever heard.'

'It's happened again,' Kathi said. 'Another delivery and a new note.'

I hadn't noticed how sombre they both looked, but a second glance made my blood drain.

'A new toe? Or just a nail?' I said. 'And whose?'

'A new body part,' said Kathi. 'It's a belly button.'

'That's . . .' I said, before I had to sit down suddenly on one of the uncomfortable little café chairs where unsuspecting motel guests sometimes ate the microwave porridge on their first morning. 'How would you even . . .? That's a big step up from an acrylic nail.'

'It's not Brandee's,' said Todd. 'It's not anyone's. It was cut off a fibreglass statue of a pregnant Asian woman at a memorial in Utah, away in the armpit of nowhere, and sent to some kid in a boot camp in the asshole of nowhere. But he put it online and it's the same words in the note.'

'Nine more where this came from?' I said. 'But that must be a copycat! No one's got ten belly buttons.'

'I'm just telling you what's on the wire,' Todd said. I was sure he meant Twitter but he has a definite flair for the dramatic.

'Another stolen statue – she's called Hope – another delivery and an identical note. God knows what it's got to do with our stuff. If anything.'

'A statue of a pregnant woman though,' I said. 'And a minority too? It's not random.'

'Another day, another hate crime,' said Kathi. 'Is Brandee some kind of radical feminist, Lex? Is that the connection?'

I tried hard not to laugh. After all, the woman had either been kidnapped or killed, or had fled her home. 'A radical feminist dentist?' I said. 'Who married Bran? Twice?' I added when I saw Noleen open her mouth to point out the obvious glassiness of my house.

'Is she involved in . . . public art projects in any way?' Todd said, which was a pretty decent suggestion, actually.

'Eh, no,' I said. 'She's a hairdo. She's a monthly manicure. She would flatten the whole of downtown for more parking, if she could get the votes. And anyway Noleen and I just worked out that Bran knew about Mama Cuento and we think he faked the nail and note on the doormat to get the police to take him seriously.'

'Unless he chopped her up,' said Noleen.

'And fed her to the hogs,' added Kathi. They had been married for a very long time.

'Making it a double bluff,' said Todd. 'And an insult to the collective intelligence of Trinity Solutions' investigation wing.'

'That's what I said!' I said. 'Only . . . he really did look upset when he was down here and when we were up there. Didn't he?'

Todd was no fan of my ex-husband. He was a good friend that way: never neutral when what you needed was bias in your favour. And Kathi was no fan of the entire category of straight white guys with perfect teeth, so a Cuento dentist would have to be something pretty special to get a fair shake from her too. But both of them nodded.

'He gave us everything,' Kathi said. 'Wait – make that, he gave us a whole lot and there didn't seem to be anything missing. We've got her passwords for her bank, doctor, email, social media . . .'

'Really?' I said. 'He knew them?' He'd never known mine.

'He told us pretty straight out what her relationships were with everyone at the business,' Todd said. 'She got a little lit at the holiday party and went behind the X-ray screen with a receptionist. Told us that loud and clear, didn't he?'

Kathi nodded. 'So we think she really went missing and he really cares, but maybe the note is a red herring? So, maybe we can forget that and concentrate on the job we're getting paid for?'

'The case of the missing manicure,' said Todd. 'Is that mean?'

'Yes it is,' I said. 'But, yes, we can. Let the California cops find Mama Cuento.'

'And the Utah cops find Hope,' said Noleen.

'And the Idaho cops interview the kid,' Todd said.

Noleen and I flashed a look between us. 'Spooky coinc—' I started to say.

But Noleen knew more than me about life in these her United States, as she had just been so keen to point out. To me 'boarding school' spoke of money and power, toddlers in top hats and a short downhill path to the top tiers of government. Noleen understood, however, that a boarding school and a correctional boot camp were probably the same thing.

'The belly button got sent to a kid at school in Idaho?' she said. 'Did you get a name?'

'Uhhhhhhh,' said Todd. 'Blaize? Blaine? Blair?'

'Blaike,' I said. 'Blaike Kowalski. He's Brandeee's son.'

We all stood there in silence for a moment, letting our thoughts shift and resettle to accommodate this minor thunderbolt. It made me feel proud. In my own quiet way, I had managed to pass on a fair few healthy mental habits to my friends. I might not have cured Todd and Kathi's specific problems, nor got Noleen to admit she had any, but I'd made all three of them stronger, more resilient, more reflective individuals.

'So who got kidnapped from the school?' said Noleen, breaking the silence. 'If dicking around with statues is a calling card, then I betcha someone's gone missing from Asshole, Idaho, same as someone vanished from Mama Cuento's backyard.'

'Nah,' said Kathi. 'Bran's on a rampage. He's warning his kid not to make waves or he'll end up in the hog pen with his mom. Sick bastard.'

'I reckon the kid offed his mom,' said Todd, 'and sent himself a belly button to throw us off the scent.'

'What the hell are you all talking about?' I said, thinking, reflective individuals, my arse. 'Are you high? Why would a seventeen-year-old kid break out of some borstal in the middle of nowhere, drive thousands of miles in a pickup that must be stolen and kidnap a statue from the same town as he was just about to kill his mother in? Then drive all the way back and point the finger at himself with a belly button? There isn't even time. He would have had to fly and hire the truck – plus a crane – and then fly back. Meanwhile, where's his mother?'

'See what I mean?' said Noleen. 'She's got no clue where Idaho is.'

'Why? Where is it?' I said.

'Just up a ways and turn right till the real estate gets less pricey,' Kathi said. 'Exactly where some Cuento bad boy would get banged up when his parents couldn't take it anymore.'

'Yay,' said Todd. Then, at our puzzled looks, he went on: 'Road trip!'

'Oh,' I said. 'Yay.'

NINE

We never got there.

When I told the others we had permission from Blaike's stepfather – not even permission; a request – to go and talk to him, Todd started cancelling clients left and right and Kathi texted Devin at college, offering bonus pay if he would take over the Skweek for a couple of days.

'He's supposed to be studying,' I reminded her.

'He can study,' she said. 'One of his buddies could film the professor and live-stream it right to Devin in the laundromat. Beats me why he ever hauls his ass all the way over town to sit in a theatre anyway.'

Me too, when she put it that way.

Todd was on the phone to Roger, saying, 'But, babe, if I don't tag along, there won't be a man for this poor kid to relate to. Just Kathi – and Lexy, for God's sake! His mom has disappeared. He needs to speak, man to man, to someone who understands.'

'How come I get a "for God's sake"?' I said. 'I'm an actual counsellor.'

'What would Todd know about a disappearing mom?' said Kathi. Which was another very good point. Todd's mother, Barb, lived in Cuento and had an alert on her phone in case her beautiful boy did anything noteworthy, such as posting a review of a pickle fork on Amazon or saying *LOL* to a cat video.

'Thank you!' Todd was saying. Of course he was. Roger was the most patient and understanding husband I had ever seen in my life. Granted, I tended to get involved with marriages when they hit the skids, but I'm including friends, family and sitcoms in my tally. 'Can I borrow your down vest?' Todd was saying into his phone now. 'And your L.L.Beans? And your green cap with the— Oh, you did? . . . Yeah, I know I did . . . Well, it was . . . Yeah, but who knew

I'd ever be going to Idaho? . . . Well, I can swing by the thrift store and re-buy it. I'm sure it'll still be there.' He hung up.

'That man's a saint,' I said.

'My rainboots have a stacked heel,' said Todd. 'I might need to stop off on the way and pick out some—'

'For God's sake!' said Kathi. 'Stop being such a cliché. Right. Are we taking the small cooler just for drinks and finding diners for meals? Or the large one and pull off at rest stops with grills?'

'No,' I said. 'I'm not spending ten hours in a car with melting ice cubes sloshing around in a box in the boot. Be normal. Why do you think God invented Starbucks?'

'Yeah, I'm not grilling at an Idaho rest stop in February,' said Todd. 'We'll all get eaten by bears.'

'Bears!' I said. I had never encountered one yet, in my few forays down to the big sequoias or up to the huge ones. 'I want to see a bear! And drive through a tree! Are there buffalo?'

'There's a casino called the Buffalo,' said Kathi. 'Just over the Oregon border. That do you?'

Even paring down the supplies to three personal coffee cups, a bag of beef jerky and a box of something called milk duds (that looked like rabbit droppings), it took us the rest of the day to reschedule our various clients, agree on the best weather forecast, translate the temperature guide to Celsius (for me) and pack enough warm clothes, hip flasks and snow chains to see us over the mountains. We were still bickering about audiobooks when the sun went down.

'*Middlesex*!' said Todd. 'Like in that movie! With Barbra Streisand!'

'Speaking of Barbra Streisand—' I said.

'I am not listening to some dude's thousand-page creep-out about gender identity,' said Kathi.

'But that's the whole point!' said Todd. 'The thousand pages. It doesn't matter what goes wrong on the road, we'll never run out of book. We could be stuck in the Donner Pass till spring and the one that ate the other two would still be listening when the thaw came.'

'Could we?' I said. 'Could we really get stuck?'

'I volunteer to be eaten first if we're listening to *Middlesex*,' said Kathi. 'And don't leave me to starve to death. That's why so many of the Donner Party died. They ate victims of starvation with no fat left on them. Died of protein poisoning. Kill me good and early. Kill me now if you're serious about that book.'

'Yeah, but could we?' I said. 'Maybe we should take the big cooler, after all. Maybe we should throw in a couple of instant barbecues?'

'I don't want to listen to SNL sketches,' Todd said. 'Or David Sedaris.'

'You better turn in your card,' said Kathi. 'Why don't we let Lexy choose?'

'BBC Radio 4 podcast,' I said, without a moment's hesitation.

Todd made a great fake-puking noise. 'Baking with Dickens!' he said. Which was accurate enough to put me in a huff, so I flounced off to the boat to download a good haul, planning to sit with my earbuds in, looking out of the window all the way to Iawherevero – then they'd be sorry.

Diego was outside his and Della's room, scuffing around the edge of the car park like a kid from the thirties sparking his clogs on the cobbles. He was six now, and just beginning to stretch out, his legs getting a bit of length to them and his ribs poking sharply up out of the water when he floated on his back in the Last Ditch pool, but he was still as cute as when he'd been a chubby four-year-old, looking like a balloon animal. His eyes didn't seem to be getting any smaller as his face grew, and his hair still shone like boot buttons and now reached halfway down his back.

'You OK, baby boy?' I said. 'You waiting for someone?' It bothered me that Diego never seemed to have any little friends over, even though he was sort of a kid with a swimming pool. If any of the kids in my primary-one class had had a swimming pool (indoor and heated, obviously), we would have carried them around in a sedan chair.

'Nah,' he said. 'Just kicked out because Mom's busy with You-Know-Who.'

I tried not to react. But I was kind of shocked that Della would put him out of the room to entertain Devin. It didn't seem like her.

'Hey,' I said, 'you know if Devin and your mom need some quiet time, you can come to the boat. Only, shout from the land, OK? Don't try to jump over on to the steps if no one's watching you.'

He screwed up his eyes until they were only twice the size of average eyes. 'Devin?' he said. 'Why would Devin need quiet time with my mom?'

Shit. 'To play Scrabble,' I said. 'I know how much you hate when we play Scrabble. Bor-ing, right?'

'Nuh-uh,' he said. 'I like Scrabble, now I can spell. Does Devin play Scrabble with my mom?'

Shit. 'Maybe,' I said. 'And if I'm not there, or I've got a client, you can go to Todd and Roger.'

'Todd plays Scrabble all the time,' said Diego. 'He plays it on his phone with people who're not even there.'

'Or you could go to the office and hang out with Noleen,' I said. 'We all love you.'

'Why does Devin need me to go away?' he asked. 'Does *Devin* not love me? Did I upset him?'

Shit. 'No,' I said. 'It's just sometimes grown-up people need some time alone together.'

'IS DEVIN DATING MY MOM?' he said, louder than I knew he could say anything. 'IS DEVIN KISSING MY MOM ON HER *MOUTH*?'

Shit. And, as if that wasn't bad enough, the door of 101 opened and Devin himself emerged, reading glasses on the end of his nose and floppy textbook held open against his chest.

'I hear my name?' he asked. 'Hey, li'l bro.'

'ARE YOU DATING MY MOMMY?'

Devin gave me a look, just as Della opened the door to her room and fired a rapid burst of Spanish at her son. I caught a few words of it, including *abogada* several times. And then a young woman in a brown business suit and court shoes came to stand behind her in the doorway.

Shit. Della was talking to a *lawyer*.

'ARE YOU DATING DEVIN, MOM?' Diego demanded. He had his little fists bunched on his skinny little hips, which was just about the most adorable thing I had ever seen outside YouTube.

'Don't shout at me!' said Della. She turned to face Devin, who held the open textbook higher up on his chest like a bulletproof shield. 'Did you tell him?' she asked. I shivered. *She* didn't need to shout. She could whisper and people would still buckle at the knee.

'No,' I said. 'Sorry. It was me. It was an accident. I thought you two were in there . . . together . . . and he was waiting.' Not only my knees felt the ice of her new look. There was a shifting in the underwear department too, nether portion.

'You thought I threw my son out into a parking lot to let me—'

'It seemed surprising,' I said.

'I would never do that,' said Della.

'I know!' I said. 'That's why I was shocked.'

'*I* would never do that,' said Devin. The lawyer gave him an appraising look.

'I know!' I said. 'I'm sorry.'

'Are you a citizen?' the lawyer asked Devin. I suppose an immigration attorney has got to have a practical streak a mile wide if she's going to get anywhere, and I was glad that she had pulled focus from me at last, but I had to feel sorry for the woman as Della rounded on her, stared her down from inches away – they were still sharing a doorway – and said, in a voice colder than the Donner Pass in December, 'He's a student. Look at him!'

'Hey!' said Devin.

'He's wearing pool slides,' said Della. I didn't get the significance, personally, but the lawyer screwed her face up and nodded as if to acknowledge an inarguable point being made.

'Hey!' said Devin again. 'You wear pool slides.'

'At the pool,' said Della, and she withdrew into her room again, taking the lawyer with her.

The three of us left standing in the car park said nothing for a moment. Then Diego piped up. 'Why do you date mommies? Are you a daddy?'

It wasn't the question Devin must have been dreading, but it used quite a lot of the same words, enough to freak him out completely and send him scurrying back into room 101, hopping and scuffing to keep the fateful pool slides on his feet.

'Is he?' Diego asked me, once the door was shut.

'He's the same age as your mom,' I said. 'Pretty much.'

'I thought he was a big boy,' said Diego. 'He goes to school. Is he a man?'

'Men go to school,' I said. 'It's a special school called a college that daddies go to. Mummies too.'

'*Mummies* go?' Diego said. 'Do zombies go?'

'What? Oh! No, I mean mommies.'

'Do vampires go? Do werewolves go? Is Devin safe there?'

'He's fine,' I said. Safer than with Della, in that mood.

'He's no good at combat,' said Diego. 'I can beat him. I can beat him with a sword and a lightsaber and ninja skills and—'

'He's fine,' I said again. 'It's a very sweet thing that you care about him. I'm sure he cares about you too.' This was because I could see the shadow of Devin's feet on the other side of his door and I knew he was listening. 'You could do worse!' I said to the feet as, hand in hand, Diego and I walked away. 'I'm going on a trip,' I said to the little boy. 'With Todd and Kathi. I'll miss you till we get back.'

'You can call me,' he said, and I battled to hide my smile. Kindness in a six-year-old doesn't need flattened by smirking.

'I might just do that,' I said. 'Thank you. Now, are you coming round to the boat or into the office? Except Noleen is tidying and she might sweep you into a bin bag and put you out for the dustmen.'

'You talk funny.'

'Or are you going up to the Skweek? Kathi might squirt you with Mr Muscle and tumble you dry, though.'

'Is that a big boy or a daddy?' Diego said.

'Mr Muscle?' I said. Diego laughed as if I'd cracked the funniest joke ever, with perfect comic timing. I loved six-year-olds. This one, anyway.

'No, silly Lexy,' he said, when the paroxysm was finally over. 'Him. Is he a big boy or a daddy? Because daddies aren't supposed to cry.'

I looked over to where he was pointing, which was the

collection of outsize wheelie bins for landfill and recycling. Skulking half hidden behind the blue one was a skinny youth, with his head down and his hand going up and down compulsively as he wiped his nose and cleaned it off on his jeans. Drug dealer, I thought, and felt sorry for him. If someone was trying to do drug deals in the forecourt of Noleen's motel, he was about to get a short lesson that would stay with him for the rest of his life.

Then he looked up. I knew those ice-blue eyes.

'Blaike?' I said. I hunkered down to Diego. 'Sorry, baby boy. We can't hang out. Go and see if Kathi's got pocket treasure, eh?' There was always something small and interesting that had fallen out of an item of laundry, and Diego was usually first in the queue to scoop them up. A painted tin battleship, less than an inch long, had been his high-water mark, never to be matched for thrills, but he kept hoping.

I walked very slowly over to the bins, as if Blaike – I was sure I recognized him – was an injured animal.

'Blaike?' I said again. 'Honey? What are you doing here?'

'I can't stay there anymore. They're sadists and abusers and there's no way I should be there,' he said. 'So I came home but I can't go home home, because she won't listen and he won't even answer his phone, so I came here to see if you would come with me and tell them. They don't pay any attention to me. But you kicked their asses over the divorce that time. So maybe you could kick their asses again, for me?'

I stared at him, aghast. Was it possible that he didn't know anything about anything and he had just coincidentally left school and come to Cuento right when his mum was being kidnapped and a statue was having its toes lopped off? It certainly looked that way.

But that couldn't be right. 'Blaike, honey,' I said. 'Did someone send you an anonymous belly button?' I certainly hoped so, because it was quite a confusing sentence for him to hear otherwise.

'That was the last straw,' he said. 'I didn't know what it was when I posted it, then it started trending and these really scary women were making threats and I had to get away. Please tell me you'll help.'

What the hell was I going to do? He was a minor and, if he'd been sent to school, then I couldn't be harbouring him. I guessed. I flicked a glance back at Della's room. That lawyer in the brown suit would be able to tell me.

'You're not going to believe this,' I said, 'but we were just on our way to see you.'

'All three of you?' He had stopped crying and now he cleared his nose with a rich, liquid sniff. But he swallowed it without even looking around for a good place to spit. Maybe the boarding school had been good for him. He'd been an unpleasant brat at fifteen when I first met him, sniggering and slinking around. His only visible talent had been finishing off drinks at parties without anyone noticing, until he passed out or threw up. Two years later, even dirty and tired, he looked more . . . wholesome.

'All three of . . .?' I began. Then I got it. 'No, not your parents and me. My partners and me. Your stepdad asked us to come and talk to you.'

'What about?' he said. 'What did my mom think of that? She's weird about you still, sometimes. When you're in the *Voyager* or if one of her friends comes to see you for something. She can be kind of weird.'

I didn't hate this version of myself, always getting press coverage and amassing new clients from Brandeee's social group. But I rose above it. 'Weird?' I said. 'Just about that? Or in general?'

'My mom?' said Blaike. 'Where do I start? Do you know why she sent me away?'

'I'd like to hear,' I said. 'But I've got to tell you something.'

'And at least I know you won't judge me,' Blaike went on. 'You just said you've got two partners, right?'

'Business partners,' I told him. 'But no, I won't judge you. Of course not. But . . . I don't suppose there's any chance you're eighteen, is there?'

He was gone before I even knew he was moving, blasting past me and taking the corner of the swimming-pool chain-link like someone on a luge.

'Blaike!' I shouted after him. 'Sorry! You can . . . trust me,'

I finished under my breath. The kid had good instincts; he knew the only reason to ask his age was if I'd been planning to tell his parents where he was, unless he'd reached the magic number.

At that moment, Todd and Kathi emerged, like a cuckoo clock couple, from their two separate doors.

'Ready to rock and roll?' said Todd, holding out his key fob and chirping open Roger's jeep. 'Well, pack. Early getaway in the morning if we do it now.'

'Change of plan,' I said. 'We've been overtaken by events. In other news, I'm an idiot.'

At that moment, Noleen stuck her head out of the office door. 'Number three!' she called over. 'Some chainsawed African-American chick in Dog Patch, Oregon just lost her nose, like that blackbird-pie deal. This world keeps getting sicker.'

TEN

When we were ensconced in my living room with the wood stove lit and a pot of tea for one sitting on top of it for me to enjoy while those weirdos drank hot cider that they stirred with cinnamon sticks, I broke the news.

'And I truly do not know what to do,' I said. 'Search for him, tell the cops, tell Bran . . . What will I do?'

'He was OK until you asked if he was eighteen?' said Todd.

'And then he took off like a bat out of hell,' I said. 'He was going to tell me why Brandeee sent him away to school, and he thought I'd understand because he thought Trinity was a polyamorous threesome instead of a business partnership, and so I wouldn't judge him.'

'So the kid's gay,' Noleen said. 'Is Idaho a state where you can still sign your kids up for conversion?'

'But Brandeee wouldn't do that,' I said. 'Bran, for all his faults, wouldn't let that happen.'

I waited through a long, tense moment to see if they would close ranks and shoot me down, and it was when we were all sitting there in silence that Roger appeared. He was still in his scrubs, and if there is anything sexier than a hunk of paediatrician who dresses in Elsa-from-*Frozen* scrubs to put his little patients at ease, then I don't think I could handle hearing about it.

'Sup?' he said, kissing Todd and throwing himself down into one of my couches, with enough surrender to his exhaustion to make the boat rock back and forth a few times.

'Where do we start?' I said.

'At the end,' said Todd. 'You're right. Bran Lancer is not a toxic 'phobe.'

'No, he's not,' Roger said. 'He's a regular clueless faux-woke Cuento ally. Why?'

'How do you know that?' I said. As far as I knew, Roger and Bran lived in separate worlds, with no overlap.

'Because I'm a paediatrician and kids get their wisdom teeth taken out,' he said. 'I didn't mention him – because you're my friend – but it's a small town.'

'And I do his dry cleaning,' Kathi said. 'Every Monday. I didn't want to tell you that either. Sorry, Lexy.'

'How about you two?' I said, glaring at Todd and Noleen. 'Golf buddies?'

'Why are we talking about your ex-husband?' Roger said. 'He hasn't asked you to go back, has he?'

'His wife's been kidnapped,' I said. 'Maybe. His wife's gone anyway. And we're looking for her. But her kid's run away from some sick conversion compound in Iowa.'

'Idaho!' If they had harmonized just a bit better, they'd have been a bona fide chorus.

'Jeez, stop nitpicking,' I said. 'And he came here to ask me for help but now he's run away.'

'It's illegal in Idaho,' Roger said. It really was useful to have a children's healthcare professional on tap. 'Can you find out who his friends in town are? He'll probably go there.'

'How weird was it that Bran wanted us to go and tell the kid his mom was missing?' said Todd. He waited. 'That wasn't rhetorical, Roger. I'm actually asking. How weird is it for step-parents to get professionals to break bad news to kids?'

'Not that weird,' Roger said. 'I've done it. Not every day, but I've done it.'

'And how do we find out who his friends are?' I said. 'You didn't see the state he was in, Roger. I really want to find him.'

'And I think we should still go,' Todd said. 'Not' – he interrupted Kathi interrupting him – 'because I look cute in my down vest, which I do, but because of the belly button.'

'We're not going to find out any more than we can about the toe bandits,' said Noleen. 'We've got film of *them*. We need to forget the belly button that made the kid run and start thinking about where he ran to. Aha!'

'What?' Kathi said.

'We've got Brandee's social-media passwords, right, Todd?'

Todd had brought the folder with him and he started leafing through it now.

'So can we get in and see what other parents she messages, and all that?'

'Brilliant!' Todd said. 'Here you go. Cuento Concerned Moms. Class of 2020 parent information loop. Yep, we should be able to track down some of Blaike's friends this way, and they'll be able to point us to others. We'll find him.'

'Or,' said Kathi, 'we tell Bran he's back and leave it up to him to find his own kid.'

'Depends why they sent him there,' I said. 'Maybe he's better off away from them.'

'Oh,' Todd said, staring down at a piece of paper he had just turned over in the file. 'We don't need to go to Idaho to find out.'

'Why?' I said.

'Ethical conundrum,' he said. 'Hmmmmmm.'

'Todd!' I said. 'You can be very annoying.'

'Only when he's awake,' said Roger. 'What are you looking at, hon?'

'I am looking at the answers to the security questions for White Pine Academy. It says here no discussions will take place between academy faculty and parents without these security questions being answered in full.'

'Fantastic!' I said. 'One of you two can phone up and pretend to be Bran.'

'Whoa, whoa, whoa, whoa,' said Roger. 'Nuh-uh. Not me. Todd, you're up.'

'Wow,' I said. 'Way to slither out of stuff.'

'I'm not on the staff of Trinity Solutions,' said Roger. 'Also – newsflash – I'm Black.'

'It's a phone,' I said. 'We're not Skyping.'

All four of them looked at me as if I had asked what to eat at a ballgame.

'I sound blacker than Dr King's mailman!' said Roger. Someone snorted.

'What does that even mean?' I said. 'Why are you laughing?'

'Lexy,' said Noleen. 'Are you telling me you can't tell if a person is Black unless you're looking at them?'

'Are you telling me you *can*?' I said. 'Seriously? What the hell? What are we going to do, then? Todd's Latino and Devin's too young.'

'What do you mean, "Todd's Latino"?' Todd said, the smile snapping off his face. 'Are you telling me you think brown people *sound* brown? Jesus, Lexy!'

'What?' I said. 'Don't they? I mean, you? How the hell am I supposed to know this stuff if no one ever tells me?'

'You got one thing right,' said Noleen. 'Devin sounds like a skateboard come to life. No way like a dentist.'

'So either you or Kathi is going to have to pretend to be Brandeee, then,' I said.

'Brandee,' said Noleen, with exaggerated patience, 'is missing.'

'But no one,' I said, with just as much, 'knows that, up at Whackjob Acres. *We* were supposed to be telling them, remember? And slap ma erse wi' a Loch Ness monster, I cannae dae it! You want to cut cards or pull straws?'

'This has got to be illegal, right?' Kathi said, when she had stopped arguing. She was sitting in my armchair, with a glass of water at her side and the sheet of security questions and answers in her lap.

'Definitely,' said Todd. 'Get dialling.'

The phone was on speaker and so we all heard the ring, then the jaunty female voice announcing that we had reached 'White Pine Residential Academy, the way home!'

'Sick!' said Noleen. We shushed her, as the jaunty voice led us through the menu. We did not know our party's extension and Kathi began to look panicked as the options stacked up: Huckleberry House, Bluebird House, Garnet House, Syringa House . . .

'Syringa House?' said Noleen. 'They trolling these kids?' We shushed her again.

 . . . Academics, Administration, Pastoral, Housekeeping, Grounds . . . And then they started on the coaches. White Pine Academy was pretty sporty, it transpired.

'Pastoral,' said Roger. 'Try there.'

Kathi took a deep breath and keyed in the extension.

'He-lope!' came a voice. 'Pastor Dave, here. How can I help you?'

'Hi,' said Kathi, using a breathy little voice, like Marilyn Monroe singing 'Happy Birthday'. 'It's Brandee Kowalski-Lancer here. Blaike's mom?'

'Well, hey, Mizz Lancer!' said Pastor Dave. There was a great deal of fluffy rustling at the other end of the phone. 'I'm just gonna go ahead and put you straight through to the principal. You have yourself a blessed day now, you hear me?'

And the line went dead.

'Blimey,' said Todd, who had taken up British exclamations purely to annoy me in the first instance and now found himself unable to ditch them. It was adding to our kitty wonderfully. I held out my hand and he slapped a ten in it.

'That was a lot of panic,' said Roger.

'For a pastor,' said Noleen.

'And he didn't run through security,' I said.

Kathi was already dialling again. 'Administration,' she said, 'if I'm going to get kicked up to the boss's office anyway.'

The jaunty voice started in on the menu again, but Kathi cut her off.

'Captain Rossoff's office,' said a slightly less jaunty real-life version of what I was sure was the same voice. 'How can I help you?'

'Hello, dear,' said Kathi. I couldn't help reacting to that – surely Brandeee didn't 'dear' people? – but Kathi gave me the finger and she had a point. If this woman had been in post long enough to have recorded the outgoing phone message, Brandeee should know her. And know her name. Which she didn't. So she couldn't use it. I gave Kathi a thumbs up.

'Who am I speaking to?' said Jaunty Voice, only she was less jaunty again. She sounded nervous.

'This is Brandee Lancer,' Kathi said. 'Blaike's mom?'

'Oh,' said the least jaunty voice I had ever heard in my life, including at funerals. 'Hello, Mizz Lancer. What can I do for you?'

'I was hoping to speak to the principal,' Kathi said.

'Oh!' Jauntiness recovered slightly. 'Certainly, I can put you right through.'

There was a short period of silence and then a gruff, booming voice came down the line: 'Rossoff's office.' He sounded exactly like that little dog who was trained to say 'sausages' that time. I had to bite my lip not to giggle.

'Captain!' Kathi purred, making it even harder not to laugh. Did she really think straight women approached every call like they worked on a chatline?

'Brandee,' he said. 'How are you? How are things down there in la-la land? What can I do for you?'

'Well,' Kathi said, 'you can run through the security questions. No one did that yet.'

There was a long pause on the other end of the phone. Had she blown it? Did no one ever actually do the security check? The principal cleared his throat at last and said, 'Of course, of course. So this isn't a social call? That's a shame.' He was lying. He sounded relieved. 'I enjoy my little chats with parents when they call to talk to their boys.'

Now there was a pause at our end. 'Well, I'm not calling to talk to Blaike,' said Kathi. 'Obv—'

He cut her off. 'Good! That's good, because I was going to have to tell you, you couldn't.'

'I kn—'

'He's in detention. Nothing serious. Just a little infraction of a pretty minor rule, but he's not taking calls right now.'

'He's . . . in detention?' Kathi said.

'He's caulking boats for Coach Roach,' the principal said. 'I'm looking at him right now. He's putting his back into it. You got a boy to be proud of, there, Brandee.'

'He's outside caulking boats in Idaho in February?' said Kathi. She had let the sex-kitten voice slip a bit and I was sure the ensuing pause was the penny dropping.

But no. It was Captain Rossoff thinking on his feet, and he wasn't a twinkletoes. 'Noooooo!' he said at last, with a kind of desperate bonhomie. 'Ho, ho, ho! He's in a nice warm boathouse. I'm looking at him on the live feed. I like to keep a close eye on things, as you know. It's part of what made you choose White Pine. So . . . what is it you wanted to discuss with me?'

'Yeah,' said Kathi. Then she paused. 'Oh! No! Gotta go! My dog's about to puke on the hardwood.' And she hung up the call.

'What a great way to get off the phone,' I said. 'I'm going to remember that and use it on my mum.'

'You'd have to buy a puppy if she decides to visit,' Noleen pointed out.

'Worth it,' I said. 'Anyway . . .'

'Yeah,' said Roger, sounding grim. He cut no slack when it came to kids being safe. He never spoke about work much but I always assumed he'd seen some things.

'White Belly Academy are hiding the fact that Blaike ran away,' said Noleen. 'Kinda puts our little game into the shade, huh?'

'You think they're scouring the woods with tracker dogs and praying they find him before they have to come clean?' Kathi said.

No one answered her specific question. But after a long quiet spell, Todd said, 'What the hell's going on?'

Operation Find Blaike was going on, that's what was going on. Kathi reprised her blonde-bombshell-cum-soccer-mom routine for every contact number she could glean from the chat boards. She got pretty good at it too. 'Hi there!' she'd breathe. 'It's Brandee. Brandee Lancer? I'm calling for news to take up to Blaike when we go visit. Anything happening I can tell him?'

If the kid had been holed up in the den of any of these houses, surely the mum would have said. Or if she'd been trying not to say, surely she'd have sounded awkward or jumpy. None of them did. They all sounded kind and concerned in exactly the smug sort of way you would sound if the mother of a boy who'd been packed off to boot camp rang you up and asked how your angel (in comparison) was doing.

'So either he didn't go to a friend,' said Todd, 'or he didn't go to a friend whose parents are in the parenting loop, or he's being hidden *from* the parents *by* a friend.'

'Or he went home,' said Noleen.

I shook my head. 'He ran off like a rabbit at the idea that I would tell Bran he was here,' I said. 'He didn't go home.'

'White Pine?' said Kathi. 'Maybe he ran back. Hey! Maybe

the reason they're hiding him running away is it's not the first time!'

'Maybe,' said Roger. 'But until he turns up there for real what we've got is a homeless kid, outside in winter, with a rainstorm forecast. We gotta find him. We gotta either find him or tell Bran and the cops, and they'll find him. Hell, maybe we gotta just tell the cops right now.'

'Or maybe,' said Noleen, 'we could call in our resident expert first. Huh? How long was Devin homeless before he came here?'

'Long enough to know some good spots we can check,' said Roger. 'Call and get him in here.'

In the time it had taken us to have our meeting, Della had finished with her lawyer, Devin had finished with his textbook, and Diego had wrapped his curly little head around the fact that someone was DATING HIS MOMMY. They all came when we texted Devin, and my heart melted to see that he was carrying a sleepy Diego in pyjamas.

'Huh,' he said, pointing at Roger. 'Are you a girl doctor?' He didn't think much of the *Frozen* scrubs, it seemed.

'I'm wearing Batman tomorrow,' said Roger. 'Girls and boys love him and they love Elsa too. Who's that on *your* PJs?'

'Pikachu,' said Diego, with a look of blistering pity for anyone sad enough not to know facts of such cultural significance.

'So, Devin,' I said, when he was settled in on the hearthrug, with Diego curled up inside his crossed legs. When did I stop sitting on the floor when there was a choice? I'd be taking a deckchair to the beach next, or eating fish and chips with a fork. 'You know, after you left the dorm, before you got here?'

'Yeah?' said Devin, with a wary look at Della.

'*Estúpido!*' said Della. 'If I was a gold-digger, I would be the worst gold-digger in the world.'

'Where did you sleep?' said Todd. 'We're looking for someone who knows Cuento but can't go home. Any ideas where we could start searching?'

'Seriously?' said Devin. 'I don't often get to be the one who says you people have no idea how lucky you are. You seriously don't know where to go in Cuento when you've nowhere to go?'

'I came here,' I said, thinking back to the night I left Bran, when I had forty dollars in my wallet and was willing to wash motel dishes to get a bed for the night.

'None taken,' said Noleen, who, if she wanted people to think she was running the Four Seasons, shouldn't advertise bug nets on her roadside sign.

'I came here too,' said Todd. 'And it was the luckiest move of my life. Best decision I ever made since my wedding day.'

Roger was staring straight ahead, clearly thinking quite a few thoughts about the fact that he lived in a motel room, but not letting any of them show on his face.

'Me too,' said Della, which counted as gushing. I'm sure Noleen got a tear in her eye.

'If it's a person who knows the town . . .' Devin said.

'He went to Tony Coelho Elementary and then Cuento High,' I said.

'No doubt about it then,' said Devin. 'You need to climb the trees.'

ELEVEN

I knew about the Cuento Treetops, obviously. They were one of the things the town was famous for, along with . . . They were the thing the town was famous for. Next to the UCC campus, a small area of Monterey pines had been taken over in the heady days of the seventies counter-culture and filled with tree houses. Students still lived there, climbing rope ladders to get home, bathing in solar-heated gravity showers and pissing off city planning officials and university modernizers alike with their composting toilets, their grey-water gardens and their general commitment to doing absolutely no harm to anyone at all, while not saying a word of complaint about the plasticky entitlements embraced by those of us with trashier lives. I could see why they annoyed everyone.

But, when Todd, Devin and I set off to discover if Blaike had rocked up there and I actually saw the place, I couldn't help but be enchanted. We were only half a mile from First Street but it was half a mile of campus and playing fields and there was a hush as if we'd been transported to another realm. Or Yosemite anyway. I saw it first as just a glow up ahead but as we kept walking I saw that the glow was made of fairy lights strung in the trees, candles burning in the windows of little wooden houses perched high up above us, and a bonfire crackling away in the cleared central area I think served as their town square.

'Good,' Devin said. 'I thought we might be too late, but there's plenty of folks still sitting around.'

He had told us that the permanent residents of the trees cooked a big meal every night to share amongst themselves and with anyone who turned up and needed food.

'Free?' I had asked.

'If you've got money, they'll take it,' said Devin. 'But if you don't, they won't starve you.'

'Why did you ever leave?' I whispered now, as we stood in the darkness just outside the warmth of the bonfire.

'You'll see,' Devin said softly, then stepped forward. 'Hey!'

'Dev!' came the cry from around the fire. 'Long time no see, my dude! You home again?'

'Welcome,' said a woman, the only one who had got to her feet. I recognized her. She quite often sat and drank coffee outside my second-favourite Cuento coffee shop after the Swiss Sisters drive-through, and she did a lot of ostentatious yoga poses right there on the pavement, as if she was in danger of seizing up if she left her limbs unknotted for half an hour. 'Come,' she said. 'Sit. Eat.'

'Good to see you, man,' said a child who looked no more than twelve to my eyes, but then it *was* firelight. 'Who's this you're bringing us?' He gave me a sleepy smile as we squeezed ourselves into the ring of people. Some of them were strumming musical instruments – mostly ukuleles, it has to be said – and some of them were texting on their phones, the blue from their screens uplighting their faces and turning them eerie.

'Lexy and Todd,' Devin said.

'You hungry?' said another woman. 'The stew's finished but we got some banana curry pizza.'

'That's why I left,' said Devin, under his breath, to me.

I giggled. 'I'm OK,' I said. 'I've eaten already.'

'You freelance freeganning?' said the twelve-year-old.

'Uhhh . . .' I said.

'Freegans,' said Devin. 'They eat the food that gets thrown away from stores and restaurants.'

'And hey,' said the woman who had greeted us, 'you do you, yeah? But share, don't waste, yeah?'

'In other words,' said Devin, under his breath, 'how dare you gorge yourself on the food you found in a garbage can, when you could have brought it here and added another topping to the banana curry pizza.'

'I see why you had to go,' I said, taking a joint from the twelve-year-old and passing it on without smoking any. 'Are any of them ever going to play anything, or do they just keep plinking away?'

'Is Baloo still here?' Devin asked the general company, instead of answering.

'Baloo packed his pipes and went to Portland,' a voice informed us from the other side of the bonfire.

'Bagpipes?' I whispered. 'Or pan pipes? Actually, it doesn't matter. Yeah, I take your point: it could be a lot worse.' I cleared my throat and spoke up. 'We're looking for someone. A runaway. He was supposed to be in Cuento today and we were going to look after him, but he didn't arrive and we're getting worried.'

'If he came here, he came here,' said the woman who had welcomed us.

'*Did* someone come?' I said.

The joint had got as far round as her now. She took a deep puff that made the lit end glow fiercely. Maybe it had illuminated Todd, bouncing off his diamond earrings. For whatever reason, he suddenly attracted her attention. 'Are those blood gems?' she said, pointing the joint at him.

Todd was sitting with both knees to one side like the little mermaid, instead of cross-legged like everyone else, and, as he turned to answer her, the curve of his neck and the elegant twist of his spine was swanlike. She scowled at him. I saw it. She already hated him; it was nothing to do with what followed.

'Do you grow your own weed?' said Todd. 'Or use an ethical supplier? Worker conditions in the field are so very upsetting unless you're careful, aren't they?'

'Our marijuana is all produced in California,' she said.

'Please don't use that racist term,' said Todd. 'I find it offensive to my Mexican heritage.'

'This is my home!' she said. 'You are not the boss of my talk in my home.'

'Gotcha,' said Todd. 'If you feel you own this patch of my native land I would be wasting my time to fight you. So many of my ancestors died fighting the conquerors. I choose peace, now.'

'Not cool, Devin,' said the twelve-year-old. 'Who is this anyway? And who's this one?'

'I'm just a lowly immigrant,' I said, catching Todd's wave.

'I'm used to people who've been here longer not wanting to share the bounty. I get it. There are only so many slices of pie.'

'Seriously, Devin, dude?' someone else piped up. 'Who are these assholes?'

'Oh, you're homophobes, are you?' said Todd. 'I can't believe you reduced me to an orifice to shame my sexuality.'

Personally, I thought he had gone too far. If I had a dollar for every time I've called Todd an arse, I'd be able to hire an assistant to call him it for me. But the now-not-the-least-bit-welcoming woman surprised me.

'I find your rejection of woman power personally insulting,' she said.

'Wait, what?' said Devin.

'Did you just say a gay man is an insult to you?' I asked her.

'To turn away from the eternal truth of the world—'

'Wow,' I said. 'I'm a marriage and family therapist by day, so I have heard some codswallop in my time. But that takes the biscuit, crushes it with butter and uses it as a base for a double-chocolate cheesecake. You need a smack on the back of the legs, missus. Seriously.'

'Uh, Devin?' said the twelve-year-old. 'I'm not sure this is gonna work out, my dude.'

'Maybe we should just . . .' I murmured.

'Is the "eternal truth of the world" really that bathing is optional and hairbrushes are the devil's work?' Todd was saying. 'Is the power of woman to knock a guy down with her halitosis from twenty paces?'

'I think we might just slip away now,' I said softly to the girl who was sitting on my other side.

'But you came for Blaike, right?' she said, softly too. 'Don't you want to see him?'

I felt my mouth drop open. 'He's really here?'

She shuffled back from the firelight on her bum and got to her feet in the darkness, with me scrambling after her.

'Tourmaline gets kinda dick-ish on weed,' the girl said as we edged further away. 'But she gets really dick-ish on booze and she's a nightmare straight, so what can we do? She's been through a lot and she's a great carpenter.'

'Yeah,' I said. 'I've had some bad neighbours too. I didn't have to share banana curry pizza with them, mind you.'

We were right out in the dark now, out of sight of the fire-light and out of earshot too, although we could still hear Tourmaline and Todd going at it hammer and tongs. They were on to Big Pharma now; she must have found out he was an anaesthetist. I hoped he'd find out she was a carpenter and get her on the genocide of trees.

After a moment of picking our way along in the dark, the girl switched on her head torch and leaned back, lighting up the underside of a gnarled and misshapen tree. It had a set of things that looked like mammoth nails – but which I now knew, after a trip to the Railway Museum in Old Sacramento, were railroad spikes – driven into its bark to make a staircase. About fifteen feet up, there was a wooden platform snugly lodged into the tree's crown. I could see a small hole in it that I guessed must serve as the entrance. It looked an acrobatically long way away from the topmost nail.

'Uhhhh, you go first and I'll watch,' I said.

She handed me her head torch and was off up the spike stairs before I had managed to fumble the damn thing into position. I got the beam trained on her just in time to see her disappear through the hatch as easily as a rabbit popping down its hole in the middle of a field. Briefly, I remembered the man in black sliding into the truck cab through its open window.

I put my hands on a spike as high as I could reach and pulled myself up until my feet were balanced by the instep on a pair of lower ones. No wonder she moved fast; it was excruciating, the way the metal dug into the flesh on my feet. I had to climb just to relieve the weight. And then, at the top, I had the choice of: stop climbing and let the shafts of the spikes destroy my insteps again; bash my head against the underneath of the platform; go back down; or do what I chose to do – swear under my breath, sure I was about to die if I was lucky or spend the rest of my

life in a recumbent wheelchair if I wasn't. I let go with
one hand and grabbed the edge of the hatch. Then I moved
the other hand. Then I climbed up the last few steps with
my feet, while shunting my top half into the hole and along
the floor. Then I let go with my feet and dangled half in
and half out of the tree house, bent at the waist, then
lolloped forward again, like a walrus galumphing up a
beach and finally got one knee inside and pushed myself
up to all fours, panting.

The girl was watching me and trying really hard not to
laugh. I acknowledged her kindness and straightened my
clothes, blowing upwards into my sweaty hair. Then I got
distracted. I'd never been in a tree house before and I didn't
know if this one was typical, but looking around – I was still
wearing the head torch – it felt like I had wandered into Enid
Blyton. It was tiny, like a caravan or a narrowboat – much
smaller than my place – and there was no bed as such, just a
hammock swinging diagonally across the entire space. But
there was a little pot-bellied stove with a bent tin pipe going
up through the roof and there was a window with shutters,
and a lot of shelves, all full of books. The laptop lent a bum
note but the fact that it was sitting on a little ledge made out
of the tree trunk itself helped.

'I can't believe he didn't wake up when you were climbing,'
the girl said. She was standing up in the middle of the floor,
looking down into the hammock. I got to my feet and joined
her. It was awkward to look at him and not shine the torch
right at him, so I took it off and turned it away.

Bathed in the gentle gold light reflected back from the
wooden walls, he looked like a child. He was curled up under
a patchwork quilt, still in his jacket and with his boots sticking
out at the other end.

'What did he say when he turned up?' I asked.

'Not much,' said the girl. 'He was tired and hungry and he
looked scared. He didn't need to say anything. That's not how
it works here.'

'How d'you know it's not me he was scared of?' I said.
'Or Devin? Or Todd and his blood gems?'

'You shouldn't laugh at people when they're being good to

you,' she said. 'He hitchhiked – rough work these days – so his trouble wasn't local.'

'These days,' I repeated. She looked about sixteen; these days were the only days she had ever known. 'And you're right,' I said. 'It *is* rough. I don't even know how he managed to hitchhike from . . . Ohiowado . . . and get here already.'

'Where?' said the girl. 'Nah, he flew to Sacramento and hitchhiked from the airport, but still, you know.'

'OK,' I said. I put my hand out and touched his shoulder lightly. 'Blaike?' I shook him, just a little. 'Blaike? Sorry to wake you.'

He opened his eyes and blinked. Then he tried to turn – he had forgotten he was in a hammock, I think – and flipped himself right out, landing at our feet on the hard floor.

'Oh my God,' I said, laughing in spite of my worry. 'That was perfect. I bet you couldn't do that again if we paid you. Are you OK?'

'How did you find me?' he said.

'I'm a witch,' I told him. 'Look, I'm sorry I was so by the book and freaked you out. I know you're seventeen but we're not going to report you to your stepdad or call social workers or anything. We just want to take care of you and work out what's going on.'

'What's going on with what?' said Blaike. He was still lying on the floor.

'The belly button,' I said. 'Obviously. That's not nothing. But also Mama Cuento's toe and then there's this wooden nose too.'

'This is some trippy shit you're into,' the girl said. 'What the hell are you talking about?'

'But the main thing is something much more serious than all of that,' I said. 'I don't want to tell you right here and now.' Because who was this girl? I was asking myself. She took him in, then she grassed him up?

'I'm not going back,' he said. 'To White Pine.'

'Honey, I don't think anyone will be at White Pine much longer, when we go public with what we know,' I said. I think that's what finally convinced him. He got to his feet and rubbed his face with his hands. 'So,' I said, 'you can sleep here for the night and we'll get together in the morning. Or we could just go now.'

'Go where?' he said. 'The motel?'

I took a punt on why he sounded so wistful. 'The motel,' I said. 'King-size bed, power shower, coffee machine, HBO.'

'I don't drink coffee,' he said.

'There's a Coke machine in the car park,' I told him. 'And an ice machine too.'

He turned to the girl. 'Thanks,' he said, 'for letting me have a nap in your hammock. But I think I'll go.'

She didn't look too happy about it but, even if she had had plans to join him after dinner and even if she found it entertaining to have sex in a hammock, she couldn't possibly have wanted to share one all night long. She shrugged and slipped down through the hatch, without another word. It was only then, as I watched her go, that I faced the certain fact that there was no way I could get out of this tree house without firefighters helping.

I put the head torch back on and peered down through the hole in the floor at the spike steps – even further away, I swear to God.

'Shit,' I said. 'How are we going to get out?'

'What do you mean?' said Blaike. He sat down on the floor, dangled his legs through the hole and disappeared.

I sat down on the floor as soon as he'd gone. I dangled my legs through the hole too. I told myself it wouldn't be so bad to live in a tree. I'd be like a swami. Maybe my most hippified clients would still come for counselling. That truly seemed like a more realistic option than launching myself into thin air and not dying.

When we were back at Todd's jeep, twenty minutes later, I still thought it was a semi-serious option that I could have explored further. It didn't help that Blaike wouldn't stop laughing. He tried. But he obviously kept remembering the sight, sound and smell of me and then his giggles would break out again.

Yes, smell. Because, as well as wanging around like a string of spit and praying out loud for the first time in years, I farted from sheer terror. And here's some news: when every muscle is clenched tighter than a Baptist with tetanus and yet you still manage to squeak out a fart, it is not silent. Not at all.

TWELVE

'That was fun,' Todd said, when Devin and him got back to the jeep. I had texted, *Got Blaike. Let's roll,* and they'd appeared through the trees, minutes later.

'What was?' I said, carefully reversing along the narrow space between pine trees, ignoring the roots under the jeep wheels and the scrape of needles on the paintwork. 'The pizza? The company? The thick cloud of smoke from unethically sourced pot? The rampant hypocrisy?'

'Locking horns with Tourmaline,' said Todd. 'Do you want me to drive by the way? I don't meet many targets so easy. Made a nice change.'

'Who are you?' Blaike said. 'What target?'

'I'm Todd. I'm one of the private detectives your stepdad has employed to . . . talk to you.'

'Yeah, about that—' Blaike said.

'Now's not the time,' I said. I was weaving through the quiet roads of the UCC campus now – empty, for the most part. Except that there were always some pretty girls, apparently on photo shoots. I didn't understand why the multistorey car park was the most popular of all backdrops. Right now, as we passed, I saw a little band heading in there, carrying lights and reflector screens and wheeling a rack of costumes. A girl in a towelling dressing gown, with her hair in big rollers, came along behind, texting and smoking.

'Blaike,' I went on, 'why did you get sent to White Pine?'

'Arson,' he said.

That shut us all up.

'I didn't do it,' he said. 'But there was no way to convince anyone. Once they'd decided.'

'Talk us through it,' I said. I wasn't exactly scared of Noleen anymore and I'd never been scared of Kathi, but still I didn't fancy bringing an arsonist to stay in their motel and them finding out, either because someone told them or because he burned the place to a cinder. It was all right for me. I had a moat.

'I set fire to a buncha stuff,' Blaike said.

'Go on,' said Todd. 'Because I gotta tell you, so far I'm on team Mom and Dad. But I'm ready to be convinced.'

We were in downtown Cuento now, on First Street. 'Pizza?' I said, pulling in at the Brick. 'It's a wood-fired oven, if it's not too indelicate to mention such a thing. But guaranteed no bananas and no curry.'

'I set fire to a buncha stuff as an exorcism,' Blaike said. 'The point was to get rid of it, not the fire itself. But I did it in the backyard, near that big eucalyptus?'

'Ohhhhhhh,' I said. 'That was you?' I had read about it in the *Voyager* – a fire in someone's back garden in the Spanish streets, smack in the middle of the driest, deadest month of a dry, dead summer, when everyone was freaking out about the brush in the hills to the north of the state and the neglected forest inland.

'That was me,' said Blaike. 'I got kicked out of CHS.'

'Permanently?' said Todd. 'That doesn't sound like the CHS I went to.'

'No, just a semester,' Blaike said. 'I didn't even care. I could have done my work at home with a tutor, but Mom has the most suspicious mind of all moms.'

'Right,' Devin said. 'She knew you would download the assignments and spend all day playing—'

'Fortnite, yeah,' said Blaike. 'Like she doesn't use every red light to get in a game of Angry Birds. She's obsessed with it.' He spoke with the easy scorn of a child who believes his mother will always be there, annoying and dependable. I wasn't looking forward to breaking the bad news.

'What do you want on your pizza?' I said. 'Each choose one topping and veto one topping, and I'll work it out.'

'Artichokes and no anchovies,' said Todd.

'Extra cheese, no cat food,' said Devin. He meant sausage but he had a point.

'Pepperoni, no pineapple,' said Blaike.

'No pineapple is a given,' I told him. 'What a compatible carful we are tonight. One extra-large, thin-crust pepperoni, mushroom and artichoke pizza, with double cheese, coming right up. And I'll get a small spicy Hawaiian with extra anchovies for Noleen and Kathi.'

'What does Della like on her pizza, Dev?' Todd said.

'Salmon.'

Todd pulled a sharp breath in over his teeth. 'Ouch,' he said. 'Sorry, man.'

'So why not the . . . What do you call it, Todd?' I said when I was back in the jeep with the pizzas ten minutes later. 'Or, if you've already done this, don't go over it again for me.'

'Continuation high school?' said Todd. 'No, we haven't. We were talking about Steph Curry.'

'Who?' I said.

Blaike laughed until Devin told him I wasn't joking. That clued me into the fact that it must be a sports player. And if Todd *and* Devin had been discussing her, she couldn't be a figure skater or a climber.

'Right,' I said. 'Blaike, why didn't you go to the continuation high school?'

'Because my stepdad's a snob,' Blaike said. 'Sorry, Lexy, I know you were married to him.'

'Only that one time,' I said. 'We all get to make a mistake. Speaking of which, this "bunch of stuff" you set fire to? You want to say any more about that?'

Blaike was silent for a while. We chugged under the tracks, past the cop shop, drive-through and self-storage, and had turned in at the Last Ditch before he spoke. 'No offence,' he said, in the end. 'But who are *you*?' I realized he was talking to Devin.

'I'm a consultant,' Devin said. 'Bound by the same client confidentiality as everyone else in Trinity.' It was news to me.

'Since when am I a client?' Blaike said.

'This is where it's got the potential to get awkward,' I said. 'Branston is actually our client, Blaike. Remember I said earlier that he had asked us to come up to Iowada-ho and talk to you? Well, it was an official assignment. I see you with your hand on the door. Please don't run again. Hear me out.'

'After the pizza,' said Todd. 'And a beer. Ten minutes of Steph Curry, beer and pizza. We all need a break.'

'So long as she's not a sleazy reality star,' I said. 'I'm not watching some poor schmuck get exploited by a camera crew.'

'Seriously?' said Blaike.

'Seriously,' Devin said.

Turns out Steph Curry is a man and he plays basketball. Roger, Kathi and Noleen were already watching him play it when we got to Todd's room. Della had peeled off, partly because of Diego's bedtime and partly because one of the few opinions she shared with me, although neither of us would ever speak them, concerned how much fun it was to watch ten giants bouncing a ball.

When they had all finished rushing about in their squeaky shoes and both pizzas were down to crusts and greasy boxes, Roger turned off the telly and gave me a significant look.

'I've been thinking, Blaike,' I said.

'When?' he asked, truly mystified that I'd had a brain cell to spare while those enormous men had lolloped about, patting a ball into a hoop with their enormous hands.

'Yeah but before you do that,' said Noleen, 'we've been hustling. We called Branston. Poor guy snatched the phone off the hook before it even rang.'

'Oh, really?' I said, giving her a stern look. 'He must be worried about something, eh? Maybe we could talk about that later on, eh?'

'Oh!' Noleen said. 'Right. Yeah. So anyway I'm real proud of what I thought up to say to him.' She cleared her throat. '"Trinity Solutions calling, Mr Lancer."' I took a moment to reflect that Trinity's workforce was expanding by the minute. '"Lexy has gone to see Blaike." Neat, huh? Cos he'd think I meant gone to Idaho, but really you'd gone to the hippy commune. Anyway so I said to him, "I just wanted to check that we're cleared to talk to the kid. Those security questions and answers you gave us copies of? You did mean us to use them to gain access, right?"'

'Ohhhh, clever,' I said. 'I was worrying about that.'

'Me too,' said Kathi, 'since it was me who did the possibly illegal impersonation.'

Blaike had been following along pretty well but he was only seventeen and he had to be tired, as well as worn out from travel and upsets. He was beginning to look mightily confused.

'What's going on?' he said.

'Absolutely!' I said, robustly. 'I agree I should just tell you straight.' I took a deep breath. 'But first: why did you run away from White Pine?'

'Because they call me Smokey the Bandit,' he said. 'Not the kids; most of them are off their heads on Adderall – which is another thing. That place was soaking my mom for a shit-ton of fees like they were so great at straightening us all out but, if they'd lost the keys to the drugs closet, it would have been Armageddon. Buncha grifters.'

'So the teachers called you unkind names?' I said.

'Right. It's not like it made me cry into my pillow, you understand. It's that it made me realize they weren't so highly trained and talented and all that nonsense in the brochure. They were stiffing my mom for all this money and it might as well have been sleep-away camp. They called me Smokey the Bandit; the guy who did my one-on-ones brought his crossword book into sessions with him. *And* he looked stuff up on his phone. Guy cheated on his crossword, with me sitting right there. And he filled in all the bullshit in the world we were supposed to have discussed and explored: "Blaike is still struggling with authority. Unresponsive to suggestions and resistant to new ideas." What ideas? What suggestions?'

'So you didn't like your new school,' I said. If I hadn't heard the principal lie to me down the phone, I wouldn't have given this report a second thought. Blaike had been a whiny fifteen-year-old when I knew him. The notion that he might be a whiny seventeen-year-old two years later was no kind of bombshell. And there was still the matter of him denying the label 'arsonist' just because he 'set fire to a bunch of stuff'.

'Why Smokey the Bandit?' Noleen chipped in.

'What was the last straw?' I asked hurriedly.

'They put it in my record that I had burned my mattress because I didn't want to wash the dishes when it was my turn.'

'You didn't, right?' said Kathi.

'No! I *did* the dishes. Kind of. Thing is they always put them back in the microwave after we've eaten, to get stuff really stuck on and make it harder. So when I did them, I wiped them over with a cloth enough so if they hadn't been back in the microwave they would have been clean. Then I went to rowing practice. Because if you miss two you're off the team and I had missed the last one because we'd had spaghetti and meatballs and the tomato sauce wouldn't shift.'

'And the mattress?' I asked.

'I went to my bedroom and it was gone. There was the box spring and the blankets and a pillow, but no mattress. I asked my room-mate what happened and he said the deputy principal had come in and taken it away.'

'And they said you burned it?' I asked him. 'Did they tell you that?'

'No way,' Blaike said. 'I hacked into the records. Well, OK, I paid this kid Jeffrey to hack in. He got in first time about three months ago and they didn't catch him, so anything you want to know, you give Jeffrey a quart of bourbon and he tells you.'

'A quart . . .?' I said. 'Where the hell do you get quarts of bourbon?'

'The dark web,' said Blaike. 'It gets delivered to the chem teacher. He takes ten per cent before tax and shipping.'

'Jesus,' I said.

'Anyway so, my mattress?' said Blaike. '*Someone* burned it. I couldn't sleep, on account of laying right on the box spring, and so I looked out of the window in the middle of the night and saw it smouldering. It was under a tree. I thought that was a nice touch, if they were trying to frame me.'

'And why would that be?' said Noleen.

'You never did tell us what it was you burned in your garden under the eucalyptus tree,' I said, thinking the best thing would be to blooter right through it.

'Whoa, whoa, whoa!' Noleen said. 'You're *that* kid? Lexy, you didn't tell me he was *that* kid.'

'My dad's stuff,' said Blaike. 'My fake dad's fake stuff.'

'Go on,' said Roger.

'My dad – Leonard Kowalski? Turns out he never existed.'

'What do you mean?' Kathi said. 'You've got his name.'

'I know, right?' Blaike said. 'My mom's got his name, I've got his name, there were photographs and stuff. There was a great big picture of a baby, that looked like all the other baby pictures of me, and I'm with this guy in it and so I always thought that was my dad – Leonard Kowalski – until he died.'

'What changed your mind?' I asked him.

'My mom told me the truth,' said Blaike. 'She sat me down one Saturday morning when Bran was out golfing and said that, since I was going to be eighteen and I would be expecting my trust fund to kick in, she was going to have to tell me that there *was* no trust fund because my dad, Lenny Kowalski, who she had said set it up for me . . . never existed.'

'Why the hell did she tell you he had set up a trust fund?' I said. 'If you believed everything she told you for seventeen years, why did she tell you something that was going to bring it all crashing down?'

'She told me about the trust because she thought she would be able to sock away enough money to make it true by the time I turned eighteen. And she came clean because that didn't work out like she expected it to. She spent a lot of money divorcing Bran, then a lot more money divorcing Burt, and then because Bran is her business partner she lost a lot of money when Bran divorced you, Lexy. So, basically, you killed my daddy.'

'Hang on!' I said. 'Rewind!'

'I'm kidding.'

'No, I mean hang on and rewind to the bit where it cost your mum a packet when Bran divorced me.'

'Because he had to buy you out of the house and he set you up in a business of your own and bought you a yacht.'

'A yacht?' said Roger. 'Is that what they told you?'

'My "yacht" is moored on the slough behind this motel,' I said. 'It's a hundred-year-old wooden houseboat with a foot-pump-action tap in the kitchen and a chemical toilet. *And* I inherited it. Also, my business wasn't a drain on theirs. My business was two thousand cards from SpeedInk and a domain registration. I left the Beige Barn with a rolling suitcase, containing my own clothes. Ask these guys. I came straight here that night – fourth of July last year – with nothing.'

'She's telling you the truth,' Todd said. 'Even the roller bag wasn't worth packing, actually. Her clothes were a sin against fashion. I had to take her in hand. Sorry. Not the point.'

'So your mom told you when you were seventeen that your daddy wasn't this great guy who left you a trust and died,' Kathi said. 'I'm not being mean, but welcome to the club, kid. Who was he?'

'A sperm donor,' Blaike said.

'Huh,' said Kathi. 'That actually does suck. Why did she tell you the story?'

'I don't know,' said Blaike.

'Why did she call herself Kowalski?' I said. 'I mean, if she was making the whole thing up, she could have called herself anything. Like Tourmaline.'

'I don't know that either,' said Blaike.

'And so you took the baby pictures and other stuff from your fake childhood, and you set it all on fire?' I said.

'Under a eucalyptus tree,' said Blaike. 'Accidentally causing a bit of a mess in our backyard and the neighbour's, yeah.'

'And so, they sent you away to a military academy, for arson?' said Kathi.

'Not military,' said Blaike. 'Just real mean. And now she won't even answer her phone. Well, she might be answering it now, but mine's out of charge and I can't get in touch with her.'

No one said anything. They all just swivelled, in unison, like a team of synchronized swivellers, and stared at me.

'Thing is, Blaike,' I said, 'the reason we were coming up to White Pine, when you stopped us by coming down here, was that your stepdad wanted us to tell you something.'

'Is my mom OK?' he said.

I hadn't been feeling good about hiding the truth from him anyway. But now, now that he had asked the question outright in his suddenly tremulous voice, sounding much younger than seventeen, it was time for it to stop.

'Absolutely,' I said. What was wrong with me?

'Where is she?'

'We don't . . .' I said, '. . . think it's a good idea to tell you.' Blame me, sue me, shoot me. Do all three. The kid had been through enough for one day.

THIRTEEN

'You'd make a good dad,' I said to Todd an hour later when we were standing over Blaike, watching him sleeping, finally. It had taken a while, but he was under at last. That was the main thing. And he was on my boat too. Noleen had been very sympathetic about the shock he'd had re the sudden non-existence of his dad, leading to the fire under the eucalyptus, but she'd pointed out that he'd just had had quite an upsetting time of it again, between one thing and another. And if I thought he was house-guest material then I could guest him at my house.

'I intend to,' said Todd. 'Be a good dad, that is. Roger needs a little encouragement. Being a baby doctor, he only sees the calamities. He doesn't believe we could raise a child without medically induced comas and emergency tracheotomies.'

'Does he believe you could raise a child without a home?' I said gently.

'Why not ask Della?' said Todd. 'See what she thinks about the horrors of raising a child in a motel.'

'Why don't *you* ask Della?' I said. 'You ask her what she thinks of someone living in a motel room, who doesn't have to. You feeling lucky enough to broach that subject with her?'

'I know, I know,' said Todd. 'Of course, I know. But I'm happy here, Lexy. With you and the others. I like living with family round me. It was always only Mom and me, growing up. I never knew this. It's not an easy thing to walk away from.'

'Oh puh-lease!' I said, loud enough to make Blaike catch his breath and turn away, humping on to his shoulder. I hoped he wouldn't bang his head or his bony feet against the panels of the little box bed. I hadn't realized how short it was until I saw him fold himself in there.

'Yeah, that was too much,' said Todd. 'But I'm glad you're nagging me about long-term self-improvement even in the heart of this crisis.'

'Oh?' I said.

'Because I still think you should go on a date and I've got one lined up for you. He's the uncle of the costume manager of the Sacramento Ballet.'

'How old is he?' I said.

'Forty. Never been married. Been building his business. He's an architect.'

'No, he isn't,' I said. 'No one is an architect in real life. Are you sure he's not a vet? And a widower? With a golden retriever?'

'OK,' said Todd. 'You got me. He owns a portable-toilet rental company.'

'OK,' I said. 'That's important work. What made you think I would have a problem with it?'

'Oh my God!' said Todd. 'You're serious, aren't you? He's a goddam architect, Lexy. Take the win. Although, now you come to mention it, I do know of a single man in the toilet-rental business . . .'

By this time, Blaike was actually thrashing back and forth, presumably trying to escape the nightmare he was having that his parents were standing over his bed, bickering. So we withdrew, going along to the back of the boat to stand in my midget kitchen.

'OK,' I said. 'I'll go on a date with this clearly fictitious individual if it'll shut you up.'

'And I'll . . . What do you want in return?'

'Nothing,' I said. 'In return, I want you and Roger back in your lovely house, and you back in your proper job that your poor mother sacrificed so much to educate you for.'

'You really want this to end?' said Todd. 'Trinity? Us?'

Of course I didn't. I didn't want anything to change. I didn't want Devin to graduate and take Della and Diego away. (I kept thinking of that lawyer asking him if he was a citizen and how he didn't go white and run.) I didn't want Todd to recover and leave me alone. As much as I complained about him bursting into my bedroom in the morning, judging my choice of bedtime reading, thread count, night cream, PJs, and language when woken by intruders, I always started the day a bit flat when he was too busy to swing by. Ah, well, I'd still have Kathi and Noleen. Even if Kathi ever recovered from her germophobia, she'd only go as far as the owner's flat. And it was closer to my houseboat than the room she and Nolly usually slept in.

'Let's not get ahead of ourselves,' I said. 'We need to solve this case. And I need to go on a hilariously awful first date and come back and tell you about it, to make you sorry you pushed me.'

The boat rocked gently and I put my head out of the kitchen door just as Kathi arrived at the top of the front steps. She came through the living room and along the passageway towards us. 'You see the news?' she said. 'Someone's been shot.'

'Oh God,' I said. 'Who? Brandeee? Where? Here? Cuento?'

'South Dakota,' Kathi said. 'There's a statue. Huge great big beautiful statue of a native woman. I mean huge!'

'I've seen it,' said Todd. 'How the hell did someone steal that? It must be fifty feet tall.'

'No one stole it. But everyone got scared someone was going to. So some folks got a posse together and went to guard it. It's on public land. But it didn't go down too well with some other folks. And . . . you know how it is. He's OK, the guy that got shot. But he got shot.'

'Maybe . . .' I said. 'Don't jump down my throat, but maybe it's a good thing. It'll raise the profile of the case. Won't it? And if Bran did make it up about Brandeee's acrylic he might get cold feet and come clean. At least people will be paying attention now.'

'Because some guy shot some other guy at a roadside rest stop in South Dakota?' said Kathi. 'Ya think that'll hit the front page of the *New York Times*?'

'The vigilantism might,' I said. 'And the three statues that have gone missing. Come on! A Latina town mother in California. A pregnant Asian in' – I dug deep – 'Idaho. Yay me!'

'Utah,' said Todd. 'There weren't any internment camps in Idaho.'

'Oh,' I said. 'Right. And a Black girl in Oregon? The point is don't tell me that's not a story.'

'Unless Alice in Wonderland in Central Park gets her hair-band twanged, nobody's going to care,' Kathi said. 'Except us. What the hell's going on? That was some freaky stuff about Blaike's fake dad, wasn't it? And that school! Where do we even start with any of this?'

'I'm going to start with Brandee's co-workers,' Todd said. 'Just like Bran suggested. How's she been? How's her mood been? Who is she close to? All that. Get some sense of why she might have run. Or if she had any reason to fear her partner.'

'Speaking of which,' I said, 'I think I'll try to track down Burt.'

'Who the hell's Burt?' said Kathi.

'You know how you introduced yourself on the phone to White Pines as Brandeee Kowalski-Lancer?' I said. 'She's really Brandeee née Rumsfeld, fake Kowalski, Lancer one, Towser, Lancer two. Burt Towser took a spin between bouts of Bran.'

'Does he live in Cuento?'

'I don't know. But how many Burt Towsers can there be? Poor guy. What are you going to do, Kathi?'

'Bowling team uniforms,' she said. 'Life goes on. But while they're rinsing and spinning, I'll be on the phone trying to find witnesses who might have seen who stole the other two statues. It must be the same crew, right? Must be.'

I woke at four o'clock, to the sound of rain pattering on the wooden roof of the houseboat. Me – a Scot – woken by rain! If I stayed in this country for the rest of my life, I wouldn't know myself at all by the end. I'd be embalmed, in an open coffin, all my pals taking selfies.

As I turned over, I thought about how glad I was that we'd found Blaike and got him out of the tree house before the weather broke. Because it really had broken. It wasn't pattering now; it was hammering, drilling down like stair rods on to my roof. I made a mental inventory of windows – all shut tight – and I tried to remember if I'd left any cushions or books out on the porch. (California weather lulls you into compla-cency that way.) I couldn't think of anything, but there was a faint meep coming from the front door and I slid out of bed and went along to let one of Diego's cats in out of the rain. He had two of them, both as white as snow and distressingly fond of rolling about at the creek's edge. I hoped the other one was tucked in under one of Diego's skinny little arms and not about to get swept up in the water as it rose.

And it would, if this carried on. I used to think the storm drains were only there to freak out cowards who'd read too many horror novels – I jumped past them, always half-expecting an arm to come whipping out and grab my ankle. But when I saw my first real downpour I understood why they'd never get away with a polite little grille in the gutter, like we had back home. Storms here were like leaving the taps on and the plug in. A jaw-dropping surge of water, more like a tide than a shower of rain. And, living in a houseboat, it was even harder to ignore. I felt the floor beneath me start to shift and creak; we were on the rise already. I scooped the kitten up and went back to bed, telling myself there were lots of shelters in the parks for the homeless to get under; they were meant to be sunshades for summer barbecues but they worked for rainy nights too.

But I still couldn't stop thinking about Brandeee. I could barely imagine her on a patio, or a beach, or even a street. I certainly couldn't imagine her huddled in a doorway or lying in a row of other unfortunates, under the corrugated iron roof of the farmers' market. We should check, though. Someone should ask around. I tutted and resettled myself, earning a grumpy little miaow from the cat. We should have asked the tree people if a skinny woman with blinding blue-white teeth had been there the night before Valentine's Day.

Surely not.

But if she hadn't taken her car and she hadn't used her cards, where was she? Unless she had a different set of cards and she was using *them*. She must have some kind of talent for invention to have conjured a whole husband out of thin air, photos and all, and then killed him off again. Leonard Kowalski. He'd have been even easier to find than Burt Towser.

*   *   *

Next time I woke, heart hammering, I could hear someone moving – nay, blundering – around on the other side of the boat. Not Todd bringing coffee! I sat up, flipping the little cat, who'd been pinning my legs down. It yowled and jumped on to the floor, then trotted out of the door, which was ajar.

'Hey, kittycat!'

Blaike. I finally remembered.

'Morning!' I called out.

He put his head round the door. 'Hey.'

'I can't stop thinking about your dad,' I said. 'Lenny Kowalski? Didn't he have any other family? A granny and grandad for you? Aunts and uncles?'

'Huh,' Blaike said. 'Nope. How dumb was I, never to ask?'

'Not dumb at all,' I said. 'A kid. Did she tell you how he died?' It made no difference; only if she'd claimed he was a war hero or something I was ready to despise her even more than I did already.

'Elk hunt,' he said. He was looking more and more uncomfortable and obviously working up to saying something. I gave him an encouraging smile. 'Is it OK to use that dinky little bathroom, or should I go to the motel?'

'Um . . .' I said. How do you ask a seventeen-year-old boy you barely know if it's a number one or a number two? Because I tried not to overload my 'dinky' little bathroom, but I didn't want to start a discussion.

'No!' he said. 'Don't tell me I need to stand on the deck and pee in the slough?'

Ah, number one. 'No, no, go for it. Bathroom's all yours. Have a shower, if you like. Use my purple shampoo. It works wonders on your highlights.'

'I might just do that,' Blaike said. 'I think I got cooties from that hammock last night.'

He was gone before I realized I had just talked my way out of an early morning pee of my own. Now *I'd* have to go over to the motel.

But such is the power of the cootie card. I'd never heard of them before I got here but, because chiggers sounded made up and weren't, and no-see-ums sounded completely impossible and weren't, it took me a while to twig that cooties weren't real. People even spoke about 'cootie shots'. They weren't real either, as I realized when Diego gave me one.

Of course, it was still raining. I put a cape on at the back door and stepped gingerly along the side of the boat, on the strip of deck that runs round it. The rain plotched down from the branches overhead and chuckled in little rivulets, slowly feeding the slough, where the water was starting to swirl with brown blooms of mud from the banks and would soon be like oxtail soup till the sun came out again.

And of course, I didn't make it into the office without Todd seeing me. 'Breakfast date?' he called down from the upstairs walkway, where he was lounging in the open door of his room in his shortie pyjamas, having just waved Roger off to work. 'You really going like that?'

'Blaike's in the bathroom and I need a wee,' I called up. 'I'm not going anywhere.'

'*Au contraire*,' said Todd, stepping back and beckoning me. 'Come up and use ours and I'll tell you exactly where you're going.'

It was a tough choice. On the one hand, Todd was offering a vacant toilet – and at breakfast time in the office it was far from guaranteed that there wouldn't be a paying tourist guest shedding some of the free coffee supplied along with that microwave porridge – but on the other hand it was going to come with a side serving of intrusive bossiness about something or other.

My bladder overruled my brain and I went up the metal stairs, two at a time, and along the walkway. The rain really was shitting down. Those dead-flat roads would soon be flooded and the silty mud of the fallow tomato fields would be turning to gumbo.

'Don't you own any waterproof footwear?' Todd said as I kicked off my sodden Converse at the door to his room and scampered loo-ward. Todd and Roger's bathroom was a treasure chest wrapped in a cliché. More cosmetic preparations than two faces could possibly soak up in the course of a night and a day stood ranged in all their overpriced glory on the shelves. I gave them a good look, used a bar of white soap to wash my hands and rejoined Todd out in the bedroom. The bedroom was a treasure chest too, but wrapped in less of a cliché. In fact, it was somewhat surprising. The motel furniture had been moved out and replaced by sleek, modern design, expensive art and top-of-the-range brushed-steel appliances. Apart from the fact that it was a room, not the five-bed house with pool that they owned, it was OK. It was a lot swankier than my boat.

'So where am I going?' I said, sitting down on the grey moleskin sofa and accepting a tiny cup of bitter espresso.

'Date,' he told me, in the tone of voice that usually says, *Duh.* He necked his own espresso and shrugged out of his pyjama shorts into the sweats he wears to go to the Swiss Sisters and buy the real coffee.

I hardly blinked. There was nothing suggestive, much less aggressive, in his stripping. Todd believes his body to be a wondrous part of God's creation – he's not wrong – and thinks sharing it is like bestowing favours on the rest of humanity.

'Date. Right,' I said. 'The architect uncle. Does it have to be today?'

'Yes, it has to be today,' Todd said, putting on a scarf and then another one and then, after a look in the mirror, a third. His morning coffee-run style is very Bolshoi practice studio. 'But it's not the architect. I was puzzled about him being single and so I did a little digging. And what I learned . . . Well, I pulled you. Put it that way.'

'Do I want to know?'

'Only if the words "Margaret Mitchell slash fiction" don't worry you. But I managed to get you in with the manager at the port-a-potty rental company, since you seemed so taken with that career arena.'

'How . . .?'

'Connections,' Todd said. 'His name is Doug. He's very artistic and you're having lunch with him.'

'We're kind of busy, Todd,' I said. 'In case you didn't notice.'

'And here comes Kathi now,' Todd said. 'To split the day's tasks. Someone has to interview Brandee's colleagues and other friends, someone has to find and talk to Burt Towser, and someone has to try to get some kind of a bead on this statue insanity.'

'I said I'd do statues,' Kathi said, as she let herself in. 'It's online and I need to stick close to the laundromat. Then later I've got a whole house diagnosis for a prospective new Trinity client. I could tack some interviews on to that . . .'

She would too. She would make herself traipse round filthy dentists' surgeries and other people's revolting houses, pulling her weight like a trouper.

'I'm slammed,' Todd said. 'Back to back until after three o'clock, except for one slot. And I thought I might hang out with Blaike and get the full story of the belly button. But, if you need me to sweet-talk information out of anyone, I can work late and do it then. I do have the knack of getting people talking.'

In direct contradiction to this claim, I found myself counting to ten before I spoke. I was a therapist, for God's sake. Getting people talking was 80 per cent of my job. Plus 10 per cent providing tissues and 10 per cent providing answers. Roughly.

'So like I said, I'll find Burt *and* interview as many of Brandeee's associates as I can get round, and go on a lunch date,' I said. 'After a nine o'clock counselling session. Todd, is it OK if I send Blaike up here, to get him out of the way?'

'Lunch date?' said Kathi. 'The architect?'

Oh good. Todd wasn't just interfering; he was oversharing too.

'He's gone,' I said. 'This one works at a port-a-loo rental company.'

Kathi reared back and I could have kicked myself.

'As the manager! I'm sure he doesn't touch them. And I won't be touching *him*. No kisses on first dates.'

She was still rearing. And actually, who could blame her? Whenever I found myself behind a trailer-load of port-a-loos on the freeway, I did tend to drop back a bit, in case of sloshing.

I hurried on: 'After my nine o'clock, I'll go to Bran and Brandeee's office and start the interviews. What was the name of the receptionist he mentioned? Elsie, was it?'

'Ha HA ha ha ha ha!' said Todd. '*Elise*, but I dare you to call her that.'

*   *   *

Blaike was more than happy to go and hang out with Todd at nine o'clock, telling me he thought Todd was 'cool' and had 'way cool' games. In other words, he thought I meant Devin. I tried not to think about how 'uncool' Todd would appear to a seventeen-year-old straight boy. He went skipping off – well, slouching off but in quite a chipper fashion for a teenager – and I prepared for my nine o'clock client: a third-time woman in her forties, who was edging very slowly towards the reason she wanted to see me. Maybe this would be the breakthrough session, I told myself, as I put on the ocean sounds and set my indoor water-feature to *trickle*.

And was it ever! I don't think I opened my mouth to say a single word after 'How have you been?' and before 'Will we make another appointment?' She let rip: on the topic of loneliness, middle age and early mistakes mostly.

'I didn't want to settle,' she said. 'I dated and I even got serious once or twice, but there was always something wrong. He was too work oriented or he wasn't ambitious enough. He was too unstable or too boring – too boring! Can you believe it? Who cares if someone's boring? You can read or watch TV or stream a podcast. You can go out with your girlfriends for fun, or have a little affair on the side even. Boring! The guy I dumped because he was boring is married with three kids and a cabin at Tahoe. His wife's a Facebook friend. She doesn't look bored. She looks happy.' She sighed and shook her head. 'Sometimes I even stepped back from some guy because of his looks! His looks! I track them all, now. The ones that looked good back then are like bowls of pudding. Some of the ugly ones grew into themselves or they got better hair and teeth. And some of my gal pals are happy with Jabba the Hutt because he's funny and good with the kids.'

She sighed again and made some kind of strange scooping gesture that had to be yoga related.

'So here I am at forty-eight, all wised up. But the forty-eight-year-olds who would have had me when we were both twenty-five are still looking at twenty-five-year-olds. And the men looking at forty-eight-year-olds are seniors! White hair and pigeon chests, retired to the golf course. I'm not ready for that! Then I hear myself say so and I think I'm doing it again. And in ten years, when the only ones who want me are in electric carts, with oxygen tanks, I'll look back to now and kick myself all over again.'

For a solid hour, this went on. She left me reeling, ears ringing, brain scrambled, and with only one coherent thought: she was right, and what was I going to wear to lunch with this artistic toilet boy?

FOURTEEN

B urt Towser wasn't hard to find, although there were more of them across the land than I'd expected. I took a punt that the orthodontal surgeon based in Madding was the one I was after, and set off up there at ten o'clock.

It was still pelting rain, which usually cheers me up – bringing, as it does, memories of childhood and Scotland; of jumping in puddles, and cocoa by the fire afterwards; of life without drought and wildfires. Today though, I had been hoping to keep my hair within the normal range of acceptable styles for toilet boy but, as I drove up the state route between Cuento and Madding, I began to see the edges of it in the rear-view mirror as it grew and frizzed and grew again, like a home chemistry trick with baking soda. When I took a look at it, after parking, I thought of those bolls of killer tumbleweed that cause pile-ups in the desert, and of those fridge cakes you make by rolling cornflakes in melted toffee, except I looked like one great big one dragged across a barber's floor before it was set all the way.

Towser's office was, as so many offices in these parts are, in a big block of suites set round an atrium, with more parking than they needed (surely) and a handy little strip mall across the way, offering a Daivz coffee, a Korean barbecue, a nail salon and a juice bar. I think it's a local zoning law that these four establishments appear in every five-unit strip mall in the state. The wild card this time was a doughnut shop, all the better to make more customers for orthodontal surgeons across the way.

I was sure the receptionist could tell I still had my wisdom teeth. She stared at the hinge of my jaw as I asked whether Dr Towser had a free moment in the next hour or so.

'You don't have an appointment?' she said. 'Dr Towser is extremely busy, scheduled all day, with no breaks.' But she was still staring at a point just in front of my ears.

The sensible thing to do was to make an appointment, but I had spoken to Bran on the hands-free while I was driving.

'Brandee?' he had said breathlessly, after less than one whole ring.

'Lexy,' I said. 'You haven't heard from her then?'

'It's been four days, Lex,' he said.

'Have you had any more . . . deliveries?'

'No, thank God. Nothing.'

'And nothing by way of a follow-up to the last one? They said, "obey instructions". Have they given you any instructions to obey?'

He gasped. 'Oh God. Oh my God. That never even occurred to me. What if the instructions are lost in the mail and—?'

'Wasn't it hand delivered?'

'What if the instructions blew away from under the porch and they—?'

'Didn't you fit a camera?'

'But Lexy,' he said, and his voice had sunk to a whisper, 'what if she's dead? What if I never see her again? What if they've hurt her and she's alone and scared? What if she's crying? What if she's cold?'

So I was going to try every way I knew how to get in to see Burt as soon as I could, and then, if that didn't work, I was going to do every other thing I could think of to find Brandeee and bring her home. Bran would never be my favourite person in the world, unless a pandemic with a sense of irony wiped out everyone else except him and me, and I didn't much care for Brandeee either but he loved her, I now realized, and love is love. Look at Charles and Camilla.

'No, I don't have an appointment,' I said, putting a hand up and pressing the place where the receptionist was looking. I worked my jaw from side to side once or twice, as if it was causing me discomfort. Then I had a brainwave. 'But I do have excellent dental coverage and, if I don't use it before I go overseas, it's going to expire before I'm back again.'

Dollar signs popped up in her eyes like cherries in a slot machine, and she invited me to take a seat while she checked Dr Towser's suddenly elastic diary.

A flicker of recognition crossed Burt's face as I was shown into his office half an hour later. We had met twice while I was married to Bran and he was married to Brandeee. I wouldn't have recognized *him*. He was Mr Generic America, Type A: neat hair; tanned face; professionally ironed blue shirt, showing his vest underneath it; pale chinos; terrible, awful, heinous shoes (where do they get these shoes?); a booming voice and, of course, a dazzling smile.

'Burt?' I said.

He frowned slightly at the use of his first name, California friendliness fighting with the constant insecurity of not quite being a doctor. I remembered it from my time with Bran.

'Forgive me for tricking your receptionist. My teeth are fine.' I waited to see if the look he was giving me would give way to a voiced thought. Because of course no UK teeth are fine, in the view of an American dentist. And not just dentists. Roger and Todd had to stop watching *The Great British Bake Off* because they couldn't stand the contestants' gappy yellow smiles on their huge flat-screen.

Burt managed to say nothing about my ridged enamel, alloy fillings and lower-set snaggles. He was probably playing a long game.

'I'm Lexy Campbell. I used to be married to Bran Lancer?'

He narrowed his eyes and clamped his jaw together tight enough to give him a sexy sort of early Clint Eastwood look.

'Did you know that Brandeee was missing?'

'I knew she'd left him,' he said. 'He called me two nights ago, frantic, asking if I knew where she was. Maybe he thought she'd come back to me.'

'She didn't leave him,' I said. 'She didn't take her car and she hasn't used her cards.'

That had got his attention. He sat up straighter behind his big empty desk and then grew very still. 'Is she OK?'

'That's what we're trying to find out. Bran told the cops, so they've got alerts out for her – I think – but she's an adult so she's low priority for them. But . . . there's reason to believe she was kidnapped.'

'Kidnapped!' he said. I hadn't thought he could sit any

straighter. He was practically levitating now. 'As in . . . for a ransom?'

'As in for a ransom. They sent Bran a note, with one of her finger—'

'Oh God! They cut off—'

'—nails!' I said.

'Oh God, they pulled out—'

'Acrylic!' I said. 'Her stick-on nails.'

He slumped now. 'Oh! Of course. She was always so very well groomed. Such an attractive woman. Such a joy to come home to.'

I don't think he meant to draw a contrast with me. I wasn't on his radar at all, despite being dressed up to the nines – i.e. in my very darkest jeans and with earrings – for my lunch date, but I was intrigued anyway.

'So . . . you were happy?' I said.

'Brandee and I?' A smile spread across his face. His teeth really were fantastic. 'We were blissfully happy. She was beautiful, energetic, successful, interesting, engaged, resourceful, independent, sweet, caring and supportive. She was the wife every man dreams of.'

I honestly didn't know where to start with any of that. She'd had two husbands already – one real and one fake – before she landed in Burt's lap, all resourceful and supportive. Surely that was a bit of a dent in the credit rating? And anyway who the hell dreams of a wife who's energetic? Unless he meant in bed? Who dreams of a wife who's independent? I thought men dreamed of a wife who was beautiful and didn't nag them for eating onion Pringles. If this was what toilet boy was after, I was in big trouble come lunchtime.

'And did you keep in touch?' I asked. 'Have you spoken to her recently?'

'We didn't,' said Burt. 'Too painful for me. She didn't keep in touch with her first husband, Lenny, either. She's a remarkable woman all round, Lexy. Tough, clear, sensible. She doesn't cling or mourn, like most . . .'

Functioning humans, I said to myself, finishing it off for him when he realized, too late, that he was saying all of this to a manifestly less tough, clear, sensible, beautiful, successful, blah-blah-blah example of the fairer sex.

'Well, no,' I said. 'She wouldn't have been able to keep in touch with Lenny, would she?'

'Oh, that's right,' said Burt. 'He died.'

And she certainly kept in close touch with Bran, I thought but, being very mature, didn't say. I had seen them in very close touch that time I came back to the Beige Barn unexpectedly.

'So, you can't help me?' I said. 'Or the police, if they come?'

'Why would the police come to me?' He was sitting up very straight again, not quite levitating yet but definitely activating boosters.

'Um, off the top of my head,' I said, 'because she left you and you still love her and someone grabbed her and tried to scare the husband she left you for. I'm just guessing.'

I swear it was only his knees under the desktop that were stopping him from floating up to the ceiling. 'Do I need a lawyer?' he said in a small voice.

'I'm the wrong person to ask,' I said. 'But where were you the night before Valentine's Day? After ten o'clock?'

This time when he slumped, he almost slithered out of his chair completely. 'I was doing a night shift in a parking lot,' he said. 'All night. Three dozen witnesses.'

'You're a car-park attendant? As well as an oral surgeon?'

'The parking-lot health centre,' Burt said. 'Oral division.'

'The what-what where, now?' I said. 'Night-shift car-park orthodontistry?'

'Not really,' he said. 'Pretty basic dental work, in fact. For the homeless and destitute. The uninsured. We've got a couple of trailers we move around. I do a night a week, usually, and that night was my last one.'

See, this is why I love American people. They're just better than us. Every Thanksgiving, they're handing out soup, and they're forever coughing up five hundred smackers for a shitty dinner to keep a library open. They don't spend nearly as much time as I do slumped on a couch, half-cut and re-watching *Buffy*.

Of course, like any other affluent American, Burt would have a gardener, ironer, general cleaner, window cleaner, carpet cleaner, pool cleaner, accountant, financial adviser, five different doctors, that lawyer he was itching to phone and probably a therapist. If he had a dog, he'd have a dog therapist too. So obviously if he was going to kidnap his ex-wife, he'd rely on a kidnapper.

I didn't say any of that. Instead, I said, 'Well, thank you for your time. I'm sorry to be the bearer of such troubling news. And if you do hear anything, if Brandeee gets in touch, could you phone Bran and put him out of his misery?'

He nodded. He really would. He would phone the guy his wife left him for, to spread relief and remove worry. This country would never cease to amaze me. I thanked him again and made my way to the door.

'If she had come back to you,' I asked, stopping before I opened it, 'would you have taken her?'

'Of course,' he said. 'In a heartbeat. She's the perfect woman.'

Her perfection meant that I wasted the time I could have spent starting to grill Elsie and the rest of Bran and Brandeee's employees on trying to find a hairdresser to fix me up before lunch. They were all fully booked except for one that had had a timely cancellation but who looked at me and said, 'It's going to take more than a blow-dry.'

So, I went early to the restaurant, thinking I could maybe do something myself in the ladies' loos, but just looking at it made me feel overwhelmed. If I'd had a do-rag, I would have toughed out all accusations of cultural appropriation and just covered that sucker up. As it was, water made it look like a patch of heather; the bottle of finisher I had shoved in my bag made it look like a patch of heather that had been sprayed with glitter; and brushing it turned it into a perfect halo of sticky frizz.

One of the waitresses came in while I was staring at it.

'I don't suppose you've got any kirby grips?' I said.

'Any what?' She was rushing to get her apron off before she went into the cubicle.

'Ummmmm, bobby pins?' I said.

She laughed and shut the cubicle door.

'Or are there any hats in the lost and found?'

'Ew,' she said. 'Cooties.'

Would make-up help? I wondered. Or would showing that I cared what I looked like make this mad hairdo seem deliberate and all the more weird? If I left it, I'd maybe come over like Frances McWhatsit, mind on higher things. But would toilet boy be looking for a girlfriend with her mind on higher things? I kept remembering Burt waxing on about Brandeee – resourceful, energetic, successful, supportive and sweet – and I tried to imagine what someone would say about me – disorganized, lazy, struggling, snarky and a bit shit.

'Every pot's got a lid,' I told my reflection.

'*What?*' said the waitress, through the cubicle door.

He was already at the table when the hostess showed me over and, since he was looking down at his phone, I had plenty time to study him. His overall aesthetic was certainly more towards the 'manager of a toilet rental company' aspect of his make-up than the 'artistic' bit: he had a buzz cut, tidy facial hair, T-shirt advertising a brewery, and jeans as dark as my own. On the table beside him, his baseball cap, advertising a different brewery, sat upside down with a pair of sunglasses and a wallet inside it. He was, in short, that category of American male I've come to think of as a walking truck payment. The only thing that stopped my heart sinking into my soggy Converse was the fact that his Scottish equivalent would have had worse hair, a scragglier beard, an unfunny slogan on his T-shirt, exactly the same jeans, and no hat or sunglasses because it was never good enough weather to need them. On the other hand, his Scottish counterpart would have been either funny or quiet, understanding that those were the choices. This guy, I was willing to bet, would talk very long and very loud even if the last time he had made anyone laugh was accidentally, by falling over.

'Oh God,' I said to the hostess. 'How do I get out of this?'

She spoke out of the corner of her mouth, like an old pro.

'Gimme your phone. I'll take your number and call you in ten minutes with a family emergency.'

'Thank you,' I said. 'But make it twenty. I'm hungry. Hi!' I went on, in a louder voice, getting to the table. 'Doug?'

'Lexy?'

We shook hands. His was large and dry and he didn't do the knuckle crunch.

'Water?' he asked, holding up a bottle of fizzy.

'Lovely. Thank you,' I said.

He stopped dead. 'Irish?'

'Close,' I said. 'Scottish.'

'Me too,' he said, sending my heart – which had climbed to my knees – back downwards. Down through my feet, through the floor, through the foundations of the building, to where the earth was still warm. 'Irish, anyway. Yeah, my maternal great-grandpa was a Dolan from County Cork.'

I buried my face in my glass and took a big drink to buy some time. I could never, ever, ever work out what I was supposed to say to any of that. It wasn't interesting. Everyone alive had grandparents and they all came from somewhere and they all had names. And that's without even thinking about the casual way he'd decided two completely separate countries were the same thing. Briefly, I considered exclaiming, *I've got friends in Canada!* to see if he'd get it, but I didn't want the evidence, as soon as this, that he wouldn't. Instead, I played it dead straight.

'My maternal great-grandpa was an Anderson from Glasgow.'

A quick frown crossed his face as if he wanted to say, *So?* but was trying not to.

A quick smile crossed mine as I decided not to say, *See?*

Then we both looked down at the menu.

'So how do you know Todd?' I said, when I had checked for steak and kidney pudding, failed to find it and settled on a salad.

'He did my sister's makeover after her divorce,' said Doug. 'You ever had one of these improbable burgers?' If he meant that, maybe he was funny after all. If he didn't, he was barely literate.

'They're pretty good,' I said, trying not to think about the ethical ramifications of Todd mining Trinity's client base for dates. 'I mean, if you're going to have raw onion, pickles, ketchup, mustard and bacon on there, why not?'

'And cheese,' he said. He really might be funny. I smiled, even though I was still deciding.

'And how is she?' I asked. 'Your sister. I'm divorced too. It's not easy, sometimes.'

'She's pretty good,' he said, then smiled at himself for nearly calling his sister a burger. He *was* funny! 'And her closet is awesome!'

'That's Todd,' I said. The server came over then and took our order for two improbable burgers with everything. I thought about how we'd call Impossible Burgers improbable forever now, and so would our kids and our grandkids without any of them knowing why. Then I got a hold of myself. 'So, you're in equipment supply,' I said.

'Actually, I own the company,' he told me. 'I say I'm the manager at work so I can tell cold callers I don't have authority to buy stuff. It's gotten to be a habit, I guess. But I'm the owner, yeah.'

'It must be a booming area,' I said. 'You see them everywhere.'

'I'm doing OK,' he said, preening slightly; the guy was only human. Now came the test. He should ask me something, if this date was going to be chalked up as successful.

He leaned in close. 'More water?'

That didn't count.

'And you're a bit of an artist in your spare time,' I said. 'Is that right?' I still couldn't square artistic ambitions with the cap full of sunglasses on the tabletop. 'Do you . . . paint?'

'Sculpt,' he said.

Ahhhhh, I thought. Scrap art. I'd have put my burger on it.

'Have you ever heard of Dora Dango?' he said.

Now, here was a first-date dilemma. I hadn't, of course, and of course I should say so. But pretending to have heard of obscure artists isn't really lying, any more than pretending to have read *Finnegan's Wake* is lying. I could look her up after lunch, or even during, on a bog break. And how amazing that he brought up a female, right out of the gate, like that. This one might actually be a keeper. I should be my best self, just in case.

'No,' I said. 'Is she a sculptor too?'

He blinked once or twice then threw back his head and laughed like a storm drain in a downpour. 'Do-ro-dan-go,' he said. 'The Japanese art of dirt polishing.'

I felt a sheen of sweat slick my neck. I had so nearly claimed to love her.

'Dirt . . .?' I said.

'You make a ball of . . . mud, and keep adding finer and finer . . . soil to fill the rough surface until there are no more pits or cracks at all and it's completely smooth. Look.' He plucked his phone out of his hat and swiped it on. His background image was something I'd have said was a planet, if I hadn't known.

'You did this?' I said.

'Uhhhhh, I made the dorodango,' he replied, slightly weirdly.

'It's . . .' *Beautiful* was obviously the missing word in the sentence, but it was a round ball of shiny dirt. Call me a philistine. 'Where is it? In your garden? Yard, I mean.'

'Oh no,' he said. 'They're far too fragile to keep outside, or even in a room with draughts and traffic. I've got these neat little round tanks, temperature controlled, in my apartment.'

'And how long have you been making them?' I said.

'For myself, five years. I took my first commission two years ago and did my first tournament in the summer.'

'T–tourn—?' I said, sitting back to let the server put my burger down. 'Competitive . . .? Like a . . .? Does that attract a crowd?' I didn't know if I was joking.

'Huge crowd,' he said. 'In Tokyo. It's nail-biting.'

I took a bite of burger and used my chewing time to decide if there was any more to say about polishing dirt balls.

'Are they always brown?' I said. 'Or grey? Do you import fancy dirt from chalk regions and all that?'

He nodded thoughtfully while he was chewing his own

mouthful. 'I've started experimenting with colour,' he said. 'Great results with beets.'

I laughed without meaning to, and then stumbled over my words to assure him I wasn't laughing at his purple mud balls. 'Something I read online,' I said. 'About having beet-root for lunch and forgetting. You go to the loo and stare at death for a minute, till you remember.'

He stared at *me* as if *I* was death, pretty much.

'Sorry,' I said. 'Gross.'

'Not at all,' he said, then took another mouthful.

I was still waiting. He swallowed and wiped his lips, the napkin scraping over the neatly trimmed ends of his moustache hairs. Another mouthful and another wait. If he didn't ask me anything about myself now, I would give him up, possible sense of humour, own business, beet balls and all.

'So what do you do exactly?' he said. 'I know you work for Todd, but in what capacity?'

'*With* Todd,' I said. 'I'm a therapist. Marriage, family, personal. A counsellor.'

'Whoa!' he said. Then he followed it up with, 'That's great.'

'Is it?' I said. 'It just as often freaks people out.'

'Not me,' he said. 'I'm guessing you're open-minded and non-judgemental.'

'I try,' I said, thinking, why is my damn phone not ringing, because this guy is seriously not OK. Who the hell admits, right out loud like that on a first date that he needs someone open-minded? What was he hinting at? What was he into? What was I going to do to Todd for getting me into it too?

'I'd like to make you a dorodango,' he was saying now.

'Aw,' I said. 'That's nice. I'd like to get you on the couch and ask about your childhood.'

His laugh was about as open and easy as it could be, which is to say it was really awkward and uncomfortable, but at least he laughed.

'How long have you been in Cuento?' he said, when he had sobered up again.

Two questions in a row. I answered him. Then I asked if he'd seen the news about Mama Cuento and if he had a theory, and long story short when my phone rang, he said: 'Your getaway?'

And I laughed and said yes, but stayed on for the rest of lunch and stretched it into coffee. He had a soy latte and I didn't even care.

When we left, it was with a plan to meet in two days' time and see a movie.

'You choose,' he said.

'Ha,' I said. 'No way. You choose.'

'I'll get it down to three,' he said. 'And you pick the winner.'

Which was so sensible and reasonable that, as I made my way to Bran's office to quiz Brandeee's colleagues, I found myself smiling as I remembered the second handshake he'd left me with after lunch, half-wishing it had been a peck on the cheek so I could have checked for aftershave before I got carried away.

Todd phoned as I was parking in another landscaped car park beside another set of office suites set around another atrium.

'How's Blaike?' I said.

'He went back to bed and he's still sleeping,' Todd said. 'But I phoned you, Lexy.'

'OK.'

'Well?'

'He knows absolutely nothing,' I said.

There was a long pause. 'That's a bit harsh. He knows everything there is to know about the Warriors.'

'I didn't know you knew him,' I said. 'And sports trivia isn't going to bring Brandeee home.'

'Oh my God!' Todd said, making the phone buzz. 'Not Burt, Lexy. Doug!'

'Oh,' I said. 'Well, he's . . . OK. He's . . . all right. He's . . . He called it an improbable burger.'

'Deliberately?'

'Don't know.'

'And?'

'We're going to the pictures the day after tomorrow.'

'What are you going to see?'

'A documentary about fungus,' I said. 'Butt out, Todd.'

'You're welcome, I'm sure,' he told me waspishly and hung up. I waited. Right enough, he rang back. 'So Burt knows nothing? And you believe him?'

'I do. He still loves her, but in a wistful way, not in a chop-her-into-three-pieces-and-store-her-in-a-freezer way.'

As I hung up and headed into my second dentists' office of the day, I prayed it was true.

FIFTEEN

You'd think a dentists' office would be dead when both the dentists were AWOL, wouldn't you? But a successful American dentists' surgery runs on a lot of nurse and hygienist energy, with the dentists themselves stopping by for a minute or two once a year to glance at X-rays. So Lancer and Lancer was going like a fair: lots of patients waiting in the plush chairs, flipping through the golf magazines; the sound of power washers emanating from all four treatment rooms; and a small child screaming lustily as a stranger in a mask approached with instruments of torture. Some things never change.

There were three young women behind the counter. One was drop dead gorgeous but had the sort of extravagantly short hair and facial piercings that would have terrified Bran. One was as plain as a pudding, with painful-looking lasered acne and a figure like a paste pot. The third one was so beautiful she didn't look real. Probably not a great deal of her *was* real – her lashes, hair colour, lips, boobs, nails and the sculptural contours of her face certainly weren't. But her tiny waist and intense violet eyes were beautiful too.

'El-ise?' I only just managed to say to her. She frowned at my mouth, as if she could tell from that angle that I'd never worn braces and only flossed after a barbecue. I ran my tongue round my teeth self-defensively. My teeth were fine and my parents hadn't had to remortgage the house for them.

'When's your appointment?' she said, batting the unlikely lashes over the unlikely violet eyes. Coloured contacts, I suddenly remembered. And she might have a corset on.

'I'm not a patient,' I told her. Then I leaned in close, so the people waiting wouldn't hear the next bit. She rolled back a foot or two in her desk chair, which was completely unnecessary. I do not have halitosis. Or cooties. Maybe she knew her contouring wouldn't stand such close scrutiny. 'My name's

Lexy Campbell,' I said, and I watched her eyebrows hook up, squeezing the immobile skin of her forehead. Surely she was too young for Botox? And for Bran. 'I'm a therapist and . . .' Oh what was the bullshit Todd had come up with to make therapy and investigation sound like a less crazy combo? 'Troubleshooter,' I said. That wasn't right, but it would do. 'I've been employed by Dr Lancer to look into the disappearance of his wife. You did know that Dr Kowalski-Lancer was missing, didn't you?'

The phone rang and she glanced at it. I gestured to her to go ahead and do her job.

'Lancer and Lancer,' she said. 'Elise speaking. Can I put you on a brief hold? My lunch break is in fifteen minutes,' she said to me. 'I'll meet you at the coffee shop between the nail bar and the Korean barbecue. Just across the street.'

'I know you're close to Bran,' I said, as she slid into the chair opposite me with her personal cup of – there was no way to tell, but I was willing to bet it was – something unspeakable. 'He told me his first instinct when he had a bad shock was to call you. So don't worry that I'm going to think there's anything dodgy going on.'

'Dodgy?' Elise said, with a pout.

I managed to make my sigh a soundless one. I'd met her type before. Cuento was full of them. She wasn't just spoiled; she was that special, coddled, peeled-grape, weep-till-you-get-your-way, affluent white girl kind of spoiled that would sulk and phone her daddy if it rained on her prom night, if anyone poorer or darker than her tried to make her understand something about their life, or like now if someone used a word she didn't know.

'Sketchy,' I said. 'Suspect. So . . . what can you tell me?'

'About what?' she said.

'About how things have been. About the atmosphere at work. The state of things between the two Lancers. Brandeee's mood. Any dodgy – suspicious – visitors or callers? Anything to get your spidey-sense thrumming? I'm just trying to build up a picture of how things were before she went away.'

Elise watched me closely as she sucked a good long draught

of her mysterious drink up a personal straw. 'Is that a trick question?' she said.

'Nope,' I assured her. 'It might strike you as a stupid one, but you have to get used to asking stupid questions in this game.'

'So you don't know?' she said. Those violet eyes were mesmerizing and she had a way of blinking, slowly, like a cat. The kid who had made her drink was still watching her from behind the coffee machine, looking as if he'd been hit on the side of the head with a shovel. The kid who'd taken her order and her money was looking over the till with an identical expression. I was probably wearing it too. We can't help it; it's in our genes. It confers an evolutionary advantage to us to be attracted to smooth skin, shiny hair and bright eyes. It helps us not mate with disease-raddled no-hopers. It's good for the species.

'I don't know,' I said, but I was beginning to guess.

'He was going to leave her,' she told me. She sat back in her seat and stretched her arms above her head, still like a cat, this time waking up in a patch of sunshine. 'He's in love with me.'

'Oh honey,' I said, unaware of deciding to speak, much less what to say. 'You know I was married to him, briefly, don't you?'

She didn't like that at all. And fair enough; it must knock some of the gloss off her catch to know he'd once been caught by the likes of me.

'And you know you'd be number four?'

She wasn't crazy about that either.

'Don't settle for a clapped-out thrice-married dentist over forty,' I said. 'My God, Elise. Go down to LA for a weekend and walk along Rodeo Drive. If you haven't got three men begging for your number by the time you have to turn and walk back again, the world's not the place it is. And it is, you know.'

'But he loves me,' she said.

'I'm sure he does,' I told her. 'Now, I'm here to gather information for a missing-person enquiry but here's some free therapy for you. Loving is what people do. Like eating and sleeping. We're monkeys – we curl up with people and pick fleas off them and love them. There's nothing unusual about it. So don't be too quick to give your heart away. How old are you, anyway?'

'Give my heart away?' she echoed, with such extreme scorn that she nearly managed to make herself look unbeautiful, for a second, until her face settled back to rest again and she returned to being a goddess. 'Thank you, Grandma! How old are *you*?'

I'm the perfect age, I thought. My morning client had waited too long; this Disney princess was crazy for thinking it was time already. But I was a bowl of medium-hot porridge. It was just the right time for me. Thinking about Doug and his beetroot balls, I felt a little smile creep over my face.

'Seriously,' I told her, coughing to get the smile wiped off again, 'Bran is not worth it for you. You need to have some fun for a while and then look for a man who is kind, funny, if you like laughing, as clever as you are – not too much dumber or smarter – and, trust me, as honest as the day is long, and up for a decent life. No addicts, no players, no drama. Watch him for ten minutes with a dog. That'll do it.'

'Uhhh,' said Elise, 'how about hot? How about ripped? How about no college loans and a car I'm not ashamed to be seen in?'

'Of course,' I said. 'All of that too.' I had done something that we're all too prone to do: I had mistaken beauty for goodness. 'Or take Bran for a spin until he's ready for wife number five,' I added. 'He's got a good pool and excellent Wi-Fi.' She didn't even know I was kidding. 'But that's not why we're here,' I reminded her. 'Tell me how Brandeee's been. Tell me anything you can to help me find her.'

'Weren't you listening?' She batted those extraordinary lashes at me again but I'd been inoculated against them via her personality now. 'He was leaving her, anyway. For me.'

'Well, I hate to be the one to break it to you,' I lied, 'but either her disappearance has made his heart grow fonder again, or the guilt of the plan to leave, butted up against getting one of her nails delivered with a ransom note, has done it, or he's had her offed and he's covering it with an extravagant display of love and heartbreak . . . Whatever. Bran is all about Brandeee now, Elise, so I think it would be a good idea for your future plans if you did everything you could to help find her.' I paused to let it sink in. 'At least if the thought of being with someone who might have killed his wife bothers you at all?'

'Does he know you're saying this about him?' she demanded.

I thought about it. 'He knows me, so . . . probably,' I concluded. 'But as I was saying, it's in your interests to tell me what you know.'

She wasn't bright, but she had such an investment in herself that it shone a clear light on the path of advantage. She nodded and took another deep suck on the straw. Either she was showing off her cheekbones or there was semolina in there.

'She hasn't been her usual self for a while,' she said. 'She's usually all about remembering to be thoughtful? Like asking after family members and remembering birthdays? Little gifts and tokens and treats for the staff. It's kinda creepy but we're all used to her.'

It didn't sound creepy. It sounded like Brandeee was a good boss. This girl was too young to be quite that cynical.

'But recently . . .?' I said, nudging her.

'Yeah. She was distracted, kept looking at her phone. She was always talking when she pulled up, and she sat in her car, finishing the call. And there were a lot of incoming texts too. More than usual.'

'Her son's been away at boarding school,' I said. 'Maybe he's been texting.'

'And then, a couple of times, she really dropped the ball,' Elise said. 'She forgot Christmas. Didn't give us any cards or presents or bonuses. And you can't really ask, when it's an extra, can you?'

'What does she usually give you?' I said.

'Five-hundred-dollar gift card, plus a little like candle or mittens or something, you know?'

'Five hundred dollars?' I said. 'That's nice. That must have been a bit of a disappointment, when it didn't turn up. Did Bran say anything?'

'He gave us his presents, same as ever,' Elise told me. 'I don't know if he knew she stiffed us.'

I wasn't sure I'd say not giving your employees a five-hundred-dollar wedge was 'stiffing' them exactly but I didn't argue.

'And, of course, Dr Lancer doesn't ever give us girls Valentine's Day gifts.'

My ears pricked up.

'That would be inappropriate. It's only Dr Kowalski-Lancer who marks that holiday.'

'And did she?' I asked. 'Or did she drop the ball again?'

'Like a rock,' Elise said. 'With an insulting Addams Family bouquet.'

I had no idea what that meant, as was so often the case with casual references to popular culture.

'Added to what happened at Christmas, it made me think she had money troubles. Real tight money troubles if it was worthwhile skimping on staff gifts. You know what I mean?'

This time, I did, but I couldn't slot it into a bigger picture any way that I was happy with. Brandeee had a son at an expensive boarding school but was cutting back on gratuities? And even if we got past that, it was hard to see why a kidnap victim would have advance money worries. A murder victim likewise. If Brandeee was in the soup financially, that pointed to her cutting ties and running away. But was I really willing to believe she had pulled off one of her own acrylics and sent it to her husband? Mimicking the ransom note from a statue heist that hadn't yet taken place when she left? And was instantly copied all over the western states?

Elise was still talking: '. . . disappointment because she's always been my role model.'

'Brandeee has?' I asked.

'Who else are we talking about? She's exactly the kind of woman I've always wanted to be. Focused, driven, self-actualized, mindful and so evolved.'

'What a sweetheart,' I said, hoping it would go over her head. Which it did, by a mile.

'Right? Anyways, I hope you find her. No, really.' My *look* hadn't gone over her head, then. 'Because, while she's missing, it would be kinda tacky for Dr Lancer to divorce her. Awkward on a practical level too, probably. Getting papers signed and whatnot?'

'And reckless,' I added, 'while the police are still trying to work out what happened to her. It's the first thing they think of, when a married woman goes missing, you know. And when a married woman whose husband wants to divorce her goes missing . . .'

'What?' she said.

'Well, put it this way: a memorial service for a missing person declared dead is a lot cheaper than a nasty divorce. No coffin to stump up for, even. Just a quick half hour in the nearest Moose Lodge, platter of little sandwiches, job done.'

'But you were kidding,' she said. Finally something had got through her foundation and contour and slapped her in the face. 'You didn't mean what you said about him having her killed, did you? Did you?'

'I'm not the police,' I reminded her.

'I need to go back to work,' she said, standing up and flipping the lid of her personal cup closed. 'I need to speak to them – I mean, my break time is over.'

'You need to speak to all the people at work that you've told about your affair and . . . untell them?' I said. I left my dolphin-killer cup on the table and hurried out after her. 'That sounds like a great plan. That'll totally work.'

She sped up when she hit the car park but so did I; we must have looked like a couple of Olympic speed-walkers, pounding over the wet tarmac as fast as feet would carry us without breaking into a run, which would have been as galling an admission here as it would have been an infraction against sportsmanship in the Games. As long as she kept one foot on the ground at all times, she could pretend to herself, me and any onlookers that she was just going back to work after her break and not hanging about, given the weather. She wasn't desperately trying to stop me talking to her colleagues before she had a chance to tell them . . . what?

'What would you say, anyway?' I panted, as we got to the door of Bran's building.

'That I was just dreaming,' she said, as she pushed the

button for the lift. 'He'll never leave her. He loves her. I was just a bit fun to him. He sometimes needs to turn away from her light, you know? She's too perfect for anyone to deal with non-stop. It's overwhelming.'

'Oh, you're good,' I said. I didn't even know how good. When the lift arrived, I stepped in; she *reached* in, pushed the 'door close' button, then took off at a sprint for the stairs.

'Slowest lift west of the Rockies!' she said as her long legs started hurdling up the stairs, taking three at a time.

She wasn't wrong. It groaned like Chewbacca and lurched like a zombie and, when I arrived on Lancer and Lancer's floor, Elise was sitting away back from the reception desk, with the other two girls clustered round her and her face buried in a hanky.

'I don't know what she's told you,' I began.

'You just came right out and called her a kidnapper in the middle of a coffee shop?' said the dumpy one. 'Right in front of Kyle?' Then she blushed and put her head down again, while I wondered which poleaxed barista Kyle was and if he had ever noticed her loving him as she ordered her macchiato.

'I'm not in the business of accusations,' I said. 'I'm gathering information for Dr Lancer, who is currently at home climbing the walls with anguish about the disappearance of Dr Kowalski-Lancer. Anything anyone can tell me about Brandeee's mood, or any of her calls, visitors or other actions in the run up to Valentine's Day, could be very helpful.'

I hadn't checked behind me to see if there were any patients waiting. With hindsight, I could have been a bit more discreet.

'So who's going to cast my implant?' said a voice, and I turned to see a man who looked vaguely familiar, sitting with an open *National Geographic* abandoned on his lap. 'She didn't turn up then?' he said to me.

'I can't comment on my client's case,' I said.

'My mother took quite a shine, you know,' he said.

'To . . . Brandeee?' I asked him. 'That's nice. Sooooooo important.' I was spouting accepted wisdom with that line. Actually, I didn't see why you had to form a close personal

bond with your doctor, dentist, podiatrist, optometrist, gynae-
cologist, dermatologist, proctologist and physio, even if you
needed all those different specialists. Which you didn't. Don't
get me wrong; I had a doctor. I'd seen her once for a contra-
ceptive prescription while Bran and I were married and I was
on his insurance, and then once for a nasty set of mouth ulcers
when Bran and I were newly divorced and I was stressed, not
sleeping well and saving on my supermarket bills by eating
mostly tinned soup and sliced bread. Incidentally, I could have
been eating fresh pineapple washed down with coconut milk
straight from the shell for breakfast, lunch and dinner, because
that one ten-minute appointment with no insurance card had
set me back 200 dollars, and all she told me to do was wash
my mouth out with salt water and keep off the chillies till the
lesions healed.

My point is, whenever anyone asked me if I liked my
doctor – and they did, a lot – I always answered that she
had a degree in medicine and so she seemed ideal. But my
other point is that I wasn't surprised when a random bloke
in a waiting room offered the information that members of
his family thought highly of their provider. They really care
about all that stuff.

In this instance, I had got him bang to wrongs.

'Not Brandee,' he said. 'She took a shine to *you*.'

'I don't work here,' I told him.

'I know,' he said. 'You own your own business and you're
trying to find her but I've got to tell you, you don't seem
well suited to the work. You might have walked past her in
the street and not realized who it was. Like you've just
done with me.'

God, that was annoying. But he was right. I had no clue
where I knew him from. A client? Surely not. I would have
remembered an out-and-out client. And Todd had clearly
never been set loose on him. The man was wearing an anorak
with arm pockets. Did he use the launderette? Again, no.
Kathi had had no hand in the wavering crease that meandered
up the front of his cargo pants, carried on clean through the
pockets, but packed in completely, far below the waistband.
Did he work in a business I frequented maybe? I didn't think

so, because he had a long, grey ponytail and if he was a
waiter he'd have been forced to keep a hairnet over it. I
always remember those hairnets because they spook me.
Correction: the hairs they don't cover spook me. Anytime I
see a deli-counter dude or a pizza-oven shoveller with his
do and his beard in a net, I can't help thinking about
his eyebrows, nostrils and knuckles, wondering if I'd be able
to tell what un-netted bit of him a hair had come from if
I found one.

So, who did I know who had a mother I also knew? I
asked myself. Todd. Diego. Blaike. I'd never met Bran's
mum in our short marriage. She lived in Florida and the
pair of them were in a holding pattern whereby he invited
her to come to California every time they spoke and she
invited him to come and see her in Orlando. And neither of
them ever did. It had seemed strange to me, but then I wasn't
overly keen to have a mother-in-law come and stay in the
brutally open-plan Beige Barn when I was, let's face it, a
newlywed.

Wait!

I chased the thought. Marital communion overheard.
Through an open window. By a mother.

'Barbra Streisand!' I said.

'That's me,' said Anorak Man.

'How is she?' I asked.

'Still dead,' he told me. 'Princess Elizabeth and Dick Clark
aren't looking too good either.'

'Your poor mum,' I said. 'Did the gardenmaster find out
what's wrong?'

'The "gardenmaster" got kicked out with a boot in her
keister,' he said, 'after telling my mother she had killed
her roses through poor husbandry and there were other shrubs
more suited to a gardener with her disability.'

I was sharing in this enormity when someone at my elbow
cleared her throat and I turned to see a dental nurse, whose
name I could never remember.

'We're ready for you now, Taylor,' she said.

'Yeah, who's ready?' he asked, closing the *National
Geographic* and stowing it in one of his many pockets. 'If

both dentists are off the grid, who's going to put a knee on my chest and get the pliers flying?'

I laughed. It was a good question. Also, he'd brought his own *National Geographic* to read in the dentists' waiting room. Americans were strange.

SIXTEEN

'Have you found her?' Bran hauled the door open and stood framed on the threshold, a picture of dejection. He was wearing a cut-off sweatshirt with no logo. I had never before seen him in any sweatshirt-fabric garment that didn't boast the name of his college or favoured sports team. He was also wearing a pair of striped pyjama trousers and mismatched socks – one black with diamonds and one a Christmas novelty with candy canes and cardinals. His hair was greasy, his breath as he started to sob was an affront to dumpsters, and he smelled of onion sweat, a smell I would never have dreamed he was capable of producing.

'I haven't,' I said. I considered telling him I'd found Blaike, but then remembered he didn't know the kid was missing. So I decided that if he said a word about needing to speak to his stepson and not being able to, I would blow the story. But if, as I suspected, poor Blaike didn't cross his mind once, I would keep shtum. I followed him back into the house, trudging through crumbs and stepping around pizza boxes and beer bottles that lay abandoned on the floor.

'You're overplaying it, Bran,' I said. 'You need to dial this down if you're going to get everyone to believe you.'

He wheeled round and stared at me out of bloodshot eyes. A muscle was pounding in his cheek. 'What are you suggesting?'

'That you know where she is or you're happy you don't, but you can't face anyone guessing as much so you're putting on a show.'

'I thought you were OK,' he said, collapsing on to the couch, where he landed in yet another pizza box. That was part of the trouble; there hadn't been enough days to account for the pizzas. 'I didn't think you hated me. But only someone who hates me would say anything so cruel. Look at me, Lexy.'

'Yeah, you look like shit on toast,' I said. 'But if you've

done something to Brandeee and you're waiting for the cops to suss you out, you're hardly going to look fresh and rested.'

'Do you . . .?' His voice ran out and he had to clear his throat and try again. 'Do you actually mean that?'

I took my time, considering it from every angle, putting it up against what I knew about him and Brandeee. 'Nah,' I said, in the end. 'So have the police been able to tell you anything?'

'No,' he said, running his hands through his hair and finishing off with a deep scalp scratch that made me want to scratch mine too. He really was filthy. He'd always taken so many long showers, back when I knew him; I'd had no idea there was this much grease waiting so close by. 'She's logged as missing. But there have been no sightings and no contact with anyone she knows. They've got no theories and no suggestions. Lexy, what if she never comes back? What if I never find out what happened?'

'I can't imagine,' I said, 'except that there must be support groups of people in the same position that you could turn to.'

'How could anyone be in the same position?' said Bran. 'What do you mean?'

'Families of missing persons who never show up,' I said. 'What's hard to understand?'

'But they're different,' said Bran, 'those deadbeat dads and wayward teens, addicted moms and bankrupt cases who run away. This is different. Brandee is an angel. She's an angel walking on earth.'

'Angels ain't what they used to be,' I said under my breath. I was getting sick of having to sit and listen to eulogies for Brandeee, although I was interested to hear Bran's in a way. See if he'd found yet another angle, different from Burt's and Elise's.

'She runs this house like a corporation,' Bran said. 'She never forgets a birthday or an anniversary. She sends condolence cards to every neighbour in a three-block radius, for spouses, parents and siblings, and sends condolence anniversary cards, three years after spouses and two for parents. She works from a spreadsheet.'

'Just like Gabriel,' I muttered.

'She supports all the school-fund drives, and libraries too.

She gives money to five churches besides her own. She goes on sex weekends twice a year and she never tags anyone on social media without asking them if they like the picture first. She—'

'Can I jump in?' I said. '*What* weekends?' I thought maybe he'd said 'tax' or 'sets' or . . . something.

'Sex weekends,' Bran said. 'Inspiration and retraining courses for focused and committed wives.'

'Are you sure?' I said. 'Because that sounds like the boldest alibi for an affair I have ever heard.'

'Absolutely, I'm sure,' he told me. 'I saw the charge go through on our joint account.'

'Wow,' I said. I'd spent an hour, just last week, telling a woman who was weaning twins and had no confidence left in her body, now that her skin was soft and her legs were veiny, that men were simple creatures and her husband would love her all the more now that she'd done this miraculous thing.

'And is there absolutely nothing you can think of at all?' I said. 'Nothing she said, or did, or that came for her in the mail? Not even any junk calls? Nothing that would cast light on her recent activity?'

'Junk calls?' said Bran.

'Yeah, you know how they target the calls to people they think are good prospects?' I said. 'So if you get Planned Parenthood, the ACLU and Amnesty, you're one kind of person, and if you get the National Police Fund, the NRA and Family First, you're probably sort of another? What do you get? Has it changed?'

'We block them,' said Bran. 'We're not cavemen.'

But something was bubbling to the top of his brain. I could see it coming. I could see him chasing it like the last pickle as it swam around out of his reach in the vinegar. I saw him tense as though to burp up a ball of gas, and I watched as he had to relax again when the gas subsided unburped.

Then I got distracted, because I was chasing a pickle burp of my own. 'Hang on,' I said. 'You told me Brandeee ran her life like a Naz— with a measure of precision? Never flaked or goofed or punted on anything?'

'She is perfect,' Bran said. 'Please use the present tense, Lexy.'

'Sorry,' I said. 'What happened at Christmas then? She didn't give out a staff bonus to Elise and the rest of them.'

'She did,' said Bran. 'Five-hundred-dollar gift cards.'

'Well, they didn't get them,' I said. 'Unless she missed Elise out. Would she have done that?'

'We laughed about Elise,' Bran said. 'She has a little crush on me and, if I'm honest, I'm flattered, but Brandee knew she had no competition for my heart or my—'

'Please don't finish that sentence!'

'Loyalty. I don't know why Elise would lie about her holiday gift.'

'Where were the vouchers for?' I asked. 'Maybe something went wrong at that end.'

Bran screwed his face up in an effort to remember. 'Some goofy place she found way out somewhere in orbit around redneck nowhere that ran courses on some crazy crap.' Then he stuffed his fist in his mouth, horrified at how he'd just spoken about his angel of a wife and her choice in gifts for underlings. I had never liked him more.

'Can you remember what it's called?' I said.

'Why?' said Bran. 'You think she emailed them to complain and they were so pissed at her that they came to her house and abducted her?'

'No,' I said. 'It's just the only thing I've heard that's even slightly out of kilter. And the word "crazy" came out of you when you weren't concentrating. Also, places away out in the armpit, or even asshole, or – as you say – orbit of nowhere keep coming up.'

'They do?'

'They do. So, how could you find out what this place is called? Credit-card bill?'

He shook his head. 'Last year's credit-card bills are stored off-site now that our taxes are done,' he said. 'It's a fire risk to keep financial documents in a residential premises. Brandee would never be so sloppy.'

'Your taxes . . . are done?' I said. 'The taxes that are due by the end of April? Never mind. Could you look it up online?'

'I can't go poking in Brandee's personal credit-card state-ment,' he said. 'This wasn't a joint expense.' He had forgotten, I think, that in his initial panic he had handed over all her passwords and PINs to Todd, Kathi and me.

'OK,' I said. 'Well, if it comes back to you . . .'

'Of course,' he said.

'So let's circle back to these junk calls you nearly remem-bered. Or was it mail?'

'It was calls,' Bran said. 'And it was nothing. Only, like you said, Lexy, you're supposed to be able to tell who someone is from the targeted junk they come in for.'

'But?' I said.

'I kept getting money-off offers from some rib joint I'd never heard of,' he said.

'A barbecue restaurant?' I said. 'That seems pretty mild.' What I was really thinking was that Brandeee, with her twice-yearly sex weekends, was lucky she wasn't getting free poles delivered in return for testimonials. I didn't understand why Bran cared so much about a downmarket eatery. But then I didn't understand why Bran cared so much about a lot of things: like the fact that driving your car put miles on it and someone might see the high number and judge you; or the fact that if I shopped in the thrift store in Cuento I might meet the original owner of my new dress at a party; or the fact that if you asked the gardener to use a rake instead of a leaf blower because you had a hangover and the noise was killing you, the neighbours would think he was a friend doing you a favour and conclude that you couldn't afford a gardener because you were a failure, with second-hand clothes and a shameful odometer, a disgrace to the American dream.

I stood. 'Try not to worry,' I said. 'And for God's sake, have a shower. Imagine if Brandeee walks back in and you're sitting there like Worzel Gummidge.'

'Who?'

'Pigpen.'

'Right,' he said. 'But what if the phone rings when I'm in the shower?'

'Have a bath.'

'OK,' he said.

'And don't eat any more pizza. What if Brandeee comes back and you're all bloated and disgusting and she takes one look at you and leaves again?'

'OK,' he said. 'I know you're trying to be kind. In your own cruel way.'

We shared a smile. It would have been a hug, if he hadn't been giving off actual waves of stink, like Pepé Le Pew.

Back at the Last Ditch, the office, launderette, Todd's room, Devin's room and Della's room were all deserted. So I squelched my way round the back to the slough, which was a lot bigger than it had been that morning – completely over its banks, so it looked like a Louisiana swamp with the bushes and scrub trees half-submerged, and the water the colour of bad instant coffee with Carnation milk in.

I stepped on the lowest stair to the porch and knew I had visitors – more than one, more than two, or one big one maybe; only, I didn't know anyone heavy enough for this. Letting myself into the living room, I could hear gentle snores from halfway back, and, as I drew level with the open door to the guest bedroom, I saw Todd, Noleen, Kathi, Devin and Della all standing, watching Blaike sleep. One of his arms was flung over a wide-awake Diego, who was looking up at his mother with anguish in his eyes.

'What's going on?' I whispered.

'There's absolutely no need to whisper,' Todd said. Boomed, actually.

'Is he OK?' I asked.

'He's fine,' said Della. 'He's just the best teenage sleeper I've ever seen in my life.'

'And that's a deep bench,' Devin added. 'Man, I thought *I* could sleep but I never pulled an all-nighter, then two naps, four hours each, the next day.'

'Diego came to wake him up after school,' said Noleen, 'but it went the other way. That was two hours ago.'

'Wriggle out, baby,' I said to the little boy.

He squirmed like a beetle on its back and managed to escape the dead weight of Blaike's arm. Blaike stopped snoring, smacked his lips and turned over. Then, after a long sigh, the snoring started up again.

'Poor kid,' I said. 'Let's leave him. We've got a lot to do.'

'And I need to get back to work,' Noleen said. She stamped off towards the front of the boat, causing it to roll and Blaike to smack his head against the box-work of the bed surround. His breathing didn't even hitch.

'A lot to do, like what?' said Todd, as the rest of us withdrew to the living room.

Diego had a skeleton crew of fantasy action figures stored under my coffee table and he settled down to renegotiate one of the treaties he'd hammered out last time, while we grown-ups shared the spoils of the day.

'Have you got the file?' I asked Kathi. 'With all the stuff Bran gave us?'

'Got it right here,' she said, slapping what I thought had been a pile of launderette invoices she'd been hugging close to her chest. 'I put them in baggies and scanned them through my printer. They're clean now. What do you want to know?'

'If I riffle through them, will they be dirty again?'

'You could wash your hands,' she said.

'If I tell you I washed them half an hour ago and haven't touched my face, and if I promise not to lick my finger while I turn the sheets, could you cope with that?'

'Or, Lexy,' Todd said, 'could you park the counsellor and let us speak to our co-worker in the investigations wing of Trinity? Is she there right now?'

'*I'll* look for whatever it is,' Kathi said. 'Todd's right: I'd rather have my therapy when it's scheduled. And in private.'

'Private!' said Devin. 'Is that for me?'

'Oh, for God's sake,' I said. 'OK. Kathi: can you get into Brandeee's personal credit-card statements for before the turn of the year and see if you can find a payment to someone that looks like a spa or a retreat or something? It's going to be for a few thou.'

'Okey-dokey,' Kathi said. 'Why?'

'Because it's the only chip in the perfection of Brandeee Lancer that I've been able to find all day. It's all I heard from everyone I spoke to: she was an angel, the perfect woman, a role model, a miracle, a machine, an inspiration, a gift from God. Except that she didn't give her staff a Christmas present this year and she gave them a weird Valentine's prezzie too. Now, Bran thinks she bought five-hundred-dollar gift vouchers' – I paused for someone to whistle, which both Devin and Kathi did – 'for some . . . I don't know . . . Paltrow-esque bunch of weirdos who run a . . . I don't know . . . centre for overpriced crap, somewhere out of town, and I'm thinking . . . I don't know.'

'Masterful,' said Todd. 'Have you ever thought of hiring yourself out as an expert witness? Grisham couldn't write stuff like that.'

'Have you ever thought of shutting up and stuffing—?' I said.

'I get it,' said Della. 'Whether she—'

'Wait,' said Devin. 'Is Della on a consultation tariff for sharing intel?'

'Intel?' I said. 'No. Insights? Yes. On a two-hundred-dollar flat rate, OK?'

'Devin,' Della said, then let out a stream of Spanish too fast for me to follow. Its general drift wasn't a mystery.

'Can't eat stubbornness,' Devin said, 'with or without pride sauce. If I'm not allowed to donate anymore—'

Kathi looked up and gave the statutory 'Ew.' She had just finished wiping down my laptop with an antiseptic towelette and now she was ready, double-gloved in latex, to start keying in details.

'—then we need all the casual work going,' Devin finished.

'Awwwww,' said Todd. 'You guys are a "we"? Totes adorbs!'

'"Totes adorbs" is on the list, Todd,' I said. 'That's going to cost you.'

'When did we add "totes adorbs"?' he said, genuinely puzzled.

'After "YOLO" and before "you do you",' I said.

'Police state,' said Todd.

Diego broke off the talks between rival kingdoms and sat back on his heels. 'You're silly,' he said. 'You say a lot and it's all silly.' Then he bent and took up the mantle of statesmanship again.

'I think I've found it,' Kathi said, raising her head from behind my laptop. 'In October, she paid out three thousand, six hundred and thirty dollars to something called PPPerfection.'

'Three thousand?' said Della. 'How many nurses do they have?'

'Three receptionists and three hygienists, I'm guessing,' I said. 'One hundred and five dollars tax and handling per five-hundred-dollar gift voucher. Sounds right. Huh.'

'Disappointed?' said Todd.

'Yeah, I thought if she was lying about it to Bran and really she had squirrelled the money away somewhere it would be evidence that she left of her own accord.'

'What about the acrylic?' said Kathi.

'She could have accidentally ripped it off and sent it as a decoy, after she heard about Mama Cuento.'

'But it was hand delivered. She'd have had to come back and walk down her own street. Kinda risky,' Devin said.

'Or she could have paid someone to place it,' said Todd. 'Speaking of short gigs for cash, Della, what were you going to say?'

'Whether she pretended to buy something because she was saving up, or she bought something that didn't arrive, it could be significant. Maybe she complained and made them angry. Maybe she went to face them and made them really angry.'

'After bedtime one night?' I said.

'And why did she not buy replacement gifts?' said Della.

'Moment passed?' Kathi suggested. 'Nah, you're right. That *is* weird. It's out of character for her to promise something, have people expect it and then not deliver.'

Her words caught at me. 'Is it?' I said. 'Is it though?' But, as I opened my mouth to say more, suddenly there was a barrage of sound as multiple pairs of feet came pounding up the steps to the porch and a cop-knock battered my front door.

SEVENTEEN

'There's a minor child in here,' Devin shouted as I made my way to open up. I didn't know whether to be enchanted that his thoughts went straight to his beloved Della's baby boy or freaked that the legalistic terminology – minor child? – came so easily off his tongue. That was a window on to something, wasn't it?

I opened the door with an 'Evening, officer,' that I amended to 'detective' when I saw Mike standing there, flanked by Soft Cop and also Mills of God, the slowest police officer in fifty states, the district and Puerto Rico. The three of them were the first Cuento fuzz I had ever encountered, away back on Independence Day. 'He-hey!' I said. 'The whole gang! We re-forming the band?'

Mike glared and Soft Cop rolled his eyes. Mills of God frowned in puzzlement. He'd chew it over at his own pace and get to the answer sometime before Easter.

'How can I help you?' I said. 'Do come in, by the way. Tea?'

'You still pushing that muck?' Mike said. She always took it as a personal affront when I offered tea. But she didn't like it any better when I learned the phrase, *Frosty one with your name on it, right there in the cooler*. There's no pleasing some people.

'Here's why we're here,' Mike began when the three of them had squeezed themselves into an awkward kick-line arrangement in front of the woodstove. My living room is not large and, Diego's diplomacy having failed and my hearthrug now being a theatre of war with battles raging on several fronts, there wasn't a great deal of room for the sudden addition of three sizable officers. Also, maybe it was the shift in weight, or much more likely the aggressive knocking, but, one way or another, Blaike had been awoken and now appeared in the doorway, scratching his belly and yawning.

'Morning,' he said. 'Or is it afternoon?' Then he opened his squeezed-shut eyes and took in the tableau.

'Mister Kowalski,' Mike said. 'I might have known.'

'I didn't do it,' said Blaike. 'What's happened?'

'Your taste in acquaintances doesn't improve,' Mike said to me, earning a 'Hey!' from both Todd and Kathi. Della usually kept her mouth shut and her head down whenever cops were near. It killed me to see it, although it was sweet to notice that Devin wore the same expression as she did and was avoiding their eyes in exactly the same way.

'Shouldn't you be at school, up in Oregon?' said Mike. 'Does your father know you're here? Does anyone here have permission to be harbouring this child?'

Blaike said, 'He's not my father.'

And Todd said, 'Yes, someone does.'

But neither of them loud enough to cover my, 'Not Oregon. Iowadihio.'

Diego, always my biggest fan whether I'm trying to entertain him or not, cracked up laughing.

'I'm going for a . . .' Blaike said. 'To the bathroom.'

'*Vamanos, papi*,' Della said, standing and holding out a hand. I loved her for speaking Spanish at that moment, a little foot-stamp of pride to offset the fact that they were hustling off the boat, with Devin following. None of the cops looked at them, but none of them looked particularly troubled by the lowered heads and scurrying feet either.

'What do you get from that?' I said. 'Don't answer. What do you want?'

'We're looking for Brandee Lancer,' said Mike. 'Mother of that little firestarter, who taught him everything he knows.'

'So are we,' said Kathi. 'How are *you* doing?'

'Pretty well,' said Mike. 'We've found her son and we can conclude that she's here with him. The only remaining question is whether she's been here all along and you've all being providing false information to a police officer. Which is a serious offence.'

'What are you talking about?' I said. 'Brandeee's not here.'

'Is that so?' Mike's smugness would have been over the top for a villain in early *Scooby Doo*. 'Well, in that case, someone in this room needs to come with me, and my guess is' – she turned to Kathi – 'you.'

Kathi scrambled to her feet, letting my laptop slide to the floor. 'To the police station?' she said. 'Am I under arrest? To go to the tank? I can't. I can't. I'll die.' And she shot off along the corridor to the back of the boat, with Todd in hot pursuit after her and me shouting, 'Catch her! She'll jump! Todd, save her!'

Both uniformed cops leaped into action, but we caught a break. Soft Cop is not a small man and Mills of God – once you add his belt with its many accessories – is thick round the middle too. Add the fact that my corridor is narrow, *et voilà*. They were jammed in the doorway like Pooh Bear, and only getting more tightly jammed for all their struggling.

'That looks like guilt to me,' Mike said. 'Jesus, Carl! Andy! Someone move backwards!'

'It's not guilt,' I said, watching them both ignore her and continue to try to fit two sizeable belted torsos into a slender passageway. I wished I had a camera running. 'It's a cleanliness phobia. Lock-up would cause her a level of trauma she's not equipped to withstand. What's she supposed to have done anyway?'

'Identity theft, hacking, offences against EFTA . . .'

'What? What the hell's EFTA?' I said.

'Electronic Funds Transfer . . .' said Mike, but then ran dry. Finally, Mills of God managed to get ahead of Soft Cop in the passageway and barrelled off along it, bouncing off my walls with a sickening scraping noise.

'If he's wrecking my antique decor . . .' I said. 'She wasn't hacking. And she definitely wasn't transferring funds. Bran gave us passwords and PINs when he hired us to find her.'

'Dr Lancer doesn't have the authority to hand out his wife's passwords and PINs,' Mike said.

'But Kathi didn't know that,' I said. 'Molly, seriously, please.' Mike bristled like a hedgehog sucking a lime in a draught. She hated being called Mike and I didn't blame her. It was a slur on her sexuality and the worst kind of locker-room talk. The only thing she hated even more was being called her actual name. Which, to be fair, didn't suit her. 'Aren't *you* scared of anything?' I said. 'Can't you give Kathi a break?

She'd need to be on suicide watch and you don't need all that paperwork, surely.'

'Did you find anything?' she said.

'OK, OK,' I said. 'Negotiating instead of empathizing, OK. Yes, we did. So will you let Kathi give a statement here? Instead of at the station?'

They were coming back. Mills, Kathi, Todd and Soft, in single file – as is best, in my passageway – followed by Blaike.

'Why the conga line?' he asked. No one answered him.

'Mrs Muntz,' Mike said, 'can you tell us what you were doing online in the last half hour?'

'Is that what this is?' Kathi said. 'How the hell did you know, anyway? Do the taxpayers of Cuento know that they're funding Bourne-level cybersecurity?'

Mike rolled her eyes. 'There's an automatic alert on her accounts and a link to our dispatch. No one's hiding in a panel van with a bugging device.'

'Under the authority of our client, Branston Lancer,' Kathi said, 'I accessed the credit-card account of his legal spouse, for the sole purpose of carrying out my contracted duty.' She glanced at Blaike, then back at Mike.

'And what did you find?' Mike said.

'Why are you snooping in my mom's account?' said Blaike. 'Does she know?'

Kathi ignored him. 'She paid three thousand dollars for gift vouchers for her staff, which the staff never received. It was an irregularity Dr Lancer wanted us to clear up for him. She's usually generous to a fault and it was one of the few areas of abnormal behaviour in recent weeks.'

I was braced for Mike to scoff and say that information was useless and we'd insulted her by bigging it up. But she surprised me. 'Good instincts,' she said. 'Well done.'

'Why, thank you,' said Todd, batting his eyes and putting Mike's hackles right back up again.

'You take all of us back in time to when life was harder when you pull that shtick,' she said.

'What shtick?' said Todd. 'This is me. I'm a southern belle trapped in the body of a burlesque-era stage-mother trapped in the body of a fabulous gay man.'

'Like a turducken,' I said.

'Exactly,' said Todd. 'Multilayered, brown and juicy.'

'Jesus Christ,' said Mike, which, coming from her while she was on duty, was clear evidence of how much he bugged her. 'We don't have time to waste on this. I've handed off the statues to the Feds, but there's still a break—'

'—in?' I said. 'A related break-in?'

'We don't have time to stand and chew the fat about our cases with civilians,' Mike said.

'But if it's related,' I said, 'we might be able to help. I know we're not officially detectives, but Bran's employed us and—'

'Not *officially* detectives?' Mike said. 'You're not unofficially detectives. You're not even imaginary detectives. You couldn't even go to a costume party as detectives if someone else kicked in the raincoats and fedoras.'

'But is it related?' I said.

Mike turned to Todd. 'How do you stand her?' she asked. 'She's so annoying.'

'Oh she is, she is,' said Todd, absentmindedly, as he scrolled on his phone. 'But then so am I. I'm absolutely infuriating. You just haven't spent enough time with me yet. We could go on a picnic one day. Then you'd see.'

Mike turned to Kathi. 'How do you stand them?' she asked.

'I drink,' Kathi said, and got a slow, appreciative nod in reply.

'Aha!' said Todd, looking up. 'Soccer Jew ear.'

Everyone else looked interested but not befuddled.

'You're going to have to give me a bit more,' I said.

'S-A-C-A-G-A-W-E-A,' Todd spelled out. 'There are statues of her all over the west, but not as many today as yesterday. One in Washington State got boosted overnight. They chipped her baby off and left it behind.'

'This is getting ridiculous,' said Kathi.

'Tell me about it,' said Todd. 'Lots of vigilante gatherings at the other Sacagaweas all over the place now, from the coast to Wyoming. Oh! They've got a living cordon round Phyllis Wheatley, in Boston.'

'I hope she appreciates it,' I said.

'Is my mom at a protest?' said Blaike. 'Is that why she won't answer her phone?'

'That's all outside our jurisdiction,' Mike said.

'And the unrelated break-in?' I said.

Mike heaved a huge sigh and pressed one index finger into the corner of her eye. 'On campus,' she said. 'A break-in at the . . .' Then she flicked a glance at Todd and clicked the side of her mouth, as if she was rethinking what she was going to say.

'RuPaul School of Slaying Them All Dead in Killer Heels?' said Todd.

'Not that I owe you any details,' Mike went on, 'but it's a break-in at the botany department.' Mills of God opened his mouth to object, but she swivelled a stare in his direction and he nodded instead.

'Botany department,' he said. 'Lotta valuable pe-onies gone missing.'

'Pe-onies?' I said. 'Why are you being so weird?'

'We ask the questions around here,' said Mike, and then flushed slightly. Clearly she couldn't think of one.

'What's the company name that took the payment from Dr Lancer?' said Mills of God, astonishing us all.

'PPPerfection,' said Kathi. 'I think they're some kind of . . .' But she trailed into silence when she saw the look go ricocheting around the three cops.

'We know who they are,' said Mike. 'Thank you.' She made her way to the door.

'Hey,' said Blaike. 'Are you sure my mom's OK?'

'I hope so, son,' said Soft Cop as he went out, which was no kind of answer at all.

'And *you're* sure you've got the stepfather's permission for young Mr Kowalski to be here?' Mike said, pausing in the doorway. 'So if we go there now and mention it, it won't be any kind of a surprise?'

'Ah, give us ten,' I said. 'Sorry.'

'Or we could take him home,' Mike said.

'No, we'll keep him here,' I told her. 'We're getting on like a house on fire, aren't we, Blaikey?'

'You and your mouth,' Mike said, and left us.

'We're breaking up again,' said Mills of God. 'Creative differences.' God bless him, he'd got there in the end.

It wasn't the worst phone call I'd ever had with Bran: I'd divorced him for one thing, and for another, I'd sold his golf clubs in a temper one day. Besides, when he took in the plain fact that the school he was paying so much money to had straight-up lied about Blaike being there, a day and a night after the kid had absconded, he realized he had bigger fish than me to fry, and hung up on me.

EIGHTEEN

'Well?' I said to Kathi, when I'd put the phone down and waited for my ear to stop ringing.

'Well what?' she said.

'What?' I said. 'Seriously?' I was honestly astonished. 'Haven't you been looking up what PPPerfection is? Didn't you *see* the way Mike looked at Soft and Mills when she heard the name? I reckon it's a clue to . . .' I stopped talking and looked over at Blaike.

'Hey, kid,' Kathi said. 'How's your folding? You wanna earn a quick forty bucks in my laundromat?'

I threw her a grateful smile as she gave Blaike her keys, dropping them from her hand into his, with no touching. He loped off Skweekward.

'I reckon,' I said again, when he had gone and the boat was still again, 'that it's a clue to where she's gone. We've got to tell him sooner or later, you know.'

Kathi's gloved fingers were flying over the keyboard now. '"PPPerfection",' she read. '"Are you tired, stressed, jaded and wrung out by your busy life? Work, kids, study, caring for elders, running the home, even dating! can leave you in need of a gentle oasis of clam" – I think they mean *calm* – "and pampering. Let us soothe away the cares of the twenty-first century in the peace of nature at our women-only restorative retreat. For treatment menu and to book an appointment, click here."'

She looked up.

'Huh,' I said. 'Well then. I don't know what they were reacting to. Do you?'

Todd shook his head. 'Maybe the business owners are shady,' he said. 'Or maybe it was just the idea of a five-hundred-dollar holiday gift. But that wasn't when they did the big reaction, was it? Who knows?'

'We could go and ask them,' I said.

'I don't think so,' Todd said. 'Don't you two feel like we're kind of pinballing around here? We don't have a sense of . . . If we go off to wherever this PPP is, now, to ask them . . . What would we even ask them? When we don't even know . . . what we're . . . I mean . . . you know.'

'Couldn't have put it better myself,' I said. 'What an orator you are. No!' I said, off his look. 'I'm not kidding. You've just perfectly summed up the utter fog we're stumbling around in. We need to get this straight in our heads and get a plan in place for the investigation, g—' I cut myself off.

'Nice save,' said Todd. 'Well bitten, that lip.'

'I need to say it,' I said. 'It's burning a hole in my brain.'

'It's going to cost you,' Kathi said. 'It's our highest-ticket item. Twenty-five buckaroos.'

'Worth it,' I said. I took a deep breath. 'We need to get this straight in our heads and get a plan in place for the investigation . . . going forward.' I leaned sideways to get my wallet out my back pocket and peel off banknotes for the kitty. 'OK,' I said. 'Pizza? Jug of margaritas? Cup of tea?'

'I don't want to have the summit here,' Todd said. 'I can smell *boy* seeping along the corridor from the guest bedroom. Let's go out somewhere. As long as you're willing to be the amanuensis, Lexy.'

It was insulting but practical. I had the worst handwriting out of the three of us and so I was the only one who could take notes in a bar or noodle shop, or anywhere else in public, without compromising client confidentiality.

'I thought doctors were supposed to be the ones with illegible scrawls,' I said.

'Family practitioners,' Todd said. 'It makes the scripts harder to forge, you know. But anesthesiologists? Think of the ways that could go wrong.'

'OK, OK,' I said. 'Jeez. Where will we go?'

It was Friday night in Cuento. And it wasn't just Friday night: it was the third Friday night of the month, which meant that, as well as all the college kids from UCC piling downtown to drink undrinkably hoppy IPA and pretend to like it at the various local microbreweries, then take the taste away at the various local pizza emporia, there would also be a squad of culture vultures on the prowl for the 'Third Friday' art walkabout, followed by their own version of pizzas at a different subset of emporia, with more artisanal sourdough crusts and less pepperoni. The only place we were sure of getting a table was whichever downtown eatery had most recently failed its health inspection and had to close for special cleaning, or the breakfast nook in Noleen's office.

'There's always the Lode doorway,' Kathi said.

The Lode was the poshest of Cuento's supermarkets. It had an oyster menu; it had pictures of the pastures where the steaks were raised; it had monthly olive events, invitation only. And it also had a sort of a café, by the fake street-market flower barrow just inside the front door, where the supermarkets I could afford to shop in had the cigarettes and the ice machine.

'We in time for the blue-plate special?' said Todd.

I knew what a blue-plate special was, now, like I knew what a Hail Mary outside a church was, and I was on the way to half-knowing what a caucus was too, so I knew Todd wasn't actually talking about a cheap dinner, if we got our skates on. But sometimes it still tired me out, trying to decipher the comfortable chat of my closest friends. As usual, I exacted my revenge by giving it back to them with knobs on.

'Shanks pony or jam jar?' I said.

'Can we just put all over-the-top slang on the list if it's used in open combat?' said Todd. But he didn't press it and we set off, grumbling no more than any other three people would grumble if they had to work on a Friday night again.

Kathi had chosen the Lode doorway because, being Cuento's poshest supermarket, it was preternaturally spanking clean. The floors shone and the shelves gleamed and – crucially – there was no back kitchen she couldn't see and had to wonder about. The coffee counter, bakery counter, sandwich bar and sushi-rolling station were all in full view and all as antiseptic as an operating theatre. Once she had Cloroxed off her seat and the table – top, obviously, and bottom for the gum – she sat back and even managed a smile.

'OK,' I said. 'I'll get the drinks in and you two focus your brains. Where are we, where are we going, what do we know, what do we not know, how do we find out—?'

'Iced mint mocha and a slice of salted caramel cheesecake,' Todd said. 'Were you ever going to stop talking?'

'Seriously?' I said. Todd didn't eat sugar and he didn't eat fat, and he definitely didn't suck down mint mochas.

'Absolutely,' he said. 'If I'm going to have to take refreshments in a grocery-store concession that "proudly serves" and on a Friday night too, like a nonagenarian, I'm gonna celebrate the fact that no one I know can see me.'

Finally, I got the blue-plate special dig. Todd reckoned it was uncool to be here. My God, if he ever came over to Scotland on a visit with me, Asda's all-day breakfast would finish him off completely. 'Kathi?' I said.

'Coffee and a biscotti,' she said. 'I'm a grown-up.'

'Biscotto,' said Todd. 'If there's only one.'

I rolled my eyes at both of them and went to place the orders. That was its own challenge, because part of what made the Lode so expensive was the quality of customer service. Me, I like a morose checkout assistant, picking her dry skin and shoving the stuff through the beeper for me to pack: the food-shop equivalent of the Yummy Parlor, basically. I can tolerate a friendly word and an offer of help out to the car usually. But the Lode was something else. They chatted, they enthused, they checked and double-checked and triple-checked that the exalted customer was getting every desire – reasonable or otherwise – anticipated and addressed. It was customer service set at bum-wipe level and, although Cuento-ites of longer standing seemed to enjoy the feeling it gave them of being a boy emperor, I usually ended up wanting to punch someone.

'Coffee?' the kid proudly serving asked, with a puckered brow.

'Yep,' I confirmed.

'What kind?'

'Ground coffee beans and water,' I said, 'at a guess. She didn't specify.'

'You want to go on over real quick and ask?'

'Not really,' I said. 'If you just pour some of that big jug of coffee there into a cup, that'll be fine.'

'You want *me* to go and ask?'

'What? No!'

'OK,' she said. 'Coffee. Um . . . what size?'

'Scratch all that,' I told her, 'and give me a sixteen-ounce Americano with room for cream. Thank you.' Which is why I hated the Lode, and Kathi too now. Because the thing that everyone else seemed to agree was fantastic, attentive, pampery customer service was really just passive-aggressive trolling taken to the nth degree.

When I had achieved three coffees and three sweet snacks, at the cost of my good mood and probably a month of my life on account of the blood pressure, I went back to the table and crashed the tray down, slopping mocha and not caring.

'Is that tray clean?' said Kathi, reaching for her Clorox travel pack.

I opened my mouth, remembered that actually I loved her, and hastily switched what I was about to say for 'Better give it a wipe round to be on the safe side.' Then I watched her clean the bottoms of the cups and plates and discard the tray with a wipe over her fingers. I had no idea about life being a challenge, really. I even smiled back over at the barista, who of course gave me a massive, insane Lode smile back.

'So,' I said, after a swig of latte and a bite of the rock bun they were mis-selling as a scone. It was pretty good, once you recategorized it under its accurate name. 'Where are we?'

'Brandee Lancer has disappeared,' said Todd. 'She lied about her son's father his whole life through, then had to come clean because she'd set a deadline for herself to come up with a lump sum that she failed to come up with. But she lied about why. Right, Lexy? It was nothing to do with your divorce settlement?'

'My divorce settlement was, "I don't want your money and I don't want to pay a lawyer to tell you that",' I said. 'So, yes.'

'Blaike took it badly – poor kid – and torched all the memorabilia about his fake dad that his mom had been fooling him with,' Kathi went on.

'Getting himself a name as an arsonist for his trouble,' said Todd. 'And a two-year stretch at an overpriced holding pen in Idaho.'

'Here's a question,' I said. 'It's something Mike said when she found Blaike on my boat. Remember? She called him a firestarter and said Brandeee taught it to him.'

'Did she?' said Todd.

'Didn't she?' I said. 'I think so. Let's ask Blaike what might lie behind that. It's a weird thing to say.' *QUESTION*, I printed in my notepad and scribbled down a reminder.

Todd leaned sideways and nodded. 'Yeah,' he said. 'You could write state secrets and leave them in the ladies' room at the Kremlin.'

'Carrying on,' I said. 'On the night after Brandeee disappeared, someone in a pickup truck stole Mama Cuento and accidentally – I think, after looking at the film – knocked off one of her toes while they were at it.'

'Wait, wait, wait,' said Kathi. 'We're mixing up the two threads.'

'Sticking with Brandee, then,' said Todd, 'someone sent a ransom note to Bran, along with one of his wife's acrylic nails, asking him to go along with their demands. But not stating any demands.'

'They didn't send it,' I said. 'They hand-delivered it. Shortly before we arrived. But we didn't see anyone. Can I talk about Mama Cuento now? This is where the two threads join together anyway.'

'The ransom notes,' said Kathi. 'Similar wording, similar . . . tokens. Mama Cuento's toe. Brandee's nail. Liberty's nose.'

'Liberty?' I said.

'The African-American wooden sculpture in Oregon,' said Todd.

'Hope's belly button doesn't really fit,' Kathi said. 'Much harder thing to chop off.'

'Except she was fibreglass,' I reminded her.

'I don't mean literally hard to chop off a statue. I mean it's a different . . .'

'It's not an appendage,' said Todd. 'But wasn't she pregnant? Hence "Hope", maybe? So it could have been sticking way-hay-hay out. Could have been nipped off, not gouged out. That's another thing we need to ask Blaike, Lexy.'

I jotted a note.

'And a baby,' said Todd. 'Sawn off Sacagawea and left behind. That's different too.'

'Mexican town mother,' Kathi was saying when I looked up again. 'Pregnant Asian girl, African-American girl, young Native mother. It's not just images of females, is it?'

'Isn't it?' said Todd, bristling.

'Aw, come on,' I said. 'Don't be like that. I agree. I mean, yes, wouldn't it be lovely if we didn't notice because it didn't matter, but gimme a break, Todd. It's definitely significant that no statues of . . . I don't know any famous white American women, except actresses.'

'Betsy Ross,' said Todd. 'Nellie Bly, Sally Ride.'

'Thank you,' I said. 'No statues of any of those Edwardian housemaids – seriously, if I ever have a daughter, I'm going to give her a name that is presidency-ready – have been tampered with.'

'Good to know you're not going to call a daughter "There's a fly in my throat, Jr",' said Kathi. They didn't make fun of my name being Leagsaidh every day anymore, but they didn't like to let a whole week pass. 'And you're right. Look at the statues where the vigilantes are on the warpath: the rest of the Sacagaweas, Dignity, Phyllis Wheatley. Everyone's got the message.'

'And what does that tell us?' I said.

'Misogynistic xenophobes,' said Todd.

'Maybe not,' said Kathi. 'They might be xenophobic misogynists.'

'I love the way you fling the big words about when it's me taking the notes,' I said. I looked at what I'd written; the spelling seemed wrong, but I couldn't think what to change to fix it. 'How about a snappier term?'

'Obviously,' said Todd. 'But I don't want to say it.'

'Well, *I* don't want to say it,' said Kathi.

'Why should I have to say it?' I whined. But I knew the answer and I got over myself. 'Nazis.'

'Which is good news,' said Kathi, 'whatever we call them.'

'Really?' I said.

'Oh yeah,' said Kathi. 'Nazis are *great* news.'

It was an unfortunate moment for a Lode staff member to come over and check that we had everything we needed. But it was nice to see that their commitment to customer service had limits.

'Ma'am?' the kid said. He was probably a college student, or about that age anyway. 'Were you quoting someone right then?'

'Huh?' said Kathi. 'No.'

'Were you being sarcastic?' the kid said. His voice was shaking and his neck was blotchy, but damn if he wasn't sticking to his guns.

'No,' said Kathi. 'Why?'

'In that case, I'm going to have to ask you to leave,' he said, dry-mouthed now, as well as blotched and shaky.

'What?' Kathi said.

But, before he could insist or she could twig or I could try to explain, we were all distracted by a rumpus over at the fake flower-market barrow where a customer seemed to be having a medium-sized set of what we mental-health professionals call the heebie-jeebies.

'What's up with her?' Todd asked, standing.

I went over to see if maybe I could calm her down, Kathi at my side. I had taken a short course in conflict resolution and de-escalation as part of my training back in the old country, and Kathi, from her years in a budget motel and attached launderette, was just about equally well versed in the care of people who were upset. And this woman, I thought as we got close, was acutely, maybe clinically, upset. She was breathing like Mimi in the last act of *La Bohême* and staring with a stricken face at the pail full of bouquets she'd been just about to pick from. Beside her, a Lode employee – instead of offering a glass of water and a sit-down, or asking who they could call to come and take the woman home – was stock still, saying 'Oh my God' over and over again. That was what really chilled my blood. A clean-cut Lode bag-packer not saying 'Oh my gosh,' if not 'Oh my good golly,' was societal breakdown and no mistake.

'What's wro—?' I started to say but, when I turned to face where they were both staring, my voice died in my throat. I *think* they were supposed to be irises, freesia and some kind of daisy, but what they actually were was a roiling mass of little fat yellow bugs, like popped blackhead middles, all squirming around, fighting for a place to latch on to the flower heads and chomp them to nothing, or taking off and flying around, then re-landing to try again. They'd already finished the roses in the bucket next door.

'Get Todd out of here!' Kathi said. 'Go!'

I wheeled round and charged back to the table. '*Vamanos, papi*,' I said, clamping him by the elbow and dragging him to his feet.

'What's going on?' he said, standing on tiptoe to see over the heads of the gathering crowd.

'Don't look, baby boy,' I said. 'Just come with me. *Vite, vite, vite, vite.*'

But my words didn't work. Instead of running, he stopped dead. 'Is it bugs?' he said.

'It's bugs,' I said, because I knew how important it was that I never *ever* lie to Todd about this.

'Can they fly?' he said.

'Absolutely not,' I said, because I'm not a monster.

Then we both fled for the door, the car park and the jeep, where Todd sat crying and swearing, slapping at himself to kill the imaginary insects he *knew* were crawling on him and stamping his feet to get the ones that he *knew* were swarming all over the floor. I thought about EMDR techniques – tapping and blinking and thinking about a beach – but the swearing seemed to be helping on its own. He sniffed hard and stopped sobbing. His attention seemed to have been caught by someone crossing the car park in front of us.

'Lex,' he said. 'Call me crazy, but look at that guy and tell me he's not familiar.'

I followed where he was pointing and saw what, to me, looked like a pretty random bloke, dressed in an outfit that must have made it very easy for him to sort out loads of washing: to wit a black sweatshirt, black trackie bums and a black beanie.

'He's not carrying any groceries,' Todd said.

'Maybe he only needed a toothbrush,' I countered.

'And I think he's headed to that truck,' said Todd. 'Look.'

I followed the trajectory of the guy's progress across the car park. He did indeed appear to be making for a large pickup with double back wheels, parked away in the far corner.

'Tell me that truck's not familiar too,' Todd said, sitting bolt upright and grabbing me.

'It's not,' I said. 'But I only know Mini Coopers and VW bugs.'

'I think that's the guy,' said Todd. 'I think that's the truck.'

'I think it's a bloke in a hoodie and a pickup,' I said. 'One of a thousand bloke–hoodie–pickup trios in a five-mile radius.' But even as I said it, I saw something that convinced me. When the man in black got to the pickup in the corner, instead of opening the passenger door and climbing in, he hoisted himself up like a gymnast and shot, feet first, through the window.

'Start the engine, Lexy,' said Todd, his voice quivering with excitement; bugs – both real and imaginary – quite forgotten. 'And follow that cab.'

NINETEEN

'For the seventeenth time,' Todd said, 'I know it's not a cab. But have you no sense of drama or even rhythm? "Follow that doolie" is horrible dialogue, Lexy. "Follow that doolie" is like "Make him an offer he should think about quite seriously." Or, "Put your lips together and yodel." Change lanes! They're changing lanes! Change lanes!'

'I'm *changing* lanes!' I said. 'Jesus.' We were on the main circular route round the north side of Cuento, the one that splits the grid streets off from the suburban lanes and circles, and the pickup with the lithe passenger was three cars ahead of us, doing a normal, sort-of legal, five over the speed limit. 'Phone Kathi and tell her where we are,' I said.

'I'll phone Noleen,' said Todd, frowning and daring me to argue. I wasn't planning to argue. I didn't understand why it was scary to speak to someone a mile and a half behind us, who was near some insects, but then I didn't have to understand. I just had to accept.

'Because if she's still in there someone in the background might describe them really loud,' Todd said.

'*That* would be bad dialogue,' I pointed out, and got a grudging laugh out of him.

'Nolly?' he said, clicking her to speaker as the call went through.

'Oh my God! Where are you? Are you OK? She phoned me! What the hell? Did they . . .? Are you OK, Todd?' Every so often Noleen proves that the offhand reserve is a carapace and underneath she's all love and smooshy hugs.

'Did they what? Did they what?' said Todd, right back to maximum panic again. 'Did they get on me? Did any of them get in the jeep with us? Lexy, did they? Did they?'

'No,' I said. 'They were metres and metres away from us and we skedaddled. Nothing is in this car, Todd, except you and me. So, Kathi called you?' I said into the phone. 'Tell her we're sorry we abandoned her, but she'll understand when she finds out why.'

'Yeah? Cos she's not too happy right now. How did you manage to get her barred from the Lode for being a Nazi sympathizer? That's not nothing.'

'Oh,' I said. 'Yeah. Well, we'll straighten that out. And you don't shop at the Lode anyway. You said when you wanted potatoes you bought potatoes and you didn't want a potato experience for an extra five bucks.'

'It's a long way from "Keep your lifestyle spuds, pal" to "By all means call me a Nazi".' She had a point. 'So. Why?'

'Because we're following the pickup that stole Mama Cuento,' said Todd. 'Tah-dah!'

'Following it where?' Noleen said.

'North out of town,' I said, as it peeled off the circular on to the highway. I glanced at the petrol gauge and saw a comforting three quarters of a tank. 'We're getting on the highway, now. Hey, is Blaike there, or is he still at the Skweek?'

'He finished his killer forty-minute shift at the folding table,' Noleen said. 'Making it a buck a minute, by the way. He's napping.'

'Again?' I said. 'Is he OK? Has he got narcolepsy or carbon-monoxide poisoning or something?'

'He ate a box of Cinnabons,' said Noleen. 'And licked the frosting right off the cardboard. He's probably just sleeping like a lion sleeps after eating a gazelle. But I can wake him up for you.'

'No,' I said. 'But when and if he wakes up of his own accord, can you ask him why Mike might have thought Brandeee is a bit of an arsonist? And . . . what was the other thing, Todd?'

'Was the fibreglass belly button a nipped-off outie or a gouged-out innie,' said Todd. 'And ask him what happened to it. Did he leave it behi—? Oh God, Lexy, we left the case file on the table at the Lode.'

'Kathi has it,' Noleen said. She went on, over Todd trying to interrupt her. 'She's going to check it over and give it a good ol' dusting with insecticide then leave it overnight in a zipped baggie.'

'Don't tell me anymore!' said Todd, and I killed the call.

'Breathe,' I said. 'Tap your legs. Imagine your beach.'

'How many times do I have to tell you it's not a beach?' said Todd. 'It's a café in Paris and I've just fallen into a chair to order a Perrier because I cannot carry these shopping bags any farther up the Champs-Élysées. I may have to call my driver.'

'Did you even try a beach?' I said. 'Or a woodland glade?'

'I can't hear you over the Paris traffic.'

I waited.

'OK,' he went on eventually. 'Tell me what colour they were. Unless they were yellow.'

This was the progress we had made. After an incident, once Todd had calmed down in his happy place, he asked one question he felt he could stand hearing the answer to. We thought it was foolproof.

'I can't tell you,' I said.

It wasn't.

'Oh God, they were yellow?' Todd shrieked. 'Really? They were yellow? Why didn't you say they were grey?'

'You want them to be grey?' I asked him.

'Of course not. That would be disgusting. Grey? I can't imagine anything more gross.'

If I had been a complete sociopath, I would have suggested grey and yellow stripes, but I'm not, so I didn't.

'Does it help that they were tiny?' I said.

'No! That means the car could be full of them. Stop torturing me. I need to google how to follow a car in case we pass Madding and the traffic thins out.'

'OK,' I said, slightly offended, because I was still three cars back in a different lane, and feeling pretty proud of myself. 'You do that and I'll do my thing. I need to think something through. You know that thing . . .?'

'General, much?' said Todd. It was a phrase I had long been meaning to add to our blacklist, but I didn't know what to call it.

'That thing when you know something and you don't know you know it. Or you think you know two things but it's one thing from two angles only you don't know that? Or you think maybe you need to move something you know to a different bit of your brain where it's going to fit better like unwrapping the loo roll so they can go in a drawer one deep.'

'Or,' said Todd, 'you keep following that car and I'll google how to not get lost, caught or shot.'

Shot. I still forget sometimes that that's an option.

'Deal,' I said. 'Not shot is my absolute favourite. Like I said about Earl with the ears, I don't think things should ever be able to hit you and go straight through.'

They do say there's a YouTube video for everything. In less than a minute, Todd was reading off his screen. '"Learn habits ahead of time." Well, that's not helpful. "Equip yourself with long-distance lenses, featuring night-vision capacity." This is bullshit. Wait, wait: "Don't follow too close behind."' He looked up. 'Good. What else? "Overtake and follow from the front, using your mirrors. Great! Overtake, Lexy.'

'We're on a highway, Todd,' I reminded him. 'If I'm in front and they go off at a junction, I'm not going to be able to do a U-ey and catch back up.'

'Oh, come on!' Todd said. 'The median's grass and we're in a jeep.'

'I'm not driving over the central reservation!' I said.

'It's my jeep!'

'It's my green card that'll get ripped up and stamped under the long leather boot of the Highway Patrol guy, in his tight britches,' I said, possibly getting slightly off the point as I imagined the scene.

'But they're not in their short-sleeved shirts in February, which is a real shame,' said Todd, always willing to get side-tracked with me. 'Otherwise, take me in, officer. Punish me.'

'For God's sake,' I said. 'You always go too far. Anyway, even if I bumped over the grass and went back, *and* they didn't see me do it, I'd have to break the speed limit to catch them and we'd get clocked.'

'Speeding isn't a crime of moral turpitude,' said Todd. 'You wouldn't lose residency for that.'

'Clocked!' I said. 'Seen, spotted – by the people we're following. Learn English!'

'Learn how to follow someone without being caught!' Todd

shot back. 'Because I don't think they're going to Madding, do you?'

We had passed four of the five exits that led into the Beteo county seat and the pickup ahead showed no signs of slowing and heading for the inside lane. I knew that once we were on the road north there would be no cover. There was literally nothing up there but Canada. Well, there was Oregon and Washington State and even inside California there were towns big enough to have a tractor dealership and a choice of burgers, but there was nothing that caused any Friday-night traffic. San Francisco was one way, Tahoe another, Napa a third. We were headed in the fourth direction, just the pickup full of statue nabbers, Todd and me.

I fell right back until the truck lights were a pair of distant twinkles. There was nowhere for them to go anyway. No exits for mile after mile after rice-paddied, tumble-weeded mile.

'So, will they have to shut the Lode down, do you reckon?' said Todd, coming back to it like a diva to a diss, helpless not to. 'It wasn't the food that was infested with killer . . . don't tell me! Do you think they'll be shut down by the health inspectors when it was only flowers?'

'I don't think so,' I said. 'Although, flowers . . .'

'What?'

'Big business,' I said. 'Especially this time of year, between Valentine's, Easter and Mother's Day. And then the weddings start up. If . . .'

'What?'

'I'm going to make a call now,' I said. 'And I don't want you to listen to it. OK? Put your earbuds in and crank up the sounds.'

'Why?' said Todd.

'Because I want to talk plainly and I don't want you to get upset,' I said. 'It's about what Mike said, remember? A break-in at the botany department? And now a stramash at a flower stand and there was dead Barbra and someone else said something flower-related or at least flower-adjacent . . . if only I could remember.'

'No, Mike won't mind you calling her up and saying that at all,' said Todd. 'That's not so vague it's infuriating. Not a bit.' He was scrolling through his playlist, jamming his buds in deep. 'Ahhhhhh. Paulo Londra!' he said, and sat back with his eyes closed and his head bobbing.

'Can you hear me?' I said softly. Then to double-check: 'Todd, you're nearer forty than thirty. Why are you pretending to like rap music?' There was no response. So I placed the call.

It took some persuasion to get the despatcher to put me through to Mike and I had to dangle the possibility of information on Mama Cuento before she sighed fit to blow down a brick house and hit the buttons.

'Hiya,' I said.

'Oh, great. It's the karate kid,' said Mike. '"Hi-*yah*", Lexy.'

I ignored her. 'Look, you know this break-in in the botany department?'

'Don't ever tell me I'm not a kind-hearted person,' Mike said.

'When Officer . . .' I realized I had no idea of Mills of God's real name. 'When the officer said that a lot of valuable peonies had been stolen, he seemed not too sure of his information. So, I was wondering, was it maybe freesias, irises and daisies instead? Because we were just in the Lode—'

'Oh, were you?' said Mike. 'You saw what went down?'

'And I was thinking a university botany department studies diseased and infected things, right? Not pretty posies. And those flowers certainly looked like they were in trouble.'

'It wasn't peonies,' Mike said. 'So you saw it all, did you?'

'What was it?'

'It wasn't the botany department at all,' Mike said. 'It was the entomology department. Only I didn't want to say that in front of Dr Kroger.'

'That was nice of you,' I said.

'Because if there's one thing I can't stand, it's a screaming queen who's literally screaming,' Mike said.

'Well, OK, that's not quite such an explosion in the human-kindness dairy, but still, it saved Todd a lot of anguish. And so the peonies were . . . what? Growing in the lab for beasties to eat?'

'It wasn't peonies that were stolen,' she said. 'Aren't you

listening? It was peach potato aphids. Thousands and thousands of the little boogers, in tanks.'

'Peach potato aphids,' I said. 'So nothing to do with flowers at all then? Just peaches and potatoes?'

'Let me enlighten you to the contrary,' Mike said. 'The dude in charge of the greenhouse that got looted would not stop talking. The peach potato aphid, Lexy, is one of the insect kingdom's great generalists. Like a tiny raccoon.'

'Right,' I said. 'And when you say "boogers", is that a descriptive term?'

'Yeah, they're creepy little dudes. Kinda yellow and gross-looking.'

'I think they ended up in the Lode,' I said.

'Oh, we know *some* of them ended up in the Lode,' said Mike. 'And some in Safeway, some in Costco, some in Winco . . . Any market in the city limits that sells flowers is selling flowers with added protein tonight. One of my officers is out picking up the CCTV now, and that's my Friday, unless we get a murder – watching the feed for the weirdest bioterrorists ever.'

'Did they leave notes?'

'In this instance, they did not.'

'Do you think they're dangerous?' I asked.

'If you're a carnation,' said Mike.

'So it's not a do-not-approach-or-attempt-to-subdue type situation?' I said. I was totally ready to tell her what we were up to and hand it over to the long arm of the law, depending on what she said next.

'Uh, no,' was what she said, and in a mighty sarcastic tone too. 'We won't be calling in the SWAT teams over the great peach potato aphid resettlement plan.'

Which I took as permission to carry on following the truck and not troubling the busy detective with the fact that I was doing so.

I hung up, tapped Todd on his shoulder, and then winced and swerved as he unplugged his buds from his phone instead of his ears and filled the car with a sudden deafening blast of Argentinian street music.

'Jesus, Lexy,' he said. 'Could you try to be a bit more

conspicuous to our mark, maybe? You didn't manage to swerve across all the lanes and on to the shoulder there.'

I said nothing, which was a triumph of self-restraint.

'What did you want to talk to Mike about?'

'Not important,' I said. 'Where do you think we're going?'

'How could I possibly hazard a guess when I don't have the information about what just happened at the Lode?'

'The information would cause you distress,' I said. 'But let's say it was the work of the same gang that stole the statue. It would be too much of a coincidence otherwise.'

'And you forgot the worst thing they did,' Todd said. 'Kidnapped a real live woman and ripped off one of her fake nails to send back to her husband.'

'Did they though?' I asked him. 'I still think it's more likely that Bran did that to get the cops' attention. Or Brandeee herself did it to kick dust over the fact that she left of her own accord. I don't think the disappearance of the woman and the disappearance of the statues are related, necessarily.'

'Except you forgot one crucial fact,' said Todd. 'The belly button got sent to Blaike, her son.'

'My God, so I did,' I said. 'So it did. And the toe, in contrast, just got put back at the scene with the floral tributes.'

'Where it might not have been found till they'd all withered and the city was clearing it up for composting,' Todd said. He waited for a response. 'Lexy? Are you listening?'

'Yes,' I said. 'Of course. I'm trying to think . . . what that . . . compost . . . But it won't come. What happened to the chainsawed nose? Did that get placed at the scene of the statue heist or did it get sent to someone, like with Blaike?'

Todd was already dialling. As he waited for Noleen to answer, he took the chance to give me some advance instruction in how to keep following a car on an empty road. 'You know what you could do? You could peel off at the next exit, and go up the ramp and over, then back on again. In case they think we're following them. They'll see you leave and then they'll see another car come on. They won't think it's the same one. Especially if you put full beams on when you rejoin. You're dipped now, right?'

'That's actually a great idea,' I said. 'But what if we go off and then on again, and they *do* see us at it? They'll get suspicious.'

'No they won't. They'll think you're buzzed or lost or something.'

'And what if we come back on and they've disappeared?'

'The exits are a day's ride apart up here,' said Todd. 'They're like Spanish missions. OK? Deal? Next exit, we go off, disguise our lights and come back.'

'What if they're driving to Alaska?' I said. 'We'll run out of petrol.'

'Honey, nobody drives to Alaska. I don't think there's even a road.'

'Of course there's a road!' I said. 'And, as for what nobody does, we're talking about people who cut off bits of statues and mail them—'

Todd held up a finger as Noleen finally answered her phone.

'An outie,' she said, on speaker. 'He found it in his boat-house locker – can you believe they have these kids row on a river, in Idaho, in February? – and handed it right over to the cops, right there in downtown Hicksville. Said he knew there was no point handing it to the school because they'd smother the second coming if they thought there'd be blow-back. So he hitched into town, made a statement, gave the cops the piece of plastic and kept walking.'

'And what about the wooden nose on the . . . who was it?'

'She's called Liberty and she's a kind of a centrepiece at a Girl Scouts camp up there. Let me just . . . I bookmarked all the new stories . . . Did they say . . .? Here it is. Her nose was sent to the PO box of the Girl Scouts of Oregon and Southwest Washington. That is sickness beyond sick. That's really nasty.'

'It's a big step up from what they did with Mama Cuento's toe,' I said.

'And the intermediate step is a real head-scratcher,' said Todd. 'Sending a belly button to a boy in a boarding school? That doesn't go with the overall . . . He's always been a boy, right, Lexy?'

I shrugged. 'I think so,' I said.

On the other end of the phone, Noleen covered the

mouthpiece and shouted, 'Hey, kid? Blaike? You're cis, right? Not trans.'

'Yeah,' came Blaike's voice in the background. 'Why?'

'Nothin',' said Noleen. She came back on the line. 'You hear that?'

'Yeah,' I said. 'No help there, then.' But still it gave me a warm glow. Some things in this mad world were getting better. 'The target statues are not random. Black, Native, Asian, Mexican. Hence Kathi dropping that brick in the Lode. But the targets for ransom notes are hard to put together. Left behind at crime scene, sent back to crime scene, Girl Scouts, grieving husband, oblivious son. Unless we can tie Brandeee to these Scouts in some way? Maybe the Akela is her sister.'

'The what?'

'Troop leader. Noleen, can you phone Bran and ask if Brandeee has connections in the area?'

'On it,' she said, and rang off.

'The area of Oregon and Southwest Washington,' Todd said. 'You know it's bigger than Scotland, right?'

'Yeah but there's no one there. It would be significant if she had family or close friends . . . Hang on. Are there elks in Washington?'

'Elk,' said Todd. 'Do I look like I would know a thing like that? Why?'

'Because Brandeee's fake husband, Lenny Kowalski, was supposed to have died in an elk-hunting accident. That's the story she always told Blaike until she finally admitted the guy didn't exist.'

'And he believed her?' said Todd. 'He believed a guy called Lenny Kowalski hunted elk?'

'Why not?' I said.

'You really need to keep on with your assimilation to the advanced level,' Todd said. 'Would you follow Montague Cavendish's recipe for Hoppin' John? How about going square dancing with Sofia Hernandez?'

'I don't know any of these people,' I said. 'Make your point, Todd.'

But he had spotted a junction and he shifted all his attention to persuading me to turn off, adjust the light setting and come back on again, like a proper private eye on an official tail.

And, to be honest, it got to me. Doing something so sketchy and so deliberate seemed to cement the fact that we were now right up in the buttes, surrounded by farmland on all sides and still barrelling north to God knows where, on a bona fide adventure.

'Yippy-kay-ay,' said Todd, when we were back on the road again and the lights of our mark were still there, winking at us far ahead. 'Let's do this thing!'

TWENTY

We crossed the state line.

'Does that make this . . . what does that mean?' I asked Todd.

'It means don't buy any cauliflowers and try to take them home,' he said. 'What's the gas doing?'

'It's being consumed steadily by the engine,' I said. 'Will we run out before they do? What kind of pickup was that anyway?'

'Dodge Ram 3500 HD,' said Todd. 'It's a guzzler but it's got a huge tank so it's a crapshoot.'

'If we pass a petrol station we should stop,' I said. 'And then you can take over driving and floor it to catch up so even if we get stopped it won't be me who gets into trouble.'

'Are you serious?' he said. 'You think if someone's going to speed and get pulled over it should be the brown guy?'

'Oh yeah,' I said, which really annoyed him.

'Oh yeah,' he echoed in a mocking voice. 'Systemic racism. It went clean out of my pretty blonde head for a minute there. No, Lexy. If we're going to stop for gas and floor it to catch up, you're driving. If we get pulled over, talk about *Outlander* for a woman sheriff, and golfing at St Andrews for a man sheriff, and you'll get off with a warning.'

'Deal,' I said and, leaning over to shake his hand, I missed the very moment that our prey, the car we'd been following all the way from Cuento until my eyes were gritty from watching its brake lights, suddenly disappeared.

'Where'd it go?' said Todd. 'Where'd it go?'

We both stared out into the blackness of the road ahead. There was no exit sign in sight and no pickup sitting on the shoulder with its lights off, waiting for us to catch up.

'Slow down,' said Todd. 'Slow down and let me look to see if there's any kind of a . . . Only how could there be? I mean, I know we're in the boonies, but it's still a highway. There can't be little lanes and private driveways opening off of this. Where the hell did it *go*?'

'There!' I said. I had slowed all the way down to twenty. 'Look. Off to the side.' I was sure of it. Beyond the hard shoulder of the road, the land was unfenced and, while most of it was black with blacker smudges that had to be trees and paler smudges that were probably distant hills, one bit of it seemed to be a smeary pinkish colour. Like the colour of brake lights still showing through the dust as a pickup truck travelled overland.

'We can't follow them off the road,' Todd said. 'There's no YouTube video ever made that could make that unsuspicious.'

'Throw something out the window,' I said. 'Right when we pass where the lights are and we'll keep driving, then come back once they've had a chance to get ahead.'

'Throw what?' said Todd. 'You mean like litter?'

'Anything,' I said. 'Something that won't blow away. But quickly.' We were getting close to being level with the pink blur and it was very small now as the pickup kept moving into the scrubland, away from the road.

'Antibacterial wipes, owner's manual, throat lozenges.' Todd was pawing through the glove box. 'I can't see anything suitable. Do you have anything?'

I didn't answer. I used the button on my side to open his window then I snatched up his personal go-cup with the integral mixer, for fad-hoppers who were currently dissolving all sorts of crap in their drinks, and lobbed it out to land on the shoulder with a sickening crack as we passed.

'Roger bought me that cup,' said Todd. 'Why didn't you throw yours?'

'Because my mum sent it for Christmas,' I told him. 'It's from Greggs.'

'So?'

'So it's made of very cheap plastic and it would roll away.'

'Replace mine,' Todd said, 'and I'll forgive you.' He was up on his seat, looking out the back window. 'I've lost sight of them. That was a brainwave, Lexy. Turn around now. This is getting exciting.'

I gave it another half a minute, just in case the pickup driver could still see the road even though we couldn't see them, then, as Todd instructed, I wheeled round on the empty tarmac and headed back to where his bashed-in go-cup was still leaking cold coffee on to the ground. I parked on the hard shoulder and pulled the handbrake on.

'Now we swap,' I said. 'Surely. You're the owner. If anyone's going to be driving off-road, shouldn't it be you?'

'The brown guy,' Todd said again.

'Oh, come *on*!' I said. 'Your name is Dr Todd Kroger and you're not as brown as I'd be if I had all summer to sunbathe. Todd, I'm not spitting on your proud Latinx heritage, but seriously, would a cop from away out here in the back of beyond conceivably pick up the subtle vibes of . . . I don't even know what . . . that say your dad was Mexican? I don't think so.'

'Lexy,' he said. 'We don't have time to go into this right now, but I am deeply, deeply . . . Yeah, OK.' He got out and went round, swiping up the ruined cup on his way, while I wriggled over to the passenger side.

'Apart from anything else, I've never driven overland,' I said.

'Me either,' said Todd, like every other jeep owner in California, I daresay.

It wasn't too bad. We couldn't go quickly, because we were following the tracks of the pickup truck as it wound between little scrubby bushes and past the odd boulder, like in a cowboy film. Occasionally there was a burst of sharp stink as we drove over something Todd told me was called vinegar weed, but mostly we were just bumping along, trying not to think what would happen if we ran out of petrol all the way out here.

'Call home, I suppose,' I said, when Todd first aired the question. Then I glanced at my phone. 'Oh no.'

'Dead battery?' Todd said. 'There should be a cable in the console there. Thank God no one *threw it out the window*.'

'My battery's fine,' I said. 'There's no signal. Let's see yours.' I was clutching at straws because we were on the same network and my phone was a bit newer, and right enough when he tossed his into my lap, it was wearing a grey frown emoji on its home screen and was stone dead.

'That's unsettling,' Todd said. 'I'll turn back the minute the fuel gauge bongs. That gives us forty miles.'

'Deal,' I said. 'Wait. I've got two bars back. We must be picking up on someone's Wi-Fi.'

Todd slammed the brakes on and put his hand out in a classic soccer-mom save to stop me getting whiplash.

'What the hell are you doing?' I snapped anyway.

'Duh,' he said. 'If you're picking up someone's Wi-Fi, we're probably getting close to where they were headed, don't you think?'

'We could be,' I agreed. 'So . . . what do we do now?'

'I think there's a little hill ahead,' Todd said. 'We could go up on foot and look over. If we can't see anything, then we keep on driving, following their tracks.'

'OK,' I said. 'Let's do it. Is there enough moonlight to walk by? Or can we put our phone lights on?'

'On low and trained at the ground,' Todd said. 'We don't want to advertise our arrival, if they *are* nearby. Hey, what's the Wi-Fi called, by the way?'

'"Direct 36-HPM-281",' I said, reading it off my settings menu. 'Shame. "Kidnappers R Us" would have been much more snappy.'

We climbed down and Todd locked the jeep; the beep sounded alarmingly loud in the cold, quiet air. After it stopped reverberating, we stood still and listened to perfect silence. It was a chilly night up here and not a breath of wind. Besides Todd's breathing, there was nothing. And it felt somehow as if that nothing went on forever. I looked back over my shoulder. There was a road there. But there was no one on it and it might as well have been scrub desert for a hundred miles all round. I swallowed.

'Are there any . . .?' I said. 'What's the wildlife situation like round these parts?' The cold air swallowed my voice. Maybe there was a fog starting.

'It's too cold for moths,' said Todd. 'Or I would not be standing here. Mosquitoes too.'

'Anything else?' I said.

'Rattlesnakes,' said Todd. 'Coyotes, bears. Why?'

'But no moths,' I said. 'Phew.' I looked up into the glittering navy-blue sky and told myself this was an adventure at best and a waste of time at worst, then I pressed my light setting down as low as it would go, trained the puny beam on the ground in front of my feet and started walking.

There was indeed a hill ahead, as Todd had thought, but it was so gradual that we walked and walked for what felt like half an hour and nothing about the ridge in front of us ever seemed to change.

'This dust gets in your throat,' Todd said, eventually, with a slight cough. 'And your eyes.'

'And your shoes,' I said. 'I've got grit in my insteps.'

We walked another while. Sometimes there was another patch of vinegar weed and once a scuffle as a tiny creature took off out of our way.

'Was that a snake?' I said.

'That scampering sound?' said Todd. 'Only if it had its tap shoes on. What's wrong with you? It was probably a gopher.'

'Cool,' I said. I didn't actually know how vicious gophers were and I didn't want to.

'Put your torch out and see if you can see anything up ahead,' Todd said.

We waited for our eyes to adjust, then looked all round.

'Nothing,' I said. 'And I'm not sure I like it.' I was dead sure I hated it actually: out here a hike from the jeep, with only someone else's password-protected Wi-Fi and no clue what we were walking into. If this ended as badly as it might, I was going to make a very sheepish corpse.

'You never want someone to read your obituary and say, "Well, what did she expect?"' I said. 'Ideally, if you die suddenly, you want people to say, "No way! Who could ever have foreseen that?"'

'No one's going to die,' said Todd. And I chose to believe that the break in his voice was from the dust.

We trudged on. The way was getting steeper, I was sure. It was certainly getting stonier; the bits in my shoes were too big to call grit now. And I was almost sure that there was a faint lightness coming from behind the ridge we were finally approaching.

'Put your light off again,' Todd breathed. 'Stand still and listen.'

Without the torchlight, it was unmistakable – a glow of

sodium. And without our footsteps the sound was unmistakable too – the flatulent hum of a petrol generator put-put-putting away somewhere not too far off.

'What will we do?' I breathed.

'What do you mean?' said Todd. 'We'll go and see what's what.'

'What do you think might be what?' I said.

'Why? What do *you* think might be what?'

'I don't know. And I don't think I want to.'

'Why not?' said Todd. Then before I had a chance to answer he said, 'Oh for God's sake!' And he started walking towards the light and sound.

I had the choice of following him towards the lair of a statue nabber and peach potato aphid bomber, or of being left all alone in the pitch black surrounded by snakes, coyotes and bears. And at least one gopher. And – this was the crunch – letting Todd walk into a potential nest of aphids on his own.

'Wait for me,' I hissed and scuttled after him.

Now, of course, the ridge came rushing up to us. Before another minute had passed, we found ourselves lying on our bellies, peering over it at what lay beyond.

There was a fenced compound dead ahead. It looked about the size of a small mall or large farm: a collection of buildings and a few exterior security lights. There were also a few humped shapes of various heights that might have been statues wrapped in tarpaulin, but might have been a hundred other things too.

What there wasn't was any obvious entrance. It was beyond frustrating to be this close and yet still so short of answers. We couldn't hear anything but the generator. And we couldn't see much detail through the close slats of the high fence. Todd shuffled to his left and I followed him. We still couldn't see much inside the fence, but we were on the other side of a big dead-looking sage bush now and at least we could see what *it* had been hiding from our view. Quite alarmingly close to where we lay, outside the fence, sat a row of pickup trucks, including – I was sure – the one we'd been following. Its engine was still ticking as it cooled down.

'Look at the licence plate!' Todd whispered, grabbing me.

'P-one-two-four-P-P,' I said. 'So?'

'PPP!' said Todd. 'PPPerfection!'

'Hang on, what?' I said. I sat up a bit to get a better view. 'Wait . . . what? So . . . these people steal statues, kidnap people, send ransom notes, do the thing they did tonight that we're not talking about, and run spa retreats? That's . . . puzzling. Nah, it's got to be a coincidence.'

'Really?' said Todd.

'Well, what's one-two-four?'

'I've let my Nazi numerology slip a bit, what with one thing and another,' Todd said.

'I don't think the numbers are anything,' I said. 'Look at the other two – P-two-nine-one-one-P-P and P-three-one-six-P. They're just fillers to make the plates legal. Let's see if we can find the way in.' I knew he'd never agree. Hoped not, anyway.

'We're not going in!' he hissed at me. 'Lexy, are you mad? Maybe if our phones were working . . .'

'They're working enough to film,' I said. 'They're working enough to record.' I fished my phone out of my pocket and dinged it on. 'Actually,' I said, 'it's worth a try . . . We're up to five bars on their Wi-Fi now. If we could take a guess at the password . . .'

'P,' said Todd. 'They seem pretty keen on that. Try PPP.'

'Nope.'

'P-one-two-four-P-P?'

'Nope.'

'PPPerfection?'

My phone played a long chorus of beeps, telling me about missed messages, as I furiously turned the sound right down. 'Yay!' I said. 'OK, are you willing to come with me now?'

'Wait till I get mine on and open a FaceTime with Roger . . . No, not Roger; he'll tell me not to. With Kathi. What are you doing?'

'I'm looking up the number plate,' I said. 'I can't find anything. I'll try P-one-two-four . . . Oh, Proverbs! It's a Bible verse.'

'Of course it is,' Todd said. 'God is great, but he has terrible taste in friends. What does it say?'

'Proverbs, chapter one, verse twenty-four,' I said. '"Because I have called and ye refused; I have stretched out my hand and no man regarded."'

'Not one of the greatest hits,' said Todd. 'What kind of thirsty little bitch chooses that for a vanity plate?'

'Oh no,' I said. Because I had had another thought and followed it through. I had looked up chapter twelve, verse four instead. I held my phone out, so Todd could read what it said.

'"A virtuous woman is a crown to her husband,"' he recited, '"but a disgraceful wife is as rottenness in his bones."'

'Bingo,' I said. 'Tell me that's not the mating cry of a sick bastard who'd knock down statues and chop bits off them.'

'Yep,' Todd said. 'Whatever they're selling through that website, thank God Brandee didn't give it out as holiday gifts.' He was clicking photographs of the number plates. When he had finished, he got up on hands and knees. 'Once round?' he said. 'See what we can see?'

'As long as you don't think they've got cameras trained on us,' I said.

'If they had cameras on us, they'd have us tied in a sack already,' Todd said.

Good point, well made. He had already started crawling, so I followed him, through the dust – much worse, now that our noses were closer to it – through the vinegar weed – ditto – and through some piles of dried shit that I actually prayed were coyote, gopher, snake or bear, because that was a safari kind of shit to crawl through, much better than what it felt like, which was dog. I think everyone would agree that, if you're crawling through dog shit on your hands and knees, you're not having a good night.

We saw nothing on the side where we started, and nothing on the next side once we'd turned a corner. Just that same high, slatted fence and the lighted buildings beyond. When we came round to the far side, though, facing away from the distant road, it was obvious that there was a gate halfway along. There was a bump in the fence line, like an arch, and more light spilled through wider slats. Todd, ahead of me, got his phone out again, ready to take a picture, if we could get a view into the compound itself, I think, but after a couple more feet of crawling he stopped dead in his tracks.

'What is it?' I whispered. 'Is someone there?'

'Oh God,' he said. 'Oh God. I know we said it, but I didn't really mean it. Not really. Lexy, look at the gate.'

I crawled up beside him and squinted at where he was pointing. There *was* an arch. It was made of wrought iron in a slightly wavy curve and it had writing in between its top and bottom band.

'Jesus,' I said. 'Who the hell puts three words in metal over a gate?'

I answered myself and Todd answered me too, so we spoke in unison: 'Nazis.'

Then, as quick as we could move, we scurried backwards on all fours until we were back on the safe side of the ridge. There, we stood, put our torches on full and ran hell for leather back to the jeep, sanity and the road home.

TWENTY-ONE

Roger was not pleased.

I should have been relieved there was no one to treat *me* like a child incapable of making my own decisions and scold me for recklessness. Instead, I felt unloved and sad. And so, surreptitiously, while they bickered, I texted Dirtball Doug and asked him if he'd like to have dinner the next day. Then I switched my phone off and rejoined the argy-bargy.

We were in Roger and Todd's room because Blaike was watching *Jackass: The Movie* in my living room, and while *Jackass* was far too disgusting for Kathi to bear being in the same space with it even if it was on a laptop facing the other way, Blaike was still too upset after the rollicking he'd got from Bran to be taken to task about his taste in films without hitting the road again for God knows where. And we couldn't go to the office because Noleen was in there cutting Diego's hair, and he always screamed throughout his haircuts, so loud that it gave Roger flashbacks to bad shifts in the children's ward and wasn't too much fun for anyone else either.

'But there's no way Mike would have reacted with enough commitment, babe,' Todd was saying. 'If we'd phoned up and said we saw someone jump in the window of a truck, we wouldn't have got past the dispatcher. If we'd said we recognized him but admitted we didn't see his face, and recognized the truck but didn't see its licence number, she'd have laughed.'

'We were very careful,' I said. 'Todd googled how to follow someone and we stayed well back. We didn't drive up and let them hear the car either. We got out and walked.'

'And fell over?' Roger said. 'You're filthy.'

'Again, taking every precaution,' I said, 'we crawled so they didn't see us.'

'You crawled on your bellies through wild land in the dark?' said Roger.

'We're fine!' said Todd. 'Now we need to call Mike and tell her what we saw.'

But Mike was less impressed than we'd hoped. I was the one who spoke to her and I got precisely nowhere. 'You saw the statues?' she said.

'Sort of,' I answered. 'I mean, I think so. Let's go with *yes*. Only they were hidden by tarps and behind a slatted fence, quite far off.'

'So let's go with *no*,' Mike said.

'We couldn't get a clear view,' I went on. 'It's hard to describe.'

'I'm aware of the layout up there,' Mike said. 'They're on our radar.'

'They are?' I said. 'Have you seen the gate? And it's not just the statues. One of them was in the Lode when the' – I flicked a glance at Todd – 'when the incident unfolded.'

'When it came to light,' Mike said. 'Not when the little boogers were planted there. So he did some grocery shopping? The prices are daylight robbery, but otherwise that's not a crime.'

'And they've kidnapped Brandeee Lancer!' I said. 'Have you forgotten that?'

'How do you figure?' Mike said.

'She paid them three thousand dollars but she never handed the vouchers over, presumably because she found out their so-called spa is a cult indoctrination centre and maybe she was going to expose them, so they grabbed her.'

'Cult indoctrination centre, huh?' said Mike.

'Oh, absolutely,' I said. 'You didn't see this place, Mike.'

'I bet I've seen worse,' Mike said. 'We all went on a course. I know it's creepy, but it's the price of freedom.'

'They're not free to kidnap people,' I said.

'Kidnap would be a major deviation from the usual MO,' said Mike. 'I can't see it.'

'And they're not free to break into universities!'

'Yeah, yeah, about that. Why would these guys steal aphids?'

'That I don't know,' I admitted. 'But you can ask them when you go up there and arrest the whole damn crew.'

'I will get right on that,' Mike said. 'You got it. The police department from this little California town is totally going to go up over the Oregon state line and bust in on a bunch of backwoods isolationists in case they stole a statue. In fact, I better start now, because it's getting late and it's a long way.'

'But you'll tell the FBI?' I said. 'Or should *we* phone them?'

'Go ahead,' Mike said. 'Make their night. And mine.'

I put the phone down and tuned back to Todd and Roger, who were still glaring at each other. 'Did you manage to blow up the picture?' I asked, because we hadn't been able to decipher which three words had been picked out in metal above the gate of the mysterious compound.

'Yep,' said Todd. 'Power, Purpose, Prosperity.'

'Huh,' I said. 'That sounds bland enough.'

Kathi had been quiet, but she kicked in now with a hollow laugh, looking up from her phone. 'Bland? You never heard of the prosperity gospel, Lexy?'

I shook my head.

'In a nutshell: "God wants me rich, so Ima go right ahead and trample over you to get there." Right, Todd?'

'Perfect summary,' Todd said. 'Google it, Lex. Google those three words.'

I whipped my phone out and did what he said. 'Oh God,' I said when the page had loaded. *Patriarchy*, the heading read. *The purpose of power. The path to prosperity.*

'Scroll down,' Kathi said. 'To the links for children, for "people stranded in other faiths" and finally, *riiiiight* down there at the bottom . . .'

'"Wives and wives in waiting",' I said.

'I think they mean women,' said Kathi. 'See what it says there?'

'"PPPerfection",' I said, clicking on the live link. 'OH MY GOD!' It took me right to the same page. '"Are you tired, stressed, jaded and wrung out by your busy life? Work, kids, study, caring for elders, running the home, even dating! can leave you in need of a gentle oasis of clam" – they really should update this page – "and pampering. Let us soothe away the cares of the twenty-first century in the peace of nature at our women-only restorative retreat. For treatment menu and to book an appointment click here." Ewwwwwwwww.'

'Right?' Kathi said. 'Now we know they think a wife should adorn her husband and if she's feisty she might rot his bones, it puts a whole new slant on things.'

'Escape the twenty-first century and rediscover your path to serfdom at our women-only gulag,' I said. 'Should I click? Should one of us see if we can get into a correspondence with these people?'

'Like Brandee did, you mean?' said Todd. 'I can't say I'm keen to let either of you two get in their clutches.'

'I can't believe Mike doesn't want to shut them down,' I said. 'It can't be legal to . . .' I was waiting for the page to load. 'The link's broken.'

'Maybe they want you to call them up,' Kathi said.

'And then they . . .?' I asked.

'And then they start the process that ends with your husband finding your fingernail on the doorstep,' said Todd. 'We need to tell Bran about this. Lexy, you're up.'

'Absolutely not,' I said. 'In no way am I up for *that*. Nuh-uh. I'd rather . . .' I couldn't think of anything unpleasant enough. 'I'd rather . . . phone this number.'

So I did.

And even though it was after eleven o'clock now, a real person answered. 'Patriarchyville,' he said. 'Bob speaking.' I hit the mute button just in time to disguise the explosion of laughter, then I put him on speakerphone.

'Sorry,' I said, in my best American accent. 'Could you repeat that, please?'

'Patriarchyville,' the voice said, maybe a bit impatiently. 'Bob speaking.'

I handed the phone to Kathi. My American accent wasn't up to an extended conversation. 'Uh, hi Bob,' Kathi said in a calm voice, meanwhile gesticulating furiously with her other hand about all the things she was going to do to me after the call. 'I was interested in a spa day for a group of girlfriends as part of my bachelorette party. You're in Oregon, right? But I couldn't get the menu page to load.'

'You getting married? Ain't that nice? You been married before?' said Bob.

'No,' Kathi said.

'You a virgin?' said Bob.

'Fuck you, you sick creep,' Kathi said. 'We're on to you.' She hung up and gave me my phone back. 'Sorry.'

'No, don't be,' said Todd. 'That was very interesting. So up front. So unlikely to work. What's even the game plan with that? I'm more confused than ever.'

'Me too,' I said. 'And I need a shower. I've got two pounds of Oregon dirt in my hair and the same down my bra. Let's leave all of this for tonight. After one of you tells Bran what happened to Brandeee.'

'That's not fair—!' Todd burst out.

I interrupted him. 'I'm going to have to tell Blaike. Would you really want to swap me?'

For a wonder, Blaike wasn't sleeping. He was draped on my couch, staring slack-jawed at the sort of video you find when you've gone online to share your thoughts about *Jackass*. I averted my eyes.

One day of a boy living here, I thought, looking around. There were three enormous shoes under the couch, each with a sock inside, and the coffee tabletop was littered with glasses and plates, empty crisp bags, and yoghurt pots with spoons congealing in them. White Pine Academy was a complete failure in the short-sharp-shock department, if anyone was asking me.

'So did Noleen ask you why Mike would think your mum trained you in arson?' I said. 'I know she got the belly-button info.'

Blaike blinked at me a couple of times. Which was fair enough; that wasn't something you heard every day.

'Mom's not an arsonist,' he said, 'just a believer in burning stuff to make a fresh start. It's like Buddhism.'

It wasn't very like Buddhism but I decided not to argue.

'She burned a pile of stuff any time she made a big change,' Blaike went on. 'Only she used to burn it in this one spot, but then she put a patio set on there and the only other spot that wasn't grass or paving – so's it didn't matter? – it turned out not so good, because of the tree.'

'How did the cops know your mum burned stuff?' I said.

'Neighbours at the old place,' Blaike said. 'Before she married Bran. Well, after she divorced him the first time. Before she married Burt.'

Poor kid. I had heard a lot about how perfect his mum was; no one had touched on the fact that she dragged him around from man to man like a best friend at a dull party. I had almost decided not to break the news to him tonight, let him have as much peace as he could get, for as long as he could get it, but he thwarted me.

'Where is she?' he said.

'Wh–what makes you ask that?'

'People keep talking about getting my stepdad's permission for stuff. Why not my mom's? Is she missing?'

'Oh, honey,' I answered. 'No. We think we know exactly where she is.'

'Where?' said Blaike in a tiny voice. On his screen, three men were filling their wetsuit trousers with beer, straight from the keg, via a hose jammed in the waistband. Blaike looked back at it, as though at his lost innocence, and then closed the laptop.

'We think she's at a place called . . . Well, it doesn't matter what it's called. But we think she's with some men who're . . . Well, it doesn't really matter what they're—'

'You're not helping,' Blaike said.

'OK.' I took a big breath. 'There's a place up in the woods, in Oregon, like a retreat or a spa. It's completely nuts, but probably harmless.' Man, I just could not stop lying to this kid!

'Probably?' Blaike said.

'It's not your responsibility,' I said. 'You need to leave it to us and your stepdad. You need to have a good night's . . . Well, you need to go back to White Pines. Let the adults take care of things.'

'That sounds pretty cool,' said Blaike. 'I never heard anyone say that before. Well not since I was like twelve. But is there any chance I could stay here and go back to Cuento High?'

'Of course,' I said. 'I'll take you in the morning.'

'Not Bran's house,' he said. 'Here!'

'Here as in *here*?' I asked. 'As in, on my boat?'

'It's way cool. No one else in my class lives on a boat.'

'I . . .' I said. 'It's kind of small, Blaike. And I run my business out of it.' I was trying to think on my feet and I knew I hadn't started with my strongest arguments. 'Your parents will never allow it,' I said, when it occurred to me.

'I don't have parents,' said Blaike. 'I have a missing mom who sent me to Idaho, and Bran said it was OK if I stayed tonight. So why not every night? Or I could divorce them. Her. He never adopted me, either time, and Burt didn't. And my dad doesn't exist. Plus anyway I'm eighteen in four weeks.'

'Just because Bran didn't insist on you going home when he found out you were here,' I began.

'Didn't insist?' said Blaike. 'He couldn't have cared less. So. Can I stay?'

'Tidy up the living room and I'll see what I think in the morning,' I said. Then I ran away because it was late and I was tired and I needed a shower and – OK, yes – a tiny little bit because I had a text from Doug about dinner.

'Bloody hell, Lexy,' I said to myself as I was stripping off my gritty clothes and trying not to worry about what all these little tiny rocks would do to my vintage hardwood flooring. I sat down on the toilet, which is where I do all my most important texting.

I eat dinner every night, was what Doug had texted back to me, *so it should be easy*.

That, I reckoned, was a great text. Funny, eager, and no exclamation marks.

How about tomorrow? I sent. *Too soon?*

Then I left the phone balanced on the windowsill, which is the only bit of my titchy bathroom that doesn't get wet when the shower turns on, and refused to look at it until I was scrubbed, rinsed, shaved here and there (sue me; it had been a long time since I'd been this close to an actual encounter), dried and moisturized. I worked vanilla body salve into my elephant-hide elbows and kneecaps – my heels were beyond redemption and I didn't want to slip, so I left them, planning an emergency pedicure in the morning.

When I was clean and soft, wrapped in a towel and turban, I picked up the phone again.

Dinner tomorrow is not too soon, Doug had texted me. *Lunch would be even better. Breakfast looks pushy.*

Dinner at six, I texted back. *Japanese? Like Dorodango. I've been studying!* Gah, I hated myself for that exclamation mark.

LOVE Japanese food. It's so starchy. Interested you studied. What think organic doro? Still OK?

Organic anything was OK, I thought. This was California.

Of course, I texted.

Thrilled you didn't freak, he sent me.

I read that seven times and was still wondering what to say back when the three dots started up.

Some people do not understand org doro.

Or opera, I texted. *Or ballet. Imagine what Damien Hirst got before he was famous.*

Phew! he sent me. Oh well, we were even. *Glad think not cultural approximation.* He must mean appropriation. I was now officially out of my depth. With the owner/manager of a toilet-rental company.

LOVE DAMIEN HIRST, he shouted at me for some reason, probably because our texts had crossed. The three dots started their dance again. *Andres Serrano.* I couldn't google artists and type text messages at the same time. I waited. *Gilbert and George.*

Them I had heard of vaguely, and not because their calendars would do for your granny. So I clicked away from my phone and looked up Serrano.

Then I clicked back and called Doug.

'Hi!' he said, answering after a ring. I heard the exclamation mark, plain as day. 'I was enjoying our exchange but this is even better.'

'Andres Serrano made a crucifix out of his own wee, right?' I said. 'So, organic dorodango would be . . .?'

'Where are you?' he said. 'Did you fall down a well?'

He was still funny. I wasn't ready to write him off and walk away. A lot rested on his answer. 'I'm in my bathroom,' I said. 'Sitting on the loo.'

'You're . . . on the toilet?' he said, his voice thick with something I really hoped was disgust.

'Sitting on the closed lid, I mean,' I said. 'When you say, "organic dorodango"—'

'I wouldn't have minded,' he said. 'How is your sewage processed on a boat anyway?'

OK, OK, I told myself. Professional interest, inevitable. 'Chemical digester,' I said.

'Aw,' he said. 'What a waste.'

OK, I told myself, but only once. Professional in-joke. Don't overanalyse it.

'Organic dorodango . . .?' I tried again.

'You are a goddess,' he said. 'I can't believe we've found each other. But please stop saying it to me or I will swoon.'

'Organic dorodango isn't *dirt* balls, is it?'

'No,' he said. 'It's—'

'DON'T TELL ME!' Wow, it was loud when you shouted in here. I had never done it before. 'Doug,' I went on at a more normal volume, 'you're a creep. You're not an artist. And it *is* cultural appropriation and, if the waiter in the Japanese restaurant found out, he would spit in your soup, but maybe you'd like that too. I don't want to see you again and I don't want you to text me. Now, are you too big a creep to accept that?'

There was a long pause.

'No,' he said. 'I'm not even surprised. My last girlfriend broke up with me over a skid mark.'

'Stop telling me things!' I said. Then my conscience kicked in. 'Although that's pretty hypocritical. Women leave skiddies in their underpants too.'

'It wasn't in my und—' he began, but I managed to hang up the call, leave the bathroom, sliding around a bit on escaped salve, but finding some purchase on tiny Oregon rocks too, march through the living room, ignoring Blaike's response to my towel and turban, disembark, stamp round to the front of the Last Ditch and up the stairs to Roger and Todd's room to bang on the door.

'Never, ever, ever set me up on a date ever, ever again,' I said to Todd, when he answered. 'Capiche?'

'Capiche!' said Roger from the bed. 'Sounds serious.'

'I am now celibate,' I said. 'Because I just shaved my legs etc. for a guy who . . . I can't even tell you. But it's over. I'm done. I'll adopt Blaike, if Brandeeee ever turns up and lets me. I'll get a cat. I'll open a donkey sanctuary. I'll join a convent, if there's a Unitarian Universalist one with decent healthcare. But I am never going on a date again. And it's all your fault.'

'You shouldn't shave your etc.,' Todd said. 'You'll get a rash. Let me see if I can find you some tea tree oil. Give her a hug, honey,' he said to Roger as he disappeared into their bathroom, but it was more than I could bear to accept a condolence hug from a gorgeous, half-naked doctor, who didn't even look surprised at the state of utter degradation I was in. I reached into their room and pulled the door shut with a satisfying bang.

Which is when the door of the next room down the balcony opened, and a man put his head round it.

'Don't *you* start!' I said.

'Lexy?' I took a closer look at him. He did seem familiar, although quite a lot of his face was obscured by an enormous white moustache and a matching thicket of white hair, but I could still see a pair of ice-blue eyes that stirred a recognition. 'You just said Blaike and Brandee,' he went on. 'I heard you.'

'Yeah? So?'

'I'm in town looking for them. And someone said Brandee's latest husband's ex was a Scot called Lexy.'

'Someone did, did they?' I said, running through the many people it might be.

'And here you are. I check in to get some shut-eye on a budget, to start the search in the morning, and here you are.'

'Here I am,' I said, acutely aware that I was wrapped in a towel. It was one of Todd and Roger's cast-offs, so it wasn't skimpy, but it wasn't clothes. Say what you like about Scotland, but at least it's too cold to let you cut about in the scud for most of the year. It's a great saviour of dignity. 'So, who are you working for? Burt? White Pines? Is Bran spreading his bets?'

'I'm not working for anyone,' the man said. 'I just want to find my boy.'

'Your "boy"?' I said. 'Who are you?'

He stepped forward and held out his hand to shake. 'I'm Len Kowalski.'

TWENTY-TWO

In retrospect, I could have picked a different thing to say to Todd and Roger, but I wasn't in a speech-writing frame of mind. Once I'd pounded on their door and been let back in, I blurted out, 'I've just met a man,' and then had to wait while they stopped laughing.

'That didn't last long,' Todd said. 'Want the tea tree oil?'

'Oh, Lexy,' said Roger. 'You do brighten the day.'

'Shut up, both of you,' I said. 'I just met a man in the next-door room to this—'

'Handy,' said Todd.

'Shut it. Who overheard what I said to you, before—'

'So, he knows you're single,' said Roger.

'And silky smooth,' added Todd.

'Will you shut your holes de pie,' I said, 'and let me tell you what's just happened? I met a man – don't! – next door, who overheard me saying "Blaike" and "Brandeee" and came out to introduce himself. Guess who he is you'll never guess so I'll tell you. Lenny Kowalski.'

And they *finally* shut up.

'Lenny Kowalski who doesn't exist, Lenny Kowalski?' Roger said.

'Which leaves me wondering,' I said, 'whether I can make Blaike's day by taking his miracle dad round to the boat and reuniting them. Or if maybe another ex-husband coming out of the woodwork when Brandeee has disappeared means that we've got a prime suspect for her abduction and I should call Mike. And I truly don't know which.'

'It would be kinda reckless to hang around town after you'd got away with killing or even just kidnapping someone, wouldn't it?' Roger said. 'If you're on the "non-existent" tariff, that's not something to give up easily.'

'He's looking for his son,' I said. 'He told me straight out, in as many words. What will I *do*?'

At the knock on the door, all three of us jumped.

'Quick, open it!' I said. 'It might be Blaike. We shouldn't let that guy see him.'

'It's not Blaike,' came Lenny Kowalski's voice through the door. 'I thought I should join the conversation.'

Todd opened up.

'These walls are not thick,' Kowalski said. 'And I have a stethoscope. Sorry.'

'You do?' said Roger, while slipping discreetly out from under the covers and putting a robe on. 'You a doctor?'

'Oncologist,' said Kowalski. 'You?'

'Paediatrician,' said Roger.

'First equal. Put your antlers way,' said Todd. 'Doctors are the pits.'

'He's an anaesthetist,' I said. 'I'm a marriage and family therapist.'

'By day,' said Todd. 'But, by night – oh, by night, Dr Kowalski! – we run an investigation agency along with a third partner, and one of our current cases is to find your ex-wife, Brandee Lancer, who has gone missing.'

'So I believe,' said Kowalski. 'As has my son. Or, at least, I thought so.' He gave me a hard stare.

I gave him one right back. 'As had you too,' I said. 'For years and years and years. What the hell happened for . . . how long has it been?'

'Sixteen years,' said Kowalski.

'So what the hell happened?' I said again.

'I just told you,' said Kowalski. 'Sixteen years. In Folsom.'

'What for?' said Roger. He had squared up, just ever so slightly, and tightened the belt of his robe.

'Kidnap,' said Kowalski.

Todd and Roger both gasped.

'That's one hell of a dry sense of humour you've got there,' I said.

Kowalski let go the laugh he'd been holding in. 'No flies on you,' he said. 'Nah, I've been in Hawaii. Brandee persuaded me a clean break was the best idea. She already had the new guy lined up, and he loved kids, and what can I tell you . . .? There goes Dad of the Year award.'

'Brandeee persuaded you to walk away from your kid and never see him again?'

'She's very persuasive,' said Kowalski. 'Her nickname at college was Svengalice.' He drew a hefty sigh. I was sure I saw the ends of his big white moustache rippling in the draught from it. 'I thought that was hilarious when she told me.'

'And what brings you back?' Roger said. 'Now, after all these years.'

'I had half a mind,' Lenny said, 'when they sent him up to that school. Oh yeah, I kept tabs. But then when he ran away from it and disappeared and I couldn't get a hold of Brandee, well, I just hopped on the next plane east.'

I looked at Roger and he looked at Todd and we all looked at Lenny. It wasn't exactly hard criminological data, but we all agreed: he seemed like a nice guy. He wasn't even freaked by the three of us staring at him like charmed snakes while we pondered everything.

'What's going on?' he said at last, but still pretty easy.

'That is a tough question to answer,' I told him. 'But we can start with this: Blaike is here. He's round the back, on my houseboat. We found him sleeping rough – well, up a tree – and brought him home to take care of him, till we can find out what else is going on. Because—'

But Lenny had stopped listening. 'He's here? He's right here? Well, what are we waiting for?'

He was off before I could explain that what we were waiting for was inspiration about how to introduce two people when one had been told the other one didn't exist and the one that did exist after all didn't know that. Man, he was fast. And I was barefoot in a bath towel. I managed to keep up with him, but not actually *catch* up, grab his arm and explain. Roger and Todd could both have overtaken me, but the path round the motel through the bushes is narrow and they couldn't get through. Thankfully, though far from Dad of the Year, he was still a father, and he stopped at the bottom of the porch steps, composed himself and ascended at a measured pace, before throwing my living-room door open and saying, 'Son, it's your dad. I'm here to take you away from this bullshit. Shoulda done it years ago.'

I got to the doorway in time to see Blaike sit up straight
and put his feet on the floor – which is pretty much the teenage
equivalent of a star-jump-and-fist-pump combo – and say,
'How did she get hold of you again?'

'What?' said Len, but he was bursting with a decade and a
half of thwarted paternal instinct and he couldn't wait for the
answer. 'Look at you! Look at the size of you! And you're
the dead spit of my old pops in his army photos! C'mere, son,
and let me hug you.'

'How much is she paying you for this?' Blaike said. 'Are
you a model? Are you an actor?'

Todd and Roger edged round me. I couldn't seem to get
beyond the door, literally paralysed by the impossibility of
unravelling any of this.

'Brandee told him you didn't exist,' said Roger, which got
the job done.

Lenny dropped into a chair, wearing an expression that was
the pictorial-dictionary definition of gobsmacked. 'She told
you I didn't exist?'

'Not at first,' said Blaike. 'For the first fifteen years, she
told me you died in an elk hunt and left me a trust fund. Then,
when she had spent all the money she was going to say was
in the trust fund and she didn't have time to re . . . What's
the word?'

'Amass,' said Roger.

'Right. She didn't have time to re-amass it, so she came clean.
Well, obviously not. She changed the story and told me you
were a sperm donor. Well, not you. Some guy. No trust fund.'

'So what did she spend all the money on?' said Lenny.

'All what money?' I chipped in.

'All my money!' Lenny said. 'The money I've been paying
into the fund since the day I left, to kick in on your eighteenth
birthday. Why the hell do you think an oncologist came to
stay in a shithole like the Last Ditch?' He blinked and turned
to Roger and Todd. 'Hey, why do you two . . .?'

'Long story,' Todd said.

'It would fill a book,' said Roger. 'Maybe two.'

'So what did she do with the money?' said Lenny. 'And
where is she?'

'Right,' I said. 'OK. Well, Blaike, I'm glad you've got someone here to support you while we tell you this. But, actually, I'm going to leave it to Todd, because I really need to go and get dressed.'

'We'll wait,' Todd said. 'It won't take you long, Lexy. I've seen your look. Why don't I make Blaike some cocoa and everyone else a margarita? Unless . . .?' He looked at Lenny, who looked at Blaike.

'How about it, kid? Can you handle a margarita, without throwing up on this nice lady's hardwood floor?'

'I *meant*, would you rather have cocoa too, Len?' Todd said.

I went off to my bedroom, stifling giggles. I'll never get used to the twenty-one-year-old drinking age or the wide streak of wholesomeness running through America, even California, even my pals.

It was cocoa all round when I got back to the living room. I had made a bit of an effort, stung by the disdain, choosing a pair of palazzo pants and a draped tunic, with long earrings and a messy bun.

'What took you?' Todd said, giving me a glance as he handed me a mug. There was no point getting offended though; he didn't mean it. He just couldn't look at me and see anything noteworthy. Secretly, I enjoyed knowing that about him without him knowing I knew, because he prided himself on his camp credentials and it would have killed him to know he was such a bad girlfriend, such a *guy*. Then, I would catch myself enjoying that and shrink a little, wondering if the whole of my life was going to feel like a school trip, with seats to choose on the bus and someone crying.

I sat down, took a slug of cocoa for courage, looked Blaike straight in the eye and said, 'We think your mum might have been kidnapped by Nazis.'

I was ready for anything. I wasn't ready for nothing.

'And the money went in ransom payments?' Lenny said, dead calm.

'No, the money went *before* Mom took off,' said Blaike, also doing a great impersonation of a millpond. 'Or . . . was taken. Seriously? Who gets kidnapped? In real life, I mean.'

'Why don't you tell us what you know,' said Lenny. 'Talk us through it.'

So I talked them through it. Brandeee telling Blaike his dad didn't exist, the fire under the eucalyptus tree and the packing off to White Pines. I told them about the 3,000 dollars to PPPerfection for spa days, and Roger found the website and showed them. I told them about the lack of Christmas gifts, and I even remembered the weird Valentine's Day gifts, even though I had no idea what Elsie—

'Elise! Jeez!' Todd said.

. . . Elise meant by 'Addams Family' bouquets. Then we got right down to it. Brandeee's disappearance, the night before Valentine's. The abduction of Mama Cuento and the leaving of the note with the toe. The appearance of a note on Bran's doorstep, with the ripped-off acrylic. The abduction of the pregnant Hope and the chainsawed sculpture of Liberty, along with the belly button and note sent to Blaike, and the nose and note sent to the Akela of the Oregon and whatever-it-was Washington Brownies or whoever they were.

'Assimilation is ongoing,' said Todd to Lenny.

I ignored him and carried on telling Lenny and Blaike about the break-in at the university that helped an act of vandalism in a snobby supermarket—

'She means upscale grocery store,' said Todd.

I broke off to ask him if he wanted to take over and he mimed zipping his lips. So I ploughed on, telling all about the guy who slipped in through the pickup-truck window and how we followed him to the back of beyond and crawled on our bellies, getting sharp little rocks stuck in our undergarments, but eventually saw that all the cars had *PPP* on their number plates, and we thought that there were at least three outsize statues on the compound, swathed in tarps, which made them hard to identify, but was in and of itself suspicious, wouldn't they say?

Blaike was still looking at the PPPerfection website when I finally stopped talking. 'Oh, Mom!' he said, but in a weary way, not in anguish. 'Yeah, I can believe that. That would sucker her right in. "Perfection"? What an easy sell.'

'But she didn't hand over the vouchers,' I said.

'I didn't mean the vouchers!' said Blaike. 'I meant the disappearing.'

'But Bran knows and the cops know,' said Roger. 'So, it's only a matter of time.'

'What's it got to do with the cops?' said Blaike. 'Right . . . Lenny?'

Lenny's shoulders slumped a bit at that, but he didn't say anything.

'Right?' Blaike asked again. 'If my mom wants to run away with a bunch of crazy men's-rights loons, once she's got me safely booted up to Idaho – ha! She thinks! – what can the cops do?'

'Wait,' I said. 'You think there's a chance she wasn't kidnapped by them? Are you saying you think she might have gone willingly?'

'Absolutely!' said Blaike. 'Right . . . Lenny? She surrendered to Burt, you know. A surrendered wife?'

'No way!' I said. 'Your mum? Seriously?' I only knew about these seriously creepy sub-Stepfords from browsing the so-called self-help section in the bookshop to accessorize my consulting room. I hadn't read much but the first few chapters didn't feature anyone like Brandeee.

'And she did something crazy in a warm tub of water with Bran, the first time they were married. Rebirthing as twins, or something? Or maybe not twins.'

'I hope not,' said Roger.

'Soulmates! That was it,' Blaike said.

'And this is the same woman, with the perfect hair and nails and career and skin and figure, who works out every morning and frightens me?' I said. 'I can't believe it.'

'Frightens you?' said Blaike. 'My mom frightens *you*? She's *terrified* of you. This European, who puts up with Bran for six months – a guy my mom's been obsessed with for eight years – and then moves on. To a boat!'

I liked the sound of myself in this version, but there was no real reason to dwell on it.

'Lenny?' I said. 'What do you think?'

'Well,' he said, slowly, as if he was thinking hard, 'they sound like a cult. And handing over all your money is what you do with a cult. That's how they get you – not by kidnapping.' He thought again. 'Not that it was *her* money. It was yours, son, from me.'

'But how could she raid a trust fund?' I asked. 'What about the trustees and the lawyers?'

'Our divorce was informal,' Lenny said. 'Lawyers would have had community property split down the middle, and access in exchange for child support all hammered out. We made our own deal. I thought she'd stick to it. Maybe she would have, if she hadn't fallen under the spell of these . . . You really think they're Nazis?'

'Um . . .' I said. 'I think they're big honking weirdos anyway. Lenny, setting the money aside, do you agree with Blaike? That this is the sort of thing Brandeee might do?'

'She . . .' Lenny said. 'Well, to be honest, she . . .' He ran dry. 'Son? You wanna step outside while I say this; she's still your mom.'

'I'm good,' said Blaike.

'Well, that time she was born with Bran isn't her only rebirth,' said Lenny. 'Let's leave it there.' We all waited. 'Or not. She was also reborn into the faith of limitless lemon light, at an ashram in Los Baños, about a year before we met. Not a real ashram – offensive as hell for them to call it that. It was more like a . . . I don't know what the hell it was, but they were the ones who showed her the true path. *Her* true path. Dentistry.'

We all tried really hard. Her son was there and he was just a kid; he shouldn't have to experience his mum being disrespected. I would have made it, if I hadn't been looking at Roger when Todd tried to speak.

'L–lemon?' he said, with a little crack in his voice.

Roger's held breath hissed down both sides of his teeth, like a Welsh curse. I lost it next, trying to laugh quietly and ending up snorting.

'Poor Brandee,' Lenny said, when we'd all got a hold of ourselves again. 'She's never had solid taste in religion. Or men. And I'm including me in that tally.'

'So, you think she really could have run away to join the Patriarchy?' I said. 'With Blaike's money? Why not take her own?'

'So Bran would let her go, probably,' said Roger. 'Community property, like Len said.'

'And what do we do next?' said Todd. 'How do we find out? Even if the cops raid the place, they're not going arrest everyone there, are they? They'll just bring in the crew that stole the statues. One to strap it, one to cut the bolts, the guy who hooked her up and the driver. Anyway, from what Mike said, they were only going to tell the Oregon cops as a courtesy. No doubt *they* know all about Patriarchyville – can you believe that name? – and won't want to go roaring in there, if they can help it. Not for a couple of statues. Unless the patriarchs get cocky and head to the Louvre next.'

'Why not?' I said. 'Why wouldn't the Oregon cops or the FBI just go in there and clean them out? If they've broken the law . . .'

'WACO,' said Roger. I didn't know what that stood for.

'Ruby Bridges,' said Lenny. I had no clue where *they* were.

'Wounded knee,' said Todd. And now I was sure they were talking in code.

'Huh?' said Blaike, saving me the trouble.

'All we're saying is, we can see the argument for leaving them alone up there, to do whatever it is they're doing.'

'Like brainwashing Mom?' Blaike said. 'Like conning her out of my college fund and my first car? That's so not fair.'

I wondered how Lenny would play this first fathering challenge of the last fifteen years.

'You're right, son,' he said. 'But the cops aren't the only show in town.'

Todd had been looking at something on my laptop and now he raised his head. 'How big would you say that place was, Lexy?'

I shrugged, having no idea what the average size of a creepy cult compound was. Patriarchyville might be a tiddler or a whopper; I had no frame of reference.

'Because it says here that the website was set up two years ago. Say they had a little Wix website someone's brother-in-law put together when they first started out, then they go upmarket two years back, and they've got a fleet of trucks, all less than two years old, right Lex?'

Like I would be able to tell how old a pickup truck was in broad daylight, if I was reading the manual, never mind in the dark, from behind a ridge.

'I see where you're going,' said Lenny.

'I've got a terrible feeling I see where you're going too,' said Roger. 'And I'm not sure I like it.'

'I don't see where you're going,' I said.

'Well,' said Todd, 'they're expanding, right? They're advertising for women. They've got a web presence that is not unsophisticated, even if some of their direct action is a little . . . Who trades in navels? That's just weird. So, I'm thinking they're probably in the market for recruits. We could . . . infiltrate them. We could try to join them. Go up there and see what we can see.'

'And, when you say "we",' I said, 'who are you talking about? Because I don't want to malign these fine gentlemen who hate native women and Black women and Latinas, but I'm guessing they're probably not mad keen on the gays either. Wouldn't you say?'

'I was thinking we could do a little reshuffling,' Todd said. 'There's you and me, and Kathi and Roger. Two men and two women. We could go in pairs.'

'What about me?' said Lenny. 'I'm as much a part of this as anyone. It's my money. For my son.'

'You *could* go stag, I suppose,' Todd said. 'But I'm guessing they're OK for single guys. What they'll need is couples and families.'

'Sounds like what they need is single women,' I said.

'Absolutely no way,' said Roger.

'If they want families, I could tag along,' said Blaike.

'Absolutely no way,' said Lenny. 'Shame there isn't another lady of a certain age who could be my wife for a day.'

At that moment, my door opened, after a familiar peremptory knock, and Noleen appeared, saying, 'Here you are! I've been looking for you all. Do you know you've left your phones in your room? Hey, kid,' she added to Blaike.

'Hey, *Mom!*' said Blaike, and cracked up laughing.

TWENTY-THREE

'**R**oad trip! Road trip!' Todd woke me at six o'clock the next morning, with a bucket of coffee and an eye-opening wardrobe selection.

'Where the hell did you get those trousers?' I said, sitting up groggily and reaching for the cup. 'Are they navy blue?'

'French-navy chants,' said Todd. 'Not a chino, but not quite a pant. You love 'em, don't you?'

'I almost don't love *you* anymore, simply because you're wearing them,' I said. 'We've vetoed the fashion singular, by the way. Only a dollar, though, because I've got a crush on Tan France. And did you know there's an alligator stuck to your left pec? Seriously, Todd, you look terrible. They're going to know you're not for real.'

'Wait till you see what *you're* wearing,' he said. 'I went to Target, last thing before bed last night, and got you the most adorable little calf-length shirtwaister. It's yellow.'

'Jesus,' I said.

'And you can cut that out. Taking the Lord's name.'

I sank back against my pillows and started the slow, steady sipping of coffee that gets me from a readiness to stay in bed all day and sob, to a readiness to move and face another morning. Then my eyes shot wide open. 'What's Noleen wearing?'

'Hers is pink,' Todd told me.

I threw the covers back and leaped out like a kid at Christmas.

As it turned out, I couldn't laugh at Noleen or at Kathi when I saw them in their dresses with their wool hats pulled on low to hide their short hair.

'I'm not sure she's worth this,' Kathi said. 'I feel naked. And pantyhose are just *wrong*.'

'Della's in the office and Devin's in the launderette, right?'

I said. 'And Blaike's going to cover lunchtime and hang out with Diego the rest of the time? So the motel is ticking over?'

'And we'll be back tonight, because we're going to call Mike and tell her where we are and tell her we'll call again once we're back out. So there's no way we're not getting out,' Noleen said. 'I mean, right?'

'I'm still worried about Roger,' I said. 'I don't think this place is going to be much of a rainbow, do you? Or salad bowl or chess board or whatever the expression is.'

'He's a big boy,' said Noleen. 'Plus there's no way he'd let Todd go without him.'

'My husband!' said Kathi, and we all shared a look. 'Is there any chance they're going to believe these three couples?'

'People believe what you tell them,' said Noleen. 'Blaike believed his dad died hunting elk. Then he believed the guy never existed. And we all believed Brandee had been kidnapped.'

'Why was there a ransom note?' I said. 'It raised suspicion instead of quashing it.'

'All will be revealed,' said Noleen.

'In Patriarchyville,' said Kathi. 'That's so annoying. It sounds so dumb.'

'Patriarchistan scans much nicer,' said Noleen. 'I might suggest that to them. They'd love it.'

We tried to laugh, but it was more of a groan. 'When we get back tonight,' I said, 'pizza, margarita and *Moonstruck*. OK?'

We don't usually even shake on things. It was a sign of how high feelings were running that, at that moment, we went in for a group hug. When Roger rolled up in a rented minivan, he leaped out and joined it.

I had forgotten what Todd was like on a road trip. Which is strange, because Todd is quite a lot at the best of times and confining him to a car for a couple of hours only distills it a little bit. He had bookmarked a lot of useful websites about modesty, family values, biblical living and God's plan for man, which woman should shut her face and listen to, and he regaled us all with it at length on the way up the road. I don't know what everyone else was doing, but I let it wash over me and looked out at the passing landscape, as almond trees gave way to rice fields, and rice fields gave way to mountains and forests, sudden dramatic vistas, and snow on far-off peaks. We had crested the summit and were back down on to rolling land again when, all of a sudden, he started mock interviews, based on the information he'd been sharing.

I didn't acquit myself all that spectacularly.

'If they ask you whose idea it was to change our life, dearest,' he said, 'what are you going to tell them?'

'I'm going to say we talked it over together and the plan just sort of hatched,' I answered. 'Who can say?'

'*You* can!' said Todd. 'You need to say it was my idea and you're going along with it because you're my wife.'

'OK,' I agreed.

'Is that it?' said Todd. '"OK"?'

'For God's sake!' I said. 'I was going along with what you were saying because I'm your wife. I was literally doing exactly what you said I should be doing, right that very minute! And you're still sniping at me!'

'I'm going to go the other way,' Noleen said. She was sitting right over the back, in the jump seats, with Lenny. 'There's no point in me trying to act like the perfect wife—'

'I think you're OK,' Kathi interrupted.

'—so Ima go with, I'm lost in the swamp of feminism and I need a change before my family – that's Lenny, our daughter Della and our son Devin – drown in the sins of this world.'

There was a moment of awestruck silence throughout the minivan.

'Bravo,' said Lenny. 'Were you raised Baptist?'

'Presbyterian,' said Noleen. 'But they really meant it.'

'Della and Devin,' Lenny said. 'How old are they?'

'You choose,' said Noleen. 'I thought sixteen-year-old twins, but it's up to you, oh master.'

'OK, so we're good,' Roger said. He was the antsiest out of all of us, and who could blame him? 'But what are we actually going to say, first off, when we roll up at the gate? That's what I've been thinking about. Who wants to hear?'

'Go for it, honey,' Todd said.

'We hope they don't mind us just showing up,' Roger said. 'And maybe we should have emailed first, but we just got to the point that we'd had it. Let's try and tag it to something. Pity it's not International Women's Day or Pride Month or something. But anyways the story is we decided to come and see what they've got. Because our friend Brandee Lancer talked about them before she left town and they sounded like a way forward, for people who're wandering in the desert.'

'Genius,' said Todd. 'Straight in with her name. You're an asset to the team.'

'Or,' I said, 'Todd could pretend to be a polygamist and you could wait for us in the nearest town. Aren't you scared, Roger?'

'Every day,' he said. 'But sometimes flushing 'em out is the only way to go.'

'Valentine's Day,' said Noleen, from the back. 'Not to change the subject or anything. Could we hang it off that?'

'Yes!' I said. 'Oh my God, yes, of course we can! It's sickening, fake, commercialized nonsense, commodifying romance and lumping a ridiculous burden on mums every-where to write cards out for the whole bloody class at their kid's school, and then still be in her chiffon babydoll at sundown.'

'Or,' said Todd, 'just tell us how you feel.'

'And that's not the way to go,' said Roger. 'They won't care about burdening women with the work of motherhood, and I don't think they'll care much about protecting the sanctity of romance from getting steamrollered by Hallmark.'

'You're right,' I said, and thought for a while. 'It destroys childhood innocence by forcing kids to think about sexual partners when they're too young, and it encourages young adults outside marriage to engage in dangerous mingling and ungodly thoughts.'

'There's the bunny!' said Todd.

'Five dollars,' said Kathi, who hated that expression like the dentist's drill.

'So, what did we all do for Valentine's Day, then?' said Kathi.

'I consoled my daughter about getting no cards,' Noleen

said. 'And Lenny stayed at work to avoid the pressure. You two, Kathi and Roger, you went out for dinner, but they played lewd music and you had to leave.'

'Barry White,' said Roger. 'With the bass turned up.'

'And I cooked you a nice dinner, Todd,' I said. 'Because I do love you, but I don't hold with saints. Unless this lot will be into saints, in which case we lit a candle to St Valentine.'

'And St Cyril,' said Todd. 'He invented the alphabet. It's his day too.' There was another short, impressed silence. 'Catholic school, baby!'

'Bullshit Catholic school,' I said. 'That was in the pub quiz at the Randy Shamrock, last month. And you didn't get it.'

'I don't think we should talk about saints,' said Lenny. 'If these guys have Bible-verse licence plates, I reckon they're not much for candles.'

'We'll soon find out,' Roger said. 'Because here we go.'

He had found the place on Google Earth at home and plotted the point where we needed to leave the road. Avis wouldn't be pleased about the minivan's suspension, but we knew now there was no road in any direction. This was the best way in.

At least this time we didn't have to abandon the car and crawl the last half mile; we drove up to the slatted fence as if we had every right, and then circled it until the gate lay dead ahead.

Power Purpose Prosperity

The arch didn't look any less creepy face-on in the cold, grey light of this cloudy day. Under it, the gate was shut and padlocked.

'No trucks,' Todd said. 'Someone must be out on the Saturday errands.'

'Which are God knows what,' Noleen said. 'Do you think they know what that gate looks like?'

'My great-grandma didn't make it out of the camps,' said Lenny. 'She gave her daughter – my grandma – all her food. They know.'

In the night, everything about the place had looked sinister, not just the arch writing; but today, on a damp February morning, with the scrubby grass still green from the winter rains, it looked more of a camp than a compound, like maybe they were meditating and baking sourdough in there, not drilling and plotting and burying tinned food in secret bunkers underground. It was hard to say which was more likely, and I still hoped that we were freaking ourselves out for nothing. I hoped that, in an hour or two, I'd remember how I felt in this minute – pulse pounding and palms sweating – and feel foolish for being scared.

But then the gate opened. And the guy who'd opened it had done it one-handed because, in his other hand, he was carrying the biggest, bulkiest, most over-the-top-looking gun I had ever seen in my life. And he was wearing head-to-toe cammo too – not like Todd wore it sometimes, ironically.

'Oh shit,' said Noleen.

'Enh,' said Roger. 'I'm from Stockton. And the safety's on.' He opened the driver's door and stepped down.

'And I did two years of nights in the ER in Sacramento,' said Todd, and slipped out of the passenger door.

Watching the two of them walk towards Cammo Guy, with his big scary gun, I felt my stomach turn and my guts move. I had to get out of the car before I messed it up, but I didn't know whether to lean forward or squat. And now Lenny was on the move too. He didn't give voice to his tough-guy credentials; maybe he thought the moustache would do the talking.

The three of us still in the van couldn't see a damn thing, except the three of them, like not quite half of the Magnificent Seven, strolling towards the gateway. Then Noleen shot out of the back door, and that was it for Kathi; she let herself down, out of the middle door. I had got ahold of myself, top and bottom, but I didn't want to be the only coward, and so on shaking legs I descended too, and scampered to catch up with Kathi and Noleen, who were holding hands as they walked forward. I grabbed Kathi's free one just as Lenny and Todd parted and gave Cammo McGun a view of us.

'Int that nice?' he said. 'Int that a purty thing to see?'

Yes, he said *purty*. And he meant it. I got a sudden flash of what we must look like, the three of us, in our petal-coloured dresses, holding hands and looking at the ground.

'Thought you were the press,' the man said. 'Wouldn't put it past those dirty cops to tell the enemy of the people what they done.'

'Cops?' said Todd. 'You get a lot of trouble with cops, all the way out here?'

I raised my eyes and looked past the guy, into the compound itself. There were huts with ropes of washing hung between them. A goat stood tethered to a stick in a patch of grass, and beds of dark earth looked ready to be planted up. I put my head down again.

'We did the world a solid,' the man was saying now. 'Removed some profane images from the view of the innocent. But they didn't see it that way and they came all the way out here to haul a pile of wood and iron and even plastic back out into the world.'

I didn't move and neither did the others, but I bet I wasn't the only one who did an internal fist-pump.

'And arrested four of our good men,' Cammo said. That was about right: the strapper, the sawer, the driver and the acrobat. 'So now our elders have had to go and post bail, then there's gonna be an arraignment and trial and fines and more press . . . We wanted to escape the world, not be held up in ridicule for it. We should never have strayed from our true path. We never will again.'

'That's good to know,' Roger said. 'That's exactly what we're looking for.'

'You're looking to join us?' said Cammo. 'Well, well, well. Any other day, I'd pepper your ass for even asking. But today . . .' He was looking at Roger with an expression I couldn't begin to read. 'Damn lawyer said "hate crime" about us taking those scarecrows out of view. Be hard to make that stick, with you right here.'

'What about the rest of us?' Roger said.

'Oh, sure!' said Cammo. 'Three couples, two of them young? That would be a nice little boost for our patriarchy.'

I looked up again at that. It's not often you hear the word used so mildly.

'As long as you didn't breed with your white wife,' he went on, 'we could make this work for everyone.'

Todd's feet moved in the dust, as if he was having to try hard to hold himself still.

'Oh,' said Roger. 'Hm. She didn't tell us that. That might be a sticking point then. My wife is actually four months gone, right now. Aren't you, honey?' He turned round to look at Kathi, crossing his eyes and sticking his tongue out.

'Like I said, though, the elders ain't here, right now. They might see it different. There are others here bearing the marks of old sin. Tattoos and divorces and whatnot. We wash clean when we join. Your wife could be cleansed and the baby baptized. No cleaning you off, though, huh? No offence. Just kiddin'.'

Roger frowned and then threw his head back and laughed, as if it was the funniest thing he had ever heard.

'But who's this "she"?' Cammo was saying. 'Who told you about us? We don't allow our women to go out into the world. Where would you have met one?'

'It was before she came,' Roger said. 'We spoke while she was preparing to join you. Brandee Lancer?'

Cammo's voice had been loud all along, but it really started booming now. 'Brandee Lancer,' he said. 'Brandee Lancer? That whore? That serpent? That *dentist*?'

'Uh . . .' Roger said.

'Get outta here!' he yelled. 'She came up here, weekend after weekend, talked big about moving in permanently, free dental for everyone, and all her money. Happy to marry our patriarch and start him a family. We never saw a penny, after her down payment. And she talked more than any woman ever should. Talked us into taking those statues and talked us into poisoning that shameless charade, and then she disappeared and left us to the cops and lawyers and press, and garbage like you. Go on, get outta here, before I give you what you're begging for.'

'OK, OK, we're leaving,' said Roger, and he started walking very slowly backwards, with Todd and Lenny flanking him, like a game of Grandma's Footsteps, but backwards and with guns.

'Did you send the notes with the body parts?' I said. 'Or was that her too? I've always hated her. Never trusted her. I'm only here because my husband brought me.'

'"Make a splash," she said,' Cammo spat. '"Stir up recruits," she said. Send them to her kid and her friend, and rake in free publicity for the cause.' He sniffed and spat. 'You do well to obey your husband, young woman, but your instincts were good. We strayed far from our true path, listening to a Jezebel like that. She is black-hearted and dangerous. You shoulda listened to your wife,' he said to Todd. 'Every so often, a fool of a woman can hit on something.'

This fool of a woman had hit on something else too. 'The acrylic nail,' I said.

He wasn't alight with intelligence at the best of times, but he went cross-eyed trying to work out what that meant. Which told me everything I needed to know.

Kathi and Noleen were back in the minivan. Roger was in the driver's seat. Lenny climbed in and I jumped up too. Only Todd was still standing out in the open, squaring up to the guy. Roger started the engine. Todd still didn't move.

'You coming, honey?' I said, leaning out of the window.

'Go and discipline her,' said Cammo. 'Don't let her talk to you like that in front of other men.'

For some reason, that little homily revolted Todd so much, it pushed him right over the edge. He turned away in disgust and climbed into the minivan beside me, leaning forward and kneading Roger's shoulder as he manoeuvred the van round and drove away.

When we stopped at a bar in the town of Weed – yes, really – we must have looked like the world's lamest folk band, or maybe the world's giddiest polygamists. There was a lot of hugging all round and ripping off of woolly hats to throw them in the air. Then we went inside and ordered quite a lot of whisky.

'I'll drive,' Lenny said. 'I've been sober seventeen years, and I'm staying that way.'

'Aren't you angry?' I said to Roger. 'How did you keep your shit together back there?'

'You can't stay angry all the time,' Roger said. 'It's bad for the digestion.' But he necked the first whisky in a oney and then squeezed Todd's hand.

'So,' Kathi said, 'Brandee wanted to leave and she wanted to take all of Blaike's money with her, so she decided to fake a kidnapping by that bunch of losers. My God, it almost worked too.'

'The statue heists were supposed to make them look so unhinged, no one would believe they hadn't kidnapped her,' I said.

'And who did they poison?' said Noleen. 'I wasn't really following, by then. Shameless . . . Who was it?'

'Not a person,' I said. 'It was a shameless charade. And I've almost . . . It's right on the tip of my . . . Valentine's Day! What would make a bouquet of flowers an Addams Family bouquet of flowers?'

'If they're all dead, isn't it?' Kathi said. 'Or they've got no heads on. That's it. Morticia tends her dead roses by chopping off their heads, remember.'

'And she sneaked across the road and killed her neighbour's roses before she left too,' I said. 'Barbra Streisand, Princess Elizabeth and Dick Van Clark.'

'Dyke,' said Kathi.

'Look who's— Never mind,' Todd said. 'What are you talking about?'

'The florist was sold out of flowers on Valentine's Day,' I said. 'I thought that meant business was booming but I bet if we check, we'll hear that she had to shut up early because they were all dying. And I saw a bunch of roses on a yard-waste pile on Valentine's Day and thought it was the last week's flowers, out for the bin men. But, if there were flowers at the house every week, I'd have seen them before, wouldn't I? You know that one little cottage left in the downtown, just the other side of the tracks? I pass it all the time. No, I think that was the Valentine's flowers and they were dead already. And then, of course, there was the break-in. At the department. That caused the problem. At the Lode.'

'What happened there?' Lenny said, and then was taken aback when five of us all said, '*Nothing!*'

'So I bet if we scout around,' I went on, 'we'll hear of a lot of florists and growers in Northern California and Southern Oregon that had flowers all die on Valentine's Day. Brandeee sabotaged Cuento, but the so-called patriarchs probably did the same elsewhere.'

'Ahem.' The waitress who had brought our whisky was back at the table again. 'Are you talking about the dead flowers?' she said. 'You mean it wasn't just Weed? We were scared it was something in the water table. We thought we were headed for Erin Brockovich country.'

'No, it was sabotage,' Todd said.

'Someone killed my grandma's rambling rose that my dead grandpa planted round the door? Who would do a thing like that?'

'It was a bunch of men's rights twats, up the road there,' I said.

'Oh, them!' she said. 'We call it Peckerville.'

Which was so perfect, we bought another round to toast her, and tipped her 40 per cent too.

TWENTY-FOUR

Coming down through the mountain pass between Oregon and California was like climbing out of winter into spring. The clouds parted. The sky turned blue. The air grew gentle. But the guy in the Fish and Ag. border-control kiosk, who only wanted to check we weren't bringing in diseased fruit to kill the citrus industry, insisted on breathalyzing Lenny when the minivan window rolled down and a wave of whisky engulfed him.

'When did you have your last drink, sir?' he said.

'Two thousand three,' Lenny said. 'I'm an alcoholic.'

Turns out telling a border cop you're an alcoholic *isn't* a good way to make sure he doesn't test you. Who knew?

'Seriously, man,' Lenny said. 'These guys are all hammered, but I'm as sober as a journalist.'

Turns out cracking jokes to a border cop who thinks you're drunk isn't a great idea either. Everyone knew that except Lenny. He had been too long in laid-back Hawaii and had forgotten where most mainland cops keep their night stick.

And then we were home. We had told Della we were coming, but she still came out of the office to greet us. Devin came out of the launderette at the other end of the Last Ditch U. Both were beaming.

'Hoooo, what a day we've had!' Noleen said. 'How'd it go for you?'

'Very good,' Della said, grinning even wider.

'Oh yeah?' said Kathi. 'What happened?'

'Oh, this and that, you know,' Della said casually, tucking her hair behind her ear.

Lenny Kowalski, Kathi, Noleen, Roger and me all waited to hear more, but Todd grabbed Della's hand and squealed like a greased balloon. 'Oh my God! Oh my God! Oh my Godmother's garter!'

'Yes, it's true,' Della said, laughing now. 'I'm getting married.' Now, finally, I noticed the ring.

Devin had jogged over, and now he put his arm around her and said, '*We're* getting married.'

'*Felicidades!*' I shouted, and Della was so happy, she didn't even fix my pronunciation for me. 'That's fantastic!'

'It's practical,' she said. 'It's a good idea for Diego to have a settled . . .' But she couldn't keep it up. 'Yes, it's lovely,' she said. 'I am dreaming. I pinch myself.'

'Hey, kid?' said Noleen to Devin. 'You remember when you first moved in here and that girl in your class was coiling round?'

Devin nodded.

'And I said, "You're young. Have some fun. Don't get too heavy"?'

Devin nodded again, frowning now.

'Well, that stops right here. You're in this for keeps, you hear me? That' – she jabbed a finger at Della – 'is a good woman, and if you hurt her I will destroy your life.'

'Well OK then,' Devin said. 'You definitely need to make a speech at the wedding.'

'When *is* the wedding?' Kathi shouted over her shoulder as she bustled off towards her room. 'Long engagement? City Hall tomorrow?'

'Soon,' Della said. 'Where you going?'

'Something I need to check,' Kathi said, and disappeared through her door.

'How did it go with you guys?' Devin said, peeling his eyes off his beloved and managing to remember that other things were happening in the world.

'Good,' Noleen said.

'Great,' said Roger. 'I got a little immersion tour of the fifties. It was awesome. But Trinity solved the case.'

'You found her?' Devin said.

'Nah,' said Noleen. 'But we found out there was no kidnapping. It was all Brandee's doing. She masterminded a cover story and she moved on. Again. You think it's another guy?' This was to Lenny. 'Number five?'

'Who knows?' he said. 'Who cares? Who's going to tell Bran?'

'Lexy can tell Bran,' Kathi said, coming back to join us. 'Who's going to tell the cops?'

'Tell them what?' I said. 'Thanks, by the way. I get all the fun jobs.'

'Tell them to hunt her down, indict her bony ass and sling her in Chowchilla.'

'For what?' said Roger.

'For this!' Kathi brought out from behind her back one of the many financial forms Bran had handed over to us, that first day up at the house.

'What is it?' I said. There wasn't a single piece of US official paperwork, from a PO-box rental application to a jury-duty exemption plea, that would have shaken a different question out of me, but everyone else took a single look and went, 'Ohhhhhhhhh!'

'Oh, great!' said Noleen. 'Couldn't happen to a nicer person.'

'What an idiot!' said Roger. 'What a rookie error.'

'What *is it*?' I said again.

'This, Lexy,' said Todd, 'is last year's annual statement of tax-free interest from a college savings account. She put Lenny's money where it would grow fastest and now she's cleaned it out and taken it all away.'

'And so . . .?' I said.

'Tax evasion,' said Kathi. 'They'll all be looking for her, now. The days are gone when a rich white lady could dick around with her kid's college chances and get away with it.'

'Wow,' I said. 'The cops will really care that much about her cheating on her taxes?'

'Not the cops,' said Lenny. 'The Feds. From now on we call her Svengalice Capone.'

It was me who went to tell Bran. Todd and Kathi took the tax form to show Mike. Lenny went to the boat to explain the situation to Blaike. Noleen went to look at wedding plans with Della and try to care. Diego and Devin went for fro-yo. Maybe every mid-twenties single mum of a six-year-old only child should marry a college kid. Two birds, one stone.

Bran looked terrible. He had dropped ten pounds at least, five of them off his face, leaving him haggard.

'Have you found her?' he said, when he answered the door.

'No,' I told him. 'Can I come in?' It was weird asking, when I used to live there.

At the two couches facing each other, where Bran had been sleeping judging by the nest of blankets, I took a deep breath and told him straight.

'It was a smokescreen, Bran. She's left you. I'm sorry.'

'I'll find her,' he said. 'I got another robo-call from that rib joint, by the way.'

'Uh-huh.'

'Replace Your Rib. Powerful Patriarchs for Worried Women. Think that's anything worth looking into?'

'No, as it turns out,' I said. 'A complete red herring.'

'But I want you to keep looking,' Bran said.

'I don't need to,' I told him. 'The FBI are going to be looking. Something to do with Al Capone? I didn't understand it fully. I haven't told anyone you faked the note and nail, by the way.'

He thought about denying it, but let the breath go as a sigh, in the end.

'Did you fish it out of the wheeliebin?' I asked him. 'Or nick it from a nail spa?'

'Does it matter?'

'Only because you got closer than you'll ever know to pissing off some really dodgy blokes.'

Bran frowned and mouthed the words.

'Oh, for God's sake: sketchy dudes! Dicey guys! Get a Britbox subscription!'

He scowled.

'I want you to swear one thing to me,' I added, once I'd calmed down again.

He nodded.

'Swear you haven't' – Bloody Noleen! – 'chopped her up and fed her to the hogs.'

'Of course not!' he said. 'What hogs?'

'It's only an exp—' I began. Then I bit my lip. Because, was it? Or was the Last Ditch just bone-deep in me now?

'And here's another thing,' I said. Then I ran dry. It felt too much like kicking a man when he was down. 'How do you feel . . . answer honestly . . . about . . . Blaike?'

His shoulders slumped. 'Blaike?' he said. 'I thought you were going to say "me".'

'What *about* you?' I said. 'Oh! *Me?* No.'

'Right. Blaike? Why?'

'Because his dad's turned up. Lenny Kowalski?'

'Doesn't exist. This must be more of the smokescreen.'

I shook my head. 'He does exist. He looks exactly like Blaike and he knows too much for there to be any doubt. I'm sorry, Bran. She's been telling quite a lot of lies, for quite a long time.'

'I'm sorry too,' Bran said. I wasn't sure what he was referring to. 'But Blaike. Does he want to stay with his daddy?'

'I think he might, yes,' I said. 'Sorry.'

'You've got nothing . . .' Bran said. 'You're the last person . . .' He scrubbed his face and gave me a smile brave enough to break a heart of stone. 'Well, send me your final bill.'

'We will,' I said. 'There's a car hire and there might be a bit of maintenance on it. We had to go off-road and it wasn't an off-roader.'

'Sounds exciting,' Bran said. Another smile, this one more rueful. 'You've landed on your feet, haven't you? Life's good?'

'Life's . . .' I said. 'Good, yes. Thank you. If I'd never met you, and all that.'

'You're welcome,' said Bran. 'Lex . . .?'

I waited but he was never going to say any more. It was up to me to respond to that. Or not. I thought about it. I thought about my six friends – three couples, now – and the blink of time I thought I might be fostering Blaike until Lenny turned up. I thought about Dirtball Doug and even Earl the Earhole. And I thought about the nine months that I had been with Bran.

'Look out for that bill,' I said, standing. 'Terms strictly thirty days.' Then I left the Beige Barn, closing the door gently behind me.

Standing outside, trying to recover from the skin-crawling awkwardness of it all, I found myself looking at the house of the blind rose-grower across the way and I headed off in that direction, greatly cheered, to give her the news. I would call it good news, but I wasn't sure how it would hit her ear. I'd have to go gently.

As before, her son answered. He was wearing a khaki waistcoat with approximately forty-nine pockets, each with two zips. 'Oh!' he said. 'Hi! How are you?'

'Great, good, fine,' I said. Why was I babbling? 'Taylor, right? How's your mum?'

'In mourning for Doris Day,' he said, leaning comfortably in the doorway, as if settling in for a chat.

'Still?'

'*Rosa* "Doris Day". Scented yellow hybrid tea. And we still don't know what happened.'

'That's what I came to tell you,' I said. 'It was sabotage. Deliberate vandalism. Roundup, probably. But if she replants she'll be fine. The FBI are hunting the perp down.'

'The FBI are?' he said, raising his eyebrows so high his aviator specs slipped down his nose. He was wearing aviator specs. 'That's gratifying.'

'Isn't it just?' I said. 'So. Tell her from me. From us. Trinity Solutions.' I fished out a card and handed it over, like Todd's always telling me to.

'Le . . .?' he said. 'League Sadie?'

'Lexy.'

'"Counselling and investigations"?' he said, still reading. 'Interesting work.'

'I'll never be rich,' I said. 'But I'll never be bored.'

'It's a problem, isn't it?' he said. 'I followed my heart too. I'm an ornithologist.' Of course he was. 'Down at the wetlands.'

'That must be fascinating. It was one of the weirdest things about moving over here, suddenly not knowing what any of the birds were.'

'How many do you know now?' He had stopped leaning against the door jamb. Mentioning bird identification was like jiggling his mouse, obviously.

'Oh, well, you know,' I said. 'Blue jays, orioles, hummingbirds, those shiny black ones with the red bit.'

He smiled. 'Would that be the greater shiny black one with the red bit, or the lesser shiny black one with the red bit?'

I smiled back, but found my smile fading as I saw him, for some reason, start to change colour.

'I could take you to the hide and teach you the water birds,' he said. 'If that would be a thing you would ever want to do, one day, when you weren't busy.'

'Uh . . .' I said.

'Except God knows when,' he said, 'because – like I told you – it's not well paid and I've got this second job at the Verizon store, which I hate, but what you gonna do?'

I stared. 'At the Verizon store downtown?' I said. 'Yeah, I think I saw you going in there the other day. Va–Valentine's Day?'

'Yeah, you did,' he said. 'I saw you too.'

'You did?'

'But I ignored you because . . . I'm forty-four years old and I work nights in a phone store.'

Forty-four years old, passionate about something and honest, I thought. And, from the back, I had quite liked the look of him, in his phone-shop trousers, with only four pockets and no zips. In fact, I had literally fancied the arse off him. The front – aviator frames and all that – could wait.

'Instead of a trip down to the wetlands,' I said, and I knew I was changing colour too, because in this moment of height-ened awareness that sounded filthy, 'why not a cup of coffee on your break, one night? I live quite near the phone shop. I could meet you.'

'A cup of coffee?' he said, still smiling. 'That's a modest enough plan.'

'Or,' I said, suddenly remembering, 'what about a wedding? Not ours. Ha-ha-ha-ha-ha-ha-ha!' For God's sake, Lexy, I said to myself. But, you know what? He didn't slam the door. He didn't go white. He didn't run away.

FACTS AND FICTIONS

Beteo County, the city of Cuento, its houses, businesses, streets, and residents are all fictional. But there are some Easter eggs in the Last Ditch books which residents of and visitors to Davis, CA, might have fun spotting. A list of these can be found on my website, www.catrionamcpherson.com

The statues of Mama Cuento, Sacagawea, Hope, and Liberty that get embroiled in this story are fictional but there *are* beautiful monuments to Sacagawea all over the west. The touching statue of Phyllis Wheatley in Boston and the awe-inspiring Dignity in South Dakota are well worth a look.

Patriarchyville, OR, is fictional. Thank God.